"Don't be frightened. This is the gentlest horse in my brother's stable," Major Grenville said.

He pulled her around in front of him, gripped her upper arms and captured her gaze. "Miss Newfield, you may count on me." The firm, warm touch of his hands set her heart to fluttering uncontrollably. "I will not allow you to be harmed."

"I thank you, Major Grenville. You have shown me nothing but kindness. I do trust you. Shall we begin? After all, what's the worst that can happen?"

He took her elbow and led her to the horse's head. "Miss Newfield, may I present Bella." He ran a hand down the creature's nose. "Bella, this is Miss Newfield," he murmured as he took Anna's gloved hand and guided it down the creature's nose. "Unlike poor Miss Peel, she is not the least bit nervous."

"You should not lie to her." Anna's voice wavered, but whether it was from the touch of the major's hand on hers or his deep, soothing tone, she could not tell.

Again he chuckled, and a shiver, not at all displ_____ _____ _____ _____ _____. She mentally shook it off_____ _____ _____ _____ uch a dis_____ _____ _____ _____ iles mea____

Books by Louise M. Gouge

Love Inspired Historical

Love Thine Enemy
The Captain's Lady
At the Captain's Command
*A Proper Companion

*Ladies in Waiting

LOUISE M. GOUGE

has been married to her husband, David, for forty-seven years. They have four children and seven grand-children. Louise always had an active imagination, thinking up stories for her friends, classmates and family, but seldom writing them down. At a friend's insistence, in 1984 she finally began to type up her latest idea. Before trying to find a publisher, Louise returned to college, earning a BA in English/creative writing and a master's degree in liberal studies. She reworked the novel based on what she had learned and sold it to a major Christian publisher. Louise then worked in television marketing for a short time before becoming a college English/humanities instructor. She has had eleven novels published, several of which have earned multiple awards, including the 2006 Inspirational Reader's Choice Award. Please visit her website at http://blog.Louisemgouge.com.

A Proper Companion

LOUISE M. GOUGE

Love Inspired

Recycling programs
for this product may
not exist in your area.

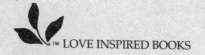 ™ LOVE INSPIRED BOOKS

ISBN-13: 978-0-373-82921-7

A PROPER COMPANION

www.LoveInspiredBooks.com

Printed in U.S.A.

For ye are all the children of God by faith in Christ Jesus. There is neither Jew nor Greek, there is neither bond nor free, there is neither male nor female: for ye are all one in Christ Jesus. And if ye be Christ's, then are ye…heirs according to the promise.

—*Galatians* 3:26, 28, 29

This book is dedicated to my beloved husband, David, who has stood by my side through my entire writing career. I would also like to thank Nancy Mayer and the Beau Monde Chapter of RWA for helping with my research into the Regency era.

Chapter One

❧

Blandon, Shropshire, England
October 1813

Amid the sea of somberly dressed mourners entering the vicarage, Anna spied a flash of crimson, and her grief lifted for the first time since *Papá*'s death three days ago. A closer look at the uniformed cavalry officer sent her emotions plunging again, for he was not Peter. But how foolish to think her brother could have returned for their father's funeral when he was an ocean away fighting the Americans. This soldier must have come to honor *Papá*. This *wounded* soldier, for the young man of perhaps five and twenty years leaned on a cane and his red-coated companion's arm. Anna lifted a silent prayer that the officer's affliction was not too severe.

The parishioners approached where she stood, each person offering a word of comfort or a memory of *Papá*, warming Anna's heart. *Papá* had been much loved, and many in his congregation would miss him as much as she. In his honor, generous neighbors had brought sprays of aromatic sage and fragrant geraniums from their autumn gardens to freshen the air in the house. The pleasant scents vied with the odors of hardworking villagers who had taken time from their harvest labors to pay their respects.

Anna bent down to kiss a small boy, and her eyes fell on the gleaming black boots of the next person in line. She straightened and found herself gazing up into the dark brown eyes of the wounded soldier.

"Miss Newfield." The tall officer bent over his cane and his pallid countenance raised her concern, as did the scent of some pungent medicine she could not identify. "I am Edmond Grenville. Please accept my condolences for your loss." At his elbow stood his companion, whose eyes were filled with worry.

She extended her black-gloved hand, glancing briefly at the stars on the officer's golden epaulettes which designated his rank. Peter had taken such pride in teaching her how to distinguish one officer from another. "I thank you for coming, Major Grenville. Did you know my father?"

He winced slightly and breathed out a labored sigh.

"Should you be seated, sir?" Anna waved a hand toward a nearby chair, wishing she could sit down, as well, for although it was only late morning the weariness of the day had already begun to settle into her.

He shook his head. "No, madam, on both counts." He inhaled deeply. "I knew *of* your father."

Anna's heart lifted. "Ah. I did not know his reputation extended beyond Blandon." She offered a smile but saw only pain in his clouded eyes.

"Very far, miss. To America, in fact." He glanced at his aide. The younger man nodded. "Your brother, Lieutenant Newfield—" His voice broke, and he cleared his throat impatiently.

Anna's heart seemed to stop and her ears hummed, blocking out the sounds around her. "Yes," she managed to murmur. "Please continue. My brother?"

The major shuddered, perhaps to shake away his weakness, for he stood taller, almost at attention. "I regret to inform you that Lieutenant Peter Newfield was wounded in battle." His words came in a rush. "To be more precise, dear lady, he saved my life, and in the process took the sword blow meant for me. After the battle, his remains were not found, and therefore he has been declared missing."

The room seemed to spin. The paneled walls closed around her. Tiny bursts of air fanned her face. Anna sat and blinked her burning eyes. Forced herself to breathe. What would *Mamá* do in this situation? Or *Papá*? Was Peter even now with their parents in the Savior's presence? Was she now truly alone?

Somewhere at the edges of her mind, she heard the cry of Job: *The Lord giveth and the Lord taketh away; blessed be the name of the Lord.* She grasped this lifeline like a drowning person. *Blessed be the name of the Lord.* This would be her hymn, her anthem, no matter what other sorrows befell her.

Friends hovered near. The major sat beside her and patted her hand.

"Dear Miss Newfield—"

"I thank you, sir." Her own voice sounded far away. "For bringing word." A tendril of hope threaded through her thoughts. "Missing, you say?"

"Unfortunately, yes." The officer leaned toward her. "You must know that I had no idea your father had died. I came to bring him word of Newfield and—"

"Missing. That means there is hope he is alive."

Major Grenville's expression softened, and he spoke as if addressing a child. "You must understand …" He sat back and shook his head. "Perhaps you need not know of such things." He returned a warm gaze to her and squeezed her hand. "We will hope, madam. We will hope."

The strength of his grip surprised Anna, as did the high color now flooding his pale face. He seemed to be making a great effort to console her, and she longed to return the kindness. "Major, the ladies of Blandon have prepared a funeral nuncheon. Will you and your companion partake?"

His brow furrowed, but his companion's face brightened. "'Twould be good to have a bite before we embark on the rest of our journey, sir."

The major eyed his aide. "I agree, Matthews. And I thank you, Miss Newfield. Your brother often spoke of your kind nature. I see it was not merely fraternal pride." His well-formed face, framed by natural chestnut curls, relaxed into a soft smile.

A wave of understanding swept through Anna. Peter had risked his life to save this friend, and that knitted him to her in a way she could not describe.

Weakness and weariness threatened to fell Edmond. He tried to rise from the chair, but even his cane did not help. Matthews touched his shoulder.

"I'll fetch you a plate, sir." The young man left the parlor, but not before he cast a concerned glance over his shoulder.

Good man, Matthews. No officer ever had a better batman to see to his personal matters. Without his tender attention, Edmond would never have survived the illness that overtook him on the voyage from America. When the seas grew violent, Matthews had cushioned Edmond with his own body against the bulkhead—and received a mass of bruises for his efforts. Yet even Matthews's valiant efforts did not protect Edmond's left leg, shattered in battle when his horse fell. Now he feared he would never ride again.

Murmured conversation drew his attention back to the gentle soul seated beside him. Poor, lovely Miss Newfield. Her dark brown hair formed a pleasing contrast to her flawless ivory complexion, and her lively green eyes exuded intelligence. Newfield had not exaggerated her beauty and grace. Or her faith. How bravely she bore her losses. Perhaps he could offer some cheering words, the kind of thing he might say to his cavalry unit after a bad sortie.

Before he could frame a thought, a pudgy, frowning man dressed in black approached the lady, followed by a woman wearing an identical scowl. A protective instinct arose within Edmond's chest.

"Miss Newfield." The man gave her a fawning bow and oily smile. "I am Danders, Squire Beamish's solicitor. He sends his condolences." His face looked anything but sympathetic. "I'm sure you understand that due to the length of your father's fatal illness, Squire Beamish has been forced to find a new cleric to minister to the good people of Blandon." He emitted an unpleasant chuckle that made the hair on Edmond's neck stand on end. Miss Newfield, however, remained serene. "Unfortunately, the new vicar and his family—" the solicitor glanced at the woman behind him "—seven children, wasn't it, Mrs. Danders? At Squire Beamish's invitation, they have all left their home in Surrey and even now are housed with us." His voice rose in pitch to a squeaky tenor. "Seven children. Heh-heh. Seems more like two dozen." He tugged at his collar. "So you will understand that they require the vicarage as soon as possible." Another shrill laugh. "Today, if you please."

Edmond found himself on his feet, leaning toward the solicitor from his own greater height. "What ails you, man, that you would intrude upon Miss Newfield's grief in this manner?" He struggled not to address this cur with the language of the battlefield.

Danders stared up at him, wide-eyed. Then he straightened his jacket, as if Edmond had given in to the temptation to grab it and shake him senseless. "I beg your pardon, um, *Major,* but exactly who are you and what business is this of yours?"

"Please, Major Grenville." Miss Newfield rose and touched his arm. "Do not trouble yourself. Just last week our village seamstress, Mrs. Brown, said I might live with her." With a nodding glance she indicated a nearby woman, whose face now filled with dismay.

"Oh, my dear." Mrs. Brown moved closer. "I didn't want to tell you so soon after dear Mr. Newfield's demise, but I've no room." She wrung her handkerchief. "My widowed sister has just come with her children, you see, and she needs a place to live."

Edmond watched with horror and amazement as this latest cannonball struck its target, for surely the young lady would crumble under this siege.

"I understand." Dry-eyed, Miss Newfield embraced her neighbor and murmured comforting assurances. A strange light shone in her fair brown eyes, and a hint of a smile graced her lips.

Edmond prayed the barrage of bad news had not commenced to drive her mad.

"Well, then," Mr. Danders said. "My wife will help you to gather your things, and you can be off."

Mrs. Danders shoved her way in front of Miss Newfield. "And don't be thinking you can run off with anything that ain't nailed down. I have a list from Squire Beamish—" she pulled a folded paper from her large reticule "—and I know every candlestick and serviette that belongs to the parish."

Now the young lady swayed slightly and her eyes lost their focus, as they had when Edmond had so brutishly announced her brother's death. But he could not help her, for his own head grew light. Rage over his weakness kept him from fainting, and he leveled a glare upon Danders. The man tugged at his collar again.

"Here, sir." Matthews was suddenly beside him, easing him back into his chair. "I've set a plate for you on this side table. Some nice cold meats, rolls, cheeses and pumpkin pie. The local housewives have made quite a feast."

"Let's get on with it, Miss Newfield." Mrs. Danders gripped the young lady's upper arm and dragged her toward the hallway.

"Yes, yes, of course." Miss Newfield's voice wavered. "Please do permit me to…"

The rest of her words were lost in the shuffling of feet as they exited the parlor door.

Edmond tried to rise and follow, but his legs betrayed him.

"Now." Danders hovered over Edmond and adjusted the spectacles resting on his pudgy nose. "Exactly what is your business with Miss Newfield? Squire Beamish will need to know *exactly* what has been going on here at the vicarage. If her character is suspect—"

Once again, anger brought Edmond to his feet. "How dare you?" Mrs. Brown's presence prevented him from speaking as he would to a scavenging mongrel. Good sense informed him that this weasel could do much harm to the young lady's reputation. Edmond suspected he was dishonest, but had no strength to investigate the matter, at least not yet. The best course was to give Danders the information he sought. "I have just arrived to inform Miss

Newfield that her brother perished in America fighting for England."

"Ah. Well, then." Danders waved away the news as he would a fly.

"'Tis the truth, Mr. Danders." Mrs. Brown continued to wring her handkerchief. "The cap'n here did just arrive. And furthermore, Miss Newfield's the soul of decency. Anyone in Blandon'll speak for her."

"Hmm." Danders lifted his nose and sniffed. "Ah, the smell of nuncheon. While my wife sees to the packing, I shall see to the kitchen. The pantry and all that's in it will of course belong to the parish." Before Edmond could respond, Danders hurried from the room.

"Will you sit, sir?" Matthews once again helped Edmond into the chair.

Frustration closed his throat. He could not think of eating. "Matthews, follow the women. See that Mrs. Danders does not mistreat Miss Newfield. If there is a dispute over any item in this house, we will not leave until this mysterious Squire Beamish has presented himself to settle the matter." *Nor will I leave until Miss Newfield is assured of a safe place to live.* It was the least he could do for the sister of the man who died to save him. And only then could he return to his family's home and begin rebuilding his own life and health. Only then could he begin to consider God's purpose for taking a remarkable man like Peter Newfield and leaving a scoundrel like Edmond Grenville.

Chapter Two

"This is the receipt for the storage chest." Anna held out the paper to Mrs. Danders. "My father purchased it for me nine years ago." She lifted a prayer of thanks for *Papá*'s meticulous record-keeping. Had he known she would one day have to give proof of ownership for her possessions?

The woman snatched the page from Anna's hand. "Hmm. Could be a forgery. But no matter. The trunk was bought with church money, so it belongs to the church." She ran a finger over the chest's finely carved lid.

"But my father purchased it with his wages. He gave it to me as a gift." Anna's head felt light, and she braced herself against the bedpost. "Surely it is mine."

"Not likely." Mrs. Danders lifted the lid and rummaged through the contents—Anna's summer dresses recently put away for the winter and a few linen towels she had embroidered in her younger days when she had hoped to marry. "Hmm. Nothing here of value." She dropped the lid, allowing it to slam against the base with a *clunk*.

Anna jumped. Her mind refused to work. *Lord, am I to lose everything?*

"What about jewelry?" Mrs. Danders's eyes narrowed. "What's that broach you're wearing?"

Anna clutched the silver filigree pin with a tiny sapphire set in the center. "My mother's." Not a lie. *Papá* had bought it for *Mamá*—with his wages.

"See here now." Major Grenville's man, Matthews, stuck his head in the door and aimed a glare at Mrs. Danders. "The major'll want an accounting of what you're up to."

Relief flooded Anna's heart. Answered prayer! "Thank you," she whispered to both the young man and the Lord.

"Indeed." Mrs. Danders balled her fists at her waist and glared back at the soldier. Then she looked about the room again. "Other than the furniture and this storage chest, there's nothing of value here. I'll see to those books in the parlor." She pushed past the aide and stomped down the hallway toward the staircase.

"We should follow, miss." Matthews waved one hand in that direction.

"Yes, of course." Anna tried to force her mind to work but other than her frantic prayers, no sensible thoughts would form. Gone were her plans to wander from room to room in a leisurely manner recalling her family's happy years in this vicarage. Gone were her hopes of packing away one or two mementos of her loved ones to carry with her wherever she went. She could cling only to God's promise that He would guide and take care of her, no matter what the circumstances. And *that* no one could take from her.

Returning to the parlor, she found the major sitting stiffly, leaning on his cane and watching Mrs. Danders like a hawk eyeing its prey. When Anna entered the room, he stood and gave her a slight bow. Before she could insist that he sit back down, she noticed Mrs. Danders pulling books from the shelf beside *Papá*'s chair. No, no longer *Papá*'s. It all belonged to the new vicar now. Anna hoped the gentleman would appreciate this small library that *Papá* had bought book by book, often instead of much-needed new clothes.

The pile of books on the floor toppled over, and *Papá*'s Bible slid across the floor.

Anna grabbed it before Mrs. Danders could. She clutched it to her chest, fighting tears. "My father brought this with him from Oxford."

The woman snorted in a most unladylike manner. "Keep it, then."

Mr. Danders hurried into the parlor with Mrs. Brown and Mrs. Pitcher, the baker's wife, hard on his heels and scolding him like magpies.

"I give that to the vicar's wife meself." Mrs. Pitcher pointed to the delicately painted porcelain teapot in the solicitor's hands. "It ain't yours. It's Miss Newfield's. And you'll give it to her now, or I'll fetch the oaken rolling pin you were so anxious to put on your list."

"And I'll be fetching that poker by the hearth, you old thief." Mrs. Brown's eyes blazed.

The two women traded a look and shook hands.

Anna's scalp tingled. God had sent her two more defenders, and perhaps in the process repaired the ancient quarrel which had long divided them. She crossed the room and grasped their still clasped hands. "Dear ladies, please do not resort to violence. Mr. Danders is merely doing his duty in cataloguing the contents of the house." Although she could not be certain that *Mrs.* Danders should be involved in the work.

Mr. Danders thrust the teapot at Mrs. Pitcher and let go. She barely had time to catch it. Muttering unintelligible words, she handed *Mamá*'s treasure to Anna. "There you go, m'dear."

"Thank you." Anna accepted the precious gift and held it close, along with the Bible, fearful of dropping them, yet just as fearful of putting either down. "Mr. Danders, I appreciate your attention to detail. Perhaps you have already settled the matter of my inheritance?" At his blank look, she hastened on. "The fifty pounds annual inheritance my father arranged through Squire Beamish?"

"What? Oh, that." He wrinkled his nose as if smelling something bad. "No, no, my dear. You misunderstood. It wasn't fifty pounds annual. It was fifty pounds, period. And unfortunately—" he traded a smirk with his wife "—only twenty pounds are available at present."

Anna's head grew light. "Only twenty?" Once again, her mind refused to work as shock overtook her. Then a memory emerged. She and *Papá* and Peter used to play a game, one that *Mamá* did not care for in the least. They called it "What's the worst thing that can happen?" Each player heaped misfortune upon an imaginary hero, all within the bounds of decency, all revealing how God could intervene and save the day. But never in their busiest imaginings had they ever burdened any fictional soul with the Job-like sorrows she had received this day. She had lost her family, her possessions and her place in the community. Now to be thrust out into the world with no place to go, she envisioned herself wandering down a muddy winter path, clutching a tattered cloth bag with her few earthly belongings, perhaps dying in a frigid snow bank on the side of the road. Picturing Peter's playful face, she wanted to laugh. Almost.

"Ah, books." Mr. Danders's eyebrows arched, and he moved toward his wife. "Yes, those are worth something."

"Hold." Major Grenville lifted his cane across the man's chest. "While Miss Newfield may be correct about your duty, I do not care for the manner in which you are carrying it out."

Instead of responding, Mr. Danders stared at Anna, his

narrowed eyes raking her up and down. "Hmm. We never did settle exactly who you are, did we, Major?" He removed his spectacles and wiped them on his sleeve, then returned them to his nose and swept another slow, critical gaze down Anna's frame and up again.

She gulped down her discomfort. No one had ever looked at her in that manner, and it somehow made her feel…unclean. She quickly dismissed the implication of his evil stare, for she had no cause for shame.

The major took a step toward the shorter man. "Watch yourself, sir." The growl in his voice sent a strange comfort shivering down Anna's back.

Mr. Danders laughed—an awful, menacing sound. "Or?"

The major returned the man's hard look. "As you can see, at present I am ill-fitted to follow through on any threat I may wish to make. However, my brother, Lord Greystone, will be very interested in the happenings in this corner of Shropshire, and you can be certain I shall apprise him of your actions."

Mr. Danders's eyes grew round again. "Lord Greystone?" The squeak returned to his voice.

"Further, sir, you will make copies of your inventory and the original list and send them to my brother without delay. Have I made myself clear?"

Mr. Danders tugged at his collar. "Yes. Very clear indeed." He waved a hand at his wife, wordlessly ordering her to put down the books she had begun placing in a leather satchel.

"Now, Miss Newfield," the major said, "we must decide on where you are to go. I have my brother's carriage at your disposal. My batman and I have just come up from Portsmouth on our way to Greystone Lodge. If you would accept the hospitality of my mother, the viscountess, we can be there in a matter of five or six hours."

Hope welled up inside of Anna. Was this the Lord's provision? "I do not know what to say, sir. Surely your mother would not welcome an unexpected guest."

A frown crossed his brow as he limped toward her. She met him halfway across the distance and experienced the full effects of his superior height and broad shoulders. My, what an impressive soldier he made. And yet, even one so well-equipped for his duty had been brought down by injury. Still, when he bent to speak quietly to her, her heart fluttered like a quaking sparrow.

"I received word upon landing in Portsmouth that my mother's elderly companion has passed away." He glanced toward the Danderses, who both stared at this innocent tête-à-tête with far too much interest. The major set a gentle hand upon her shoulder and turned her away from their prying eyes. "Mother is…she, well, hmm." His gaze lit on the two items Anna still held, and she detected a twinkle in his eyes. "Miss Newfield, I believe you may safely put down your treasures. I will make certain they are not…misplaced."

Warmth crept into her cheeks. "Oh. Yes. Of course." She set the Bible and teapot on the occasional table and returned to his side. "I am deeply grieved to hear of your mother's loss. Is there anything I can do to help?"

A note of sadness colored his soft chuckle. "What an interesting young lady you are. In the midst of your own grief, you are concerned about someone you do not even know." His intense gaze brought more heat to her face, and she could think of no response. "Mother does not like to be alone. I would be pleased to recommend you for her new companion."

"Yes." Mrs. Pitcher inserted herself into the conversation. "That's just the thing."

"Indeed it is." Mrs. Brown appeared at her former adversary's elbow. "But you cannot travel alone with this gentleman." She glanced over her shoulder toward the solicitor. "That one seems the sort who would speak ill of you just for spite."

The major nodded his agreement. "Perhaps one of you could accompany us to Greystone Lodge. You could return by the post on the morrow. At my expense, of course."

"Ah, 'twould be grand to see inside a viscount's manor house." Mrs. Pitcher sighed. "Alas, my husband cannot do without me at the bakery. Gladys, you'll have to go."

Mrs. Brown's face became a progressive comedy: Surprise, skepticism, comprehension, then utter joy danced across her countenance. "Why, I can't think of a single hindrance."

Major Grenville smiled. Grinned, actually. "What say you, Miss Newfield?"

Anna placed a hand over her mouth as hot tears flooded her cheeks. All she could manage was a trembling nod. How good the Lord was to her. Before she called upon Him, He had already answered. Before she had known of her own need, He had already prepared a place for her. She lifted a silent prayer for the dearly departed old companion, gone to her reward.

"And now—" Mrs. Pitcher raised her voice, and all heads turned her way. "Gladys and I will help you pack, m'dear." She glared at the solicitor. "And may the good Lord help anybody who tries to interfere."

The two women made decisions about what to bring, for Anna could not put together a single coherent thought. They packed the wooden chest, which the major insisted belonged to her, working quickly so the travelers could reach Greystone Lodge before nightfall. All too soon the major's carriage rumbled out of Blandon, and Anna left behind the only life she had ever known. It was all she could do not to weep aloud, even as tears blurred her vision.

No, she must not break down. Instead, she would cling to the precious promise that one day all of these trials would seem as nothing. One day she would behold the Lord, just as *Papá* now did…and *Mamá,* gone these four years…and every trial would disappear. As for Peter, she would hold out hope that he was simply missing, perhaps a prisoner of the Americans. She prayed he would be treated with kindness, just as he would treat someone kindly who was under his charge.

The Lord had left her alone for some reason. During *Papá*'s illness, she came to realize she must find an occupation, never mind the social prejudice against a woman of the gentry engaging in work. It would be irresponsible for her to starve to death when she could support herself and perhaps do some good in the process. If the major's mother did not approve of her as a companion, the Lord would give her some other employment. She simply must discover what it was.

Chapter Three

Despite the carriage's cushioned upholstery and excellent springs, Edmond felt every bump on the road to Greystone Lodge. But at least the rutted highway held none of the surprises that plagued ocean travel: sudden plunges into watery troughs or massive swells that almost capsized the ship. How good it felt to be back on land and on his way home, if he might still consider the Lodge home. Lord Greystone had always been generous to his two younger brothers and would never turn them out. But a man must establish his own residence, his own occupation. Edmond longed to return to his Oxford law studies and become a barrister, but whether or not he could do so remained to be seen. After fighting on the Continent and in America for five years, he desired peace and rest, no matter what work he must set his hands to. Surely even Mother would see he was not fit to return to war.

Ah, well, time enough to ponder those matters while he healed. For now, he must play host to the other occupants of the carriage, particularly Miss Newfield, who seemed to be struggling to contain her tears. Brave girl. For once in his life, he felt as if the hand of the Almighty had directed him. On the monthlong voyage home, he had made up his mind to deliver the news of Newfield's heroic death in person rather than by letter. But when he came upon the vicar's funeral and subsequent harassment of the poor young lady, he felt certain his plan had been God's doing. Perhaps this was the first step in his quest to discover his purpose on this earth.

On the other hand, now that they were on the way to the Lodge, he was reconsidering the wisdom of bringing her home with him. Yet what else could he have done? Like a desperate act executed amidst the chaos of battle, Edmond's offer had been the only weapon he could grasp to save Miss Newfield. And however weak a defender he might be, he could not, would not abandon her.

Of course, he must consider Mother's reaction, but he would not think about that now. Instead, he cast about in his mind how he might engage Miss Newfield in conversation. What topic might a vicar's daughter find interesting? In fact, what might any young lady wish to discuss? Edmond had never perfected the art. As a younger son, he had met with young ladies' turned backs more often than the friendly faces they offered his titled eldest brother. That painful memory dampened his spirits. Like any man, he wished to marry one day, but until he established himself in a lucrative profession, no Society lady would welcome his attentions. And he could hardly blame them. Why, even a poor gentlewoman like Miss Newfield deserved a husband who could adequately support her. Had no such gentleman resided in Blandon? Surely someone had aspired to win the hand of such a fair prize. Were they of like social rank, he might be tempted to court her himself after he regained his health.

Anna's prior experiences in wheeled conveyances were limited to clattering dog carts and bumpy hay wagons.

In contrast, the viscount's roomy carriage had cushioned velvet seats and large wheels on springs that rolled over the rutted highway more smoothly than she ever imagined. It swayed almost like a cradle, lulling her toward the solace of sleep, for she was weary in body and numbed by her many losses. But sleeping might be considered rude. In an effort to shake off her drowsiness, she took deep breaths and peered through the wide windows to view the changing scenery from fields to forests to villages and back to fields again. Harvest was underway in all parts of Shropshire, and the scents of apples and newly mown hay filled the brisk autumn air all along the route.

Mrs. Brown sat beside Anna, her knitting needles clicking softly in time with the rumbling wheels. Across from them, Matthews slumbered against the padded carriage wall. Beside him, Major Grenville grimaced from time to time, then schooled his face into a milder expression. At these brave attempts to mask his pain, Anna's heart went out to him. Perhaps she could distract him from his misery by engaging him in conversation.

What did one say to an army officer, an aristocratic gentleman whose titled brother sat in Parliament? Should she even begin a conversation with someone of his rank? In fact, the thought of meeting such an august person as the viscount set her nerves on edge. That was nonsense, of course. Did not the scriptures teach that all were equal in Christ? But while she might believe it, she had often heard that the aristocracy and, even more, the nobility considered themselves far above other mortals. She would soon find out whether Lord Greystone and his mother, the viscountess, held that opinion. Furthermore, Anna could not guess what being a lady's companion entailed. She hesitated to ask the major, lest such questions be deemed improper.

One subject did come to mind that she would venture to address.

"Major, would you mind—"

"Miss Newfield, are you—"

They spoke at the same time, each stopping midsentence.

"Pray continue, Miss Newfield." He smiled and waved his hand for her to proceed.

"I thank you, sir." Anna's cheeks warmed at his courtesy. "I wonder if you could tell me more about my brother. He is not one to write home, although we did hear from him just after he arrived in Detroit last year."

Instantly she regretted her question, for the major frowned and gazed out the window as if he had not heard her. After a moment, he turned back, his eyes filled with kindness.

"I met Lieutenant Newfield upon his arrival. He was a charming lad, full of good humor and laughter. You must have grown up in a merry and loving household, madam, for he always made light of any difficulty." Pain, which she sensed was more emotional than physical, shot across his features.

"That's our Master Peter." Mrs. Brown looked up from her knitting, her eyes misty. "The whole village loved him in spite of his boyish pranks. The mischief was never wicked, you understand, just meant to make us laugh at ourselves. And now—" She stared down at her handiwork and fell silent.

Despair crept into Anna's chest. Was Peter truly dead? No, she would not believe it. Missing did not mean deceased. "Please tell me more, Major."

The gentleman's smile seemed strained as he proceeded to recount how Peter chattered endlessly about his godly father and his "perfect" sister. She laughed and rolled her eyes, for when they were children, she had often joined her brother in his escapades.

The major's batman awoke and joined the conversation, reporting an instance of mischief so very much like Peter. Briefly the carriage rang with laughter. Then all fell silent.

Bracing herself, Anna captured the major's gaze. "You must tell me about that day."

He stared at her for a long moment, his dark eyes shadowed in the enclosed carriage. "A soldier does not like to admit defeat, madam, but unfortunately we were in retreat from the American forces. A company of their foot soldiers attacked our cavalry, and Providence was on their side. My horse was shot from under me." He winced, and Anna sensed the creature had meant much to him. "Or, I should say, on top of me. My left leg was beneath him, so of course I could not move. Several of the enemy regarded me as an easy target. One raised his saber to strike." He sucked in his cheeks and looked out the window for a moment. "Lieutenant Newfield threw himself across me. I heard him cry out." He paused as if reliving the scene, then shook it off. "That is the last thing I recall. I awoke in a field hospital some days later. No one could answer my queries about your brother. No one saw him after the battle."

Anna swallowed hard and forcefully dismissed the despair threatening to seize her. "Missing does not mean dead. Even if I never hear from him, I shall trust that God spared him. That he is somewhere in America recovering from his wounds." She tried to soften the strain in her voice, but could not. "Whyever would the Lord create such a good, gallant soul only to take him away from those who love and need him?" She stared about her small circle of companions, beseeching someone to explain the mind of God.

Beside her, Mrs. Brown sniffed. Matthews would not meet her gaze. The major reached out to touch her hand. "Indeed, dear lady, whyever would He?"

The sun touched the treetops and then sank behind their foliage before the carriage rolled up the long drive to Greystone Lodge. In the fading daylight, Edmond could see Greystone's banner raised on the flagpole above the pointed roof of the old brick manor house, announcing His Lordship was at home. After his three-year absence, Edmond felt both his anticipation and his anxiety grow with every mile. Yet his guest now wore a serene expression, as if unconcerned about the coming interview. He found it interesting that she had used their travel time to ask about Peter rather than the woman who would be her employer, if all went well. But then, no doubt she was still numb from the tragic news her day had brought. Edmond prayed she would receive no further shocks—now or ever.

The fading daylight shadowed the massive stone building as the carriage rolled up to the half-circle drive at the front entrance. In spite of the conveyance's roominess, Anna's legs felt cramped from the long drive, but she had no doubt the major's discomfort was far more intense. Still, he did not complain as they disembarked.

Grooms and servants appeared, and soon the small party found themselves in the manor house's large drawing room. There the major leaned on his cane and gazed about the room, a soft smile gracing his lean, handsome face. How good it must be for him to return to his childhood home, which now belonged to his brother, the viscount.

Anna experienced a pang of sorrow, for she would never see her own home again. Indeed, she had no home. She quickly cast aside the thought, relishing instead the scent of roses wafting from an arrangement on a nearby side table and admiring the lovely furnishings that filled the room: plush velvet chairs and settees, portraits of noble ancestors, bisque figurines and heavy draperies. She had never beheld such elegance. Mrs. Brown's wide-eyed perusal of their surroundings revealed that she was likewise awestruck.

A middle-aged butler strode into the room and announced, "Lady Greystone."

Anna's heart jolted. The moment had come. She straightened and squeezed Mrs. Brown's hand. Her friend returned the gesture and whispered good wishes.

A slender woman of medium height entered the room. Her dark grey hair was arranged in curls around her thin face, softening what some might consider hawk-like features. Anna noted her resemblance to Major Grenville and wondered whether the woman possessed his generous disposition as well.

"Edmond." The woman marched toward her son, her gloved right hand extended. "Welcome home." Despite her words of greeting, her tone rang with formality.

"Mother." Major Grenville bowed and kissed her offered hand. "You look well."

"Humph. What else would you say to me?" She stepped back and viewed him up and down. "You, on the other hand, do not look well at all." She reached up and gripped his chin, turning his head one way, then the other, and emitted another disagreeable harrumph. "Still, you will live to serve another day."

Anna's heart sank. When Peter returned to her, she would embrace him and shower him with sisterly kisses and loving affirmation. How could this woman be so cold to her wounded son who had sailed across the ocean to fight for England?

Major Grenville gave her a warm smile. "Just so, Mother, if they want a cavalry officer who may not be able to ride as he once did."

Yet another harrumph from the lady. "Nonsense. They would not dare to turn down Greystone's brother. I shall see to it."

Anna's mind spun as she observed the woman's attitude. Even Mrs. Brown must be shocked, for she gasped softly.

Lady Greystone's head whipped around in their direction, and her dark, elegant eyebrows rose. "Who on earth are these creatures? How dare you bring them into my drawing room?" She eyed the major briefly before stepping over to Anna and glaring at her up and down through the single lens of her quizzing glass. "And just what is *this* one to you?"

The major limped forward, worry creasing his forehead. "Mother, forgive me, but when I read your letter about Miss Peel's demise, I knew you would be searching for a new companion. This young lady is a vicar's daughter and—"

"How dare you?" The viscountess turned her quizzing glass toward him with a fierce glare. "Do you think you can just snatch up some dowdy creature from the roadside and bring her through my front door into my drawing room to be my companion?" Her angry stare returned to Anna.

"You." She sneered as if Anna smelled bad, and stepped back as one would from a victim of the plague. "Take your servant and get out."

Chapter Four

"Wait." Edmond leaned on Matthews's arm and limped after Mother. "Madam, I beg your indulgence. This is no stranger from the side of the road." He swallowed hard, wondering how much longer he could remain on his feet. "Miss Newfield's brother saved my life and died in the process." He glanced at the young woman, who winced at his words. He despised dashing her hopes that her brother might yet live. But Mother would respond better to a brave soldier's death than to one who simply remained missing. In the corner of his eye, he noticed the outrage on Mrs. Brown's plump face. If the woman spoke up to her betters, all would be lost.

He hastened to fill in the silence as Mother's stare continued to rake the young woman up and down through her quizzing glass. "As I said, she is a vicar's daughter of flawless reputation."

Mother's head snapped toward Edmond and then back toward Miss Newfield. "Indeed."

"Yes, madam." He sent Miss Newfield and her companion a warning frown indicating that he would speak for them. "And Mrs. Brown is a renowned and much-in-demand seamstress in her town, yet she took time from

her work to accompany her friend for propriety's sake."
At the compliment, Mrs. Brown's angry flush softened to
a pleased blush.

"Hmm." Mother's slender eyebrows, always an indicator of her mood, lowered from their aristocratic arch. She
tapped her quizzing glass against her chin, then circled
Miss Newfield as a man might circle a horse he was ap-
praising. "Hmm," she repeated. "Do you read, *gel?*"

Miss Newfield executed a perfect curtsey. "Yes, Lady
Greystone. English, French and Latin." For the first time
in their brief acquaintance, Edmond noticed her flawless
diction. Where had she learned to speak so well?

Mother's eyebrows arched again, this time in surprise.
"Indeed?" She harrumphed. "Educated by your father, I
suppose."

Ah, yes. Edmond recalled the incident with the vicar's
Bible brought from Oxford, where all Greystone sons had
attended school. Another connection with the Newfield
family formed in his mind, but he would wait to mention
that to Mother.

"Yes, my lady." Miss Newfield's demeanor was everything proper in tone and posture, at once both confident
and deferential.

Edmond felt a surge of pride, as if she were one of his
soldiers who had met the approval of a superior. Pride, and
perhaps a hint of affection such as he felt for Matthews.

"Are you a bluestocking?" Mother's contempt for those
women was evident in her haughty tone.

"I—I…" Miss Newfield glanced at Edmond, her head
tilted in a pretty, questioning pose.

"Mother, I doubt the Bluestocking Literary Society
meets in such a small village as Blandon."

Understanding filled Miss Newfield's eyes, and she gave
Edmond a grateful smile. A strange feeling filled his chest.

Once again he had found a way to help the young lady, and it gave him every bit as much satisfaction as winning a battle.

"Humph." Mother came close to sneering. "Who are your people?"

Miss Newfield's poise remained intact. "My lady, my father was the second son of a gentleman whose grandfather was knighted by Her Majesty Queen Anne."

"And your father chose to bury himself in a remote village? Could he not obtain a better living through influential friends?"

"I do not know, my lady. But his people loved him."

Mrs. Brown mumbled her agreement, but Mother appeared not to hear her and continued to stare at Miss Newfield.

"Well." She shot a glance at Edmond. "We shall see if she suits." She turned toward him. "I will forgive you for bringing servants into my drawing room because of these unusual circumstances. This one may help you." She waved a hand at Matthews. "But only as long as you require his assistance. That one—" a sniff toward Mrs. Brown "—*renowned* seamstress or not, will remain in the servants' quarters." She strode to the bell pull beside the marble hearth and gave it a yank. "You will be in your old chambers. Mrs. Dobbins will assign a room to Miss Newman...Newmarket—"

"Newfield." Edmond recognized his mother's method of putting people in their places. That was her way, as if she alone guarded the social order of England. Clearly, she thought the great-granddaughter of a knight, whose descendants received no title or lands, did not warrant any amount of attention or respect.

"Yes," she drawled. "I shall grant Newfield a time of trial. Should she prove inadequate, she will be sent away.

Should she attempt to raise herself above her station, she will be turned out."

Edmond saw alarm flicker in the young woman's eyes, followed by a glint of courage as she recovered by force of will. The sight heartened him. She would need that strength in this house. "And her pay?"

Mother sniffed. "Pay? Humph. Her needs will be met. That is sufficient."

Edmond ground his teeth at her stinginess. Nothing ever changed here. One would think he had gone out the front door just this morning and been in America for only a day.

Miss Newfield, however, curtseyed to his mother again. "Thank you, my lady. I am grateful."

Mother reached out and lifted Miss Newfield's chin. "Hmm. Your eyes are clear, your posture acceptable. Perhaps your youthful energies will be a welcome diversion. Peel never had energy. Do you ride, *gel?*"

"No, my lady." Her tone held even.

Once again, Edmond's approval soared. This gentlewoman was not easily intimidated.

"You will learn. Greystone's groom will teach you," Mother pronounced, then peered over her shoulder at Edmond.

He gave her his best smile. Unfortunately, it felt more like a grimace.

"Oh, do retire, Edmond, before you drop on my drawing room floor. I shall have supper sent up."

"If you do not mind, madam, I should like to see Greystone." Somehow he would manage to hold on if his eldest brother was about the manor house.

"He is out seeing to his tenants. I do not expect him back soon."

"Permit me, sir." Matthews nudged Edmond toward the door.

"Very well. In the morning, then." With more than a little reluctance, Edmond gave his apologies and left Miss Newfield to the care of his mother, Lady Greystone, whom he and his brothers had sometimes referred to as Lady Gorgon when they were boys.

Anna watched Major Grenville and his batman move toward the drawing room door, her heart sinking lower with his every step. Upon their exit, the room seemed to grow colder. As if she shared the same sensation, Mrs. Brown moved closer, her plump arm cushioning Anna's trembling one. Anna prayed her friend would not speak up to Lady Greystone, or speak at all, lest she cause an offense.

The people of Blandon had little to do with the aristocracy. Even Squire Beamish, a mere gentleman, rarely visited the village, although he was responsible for its care. Such neglect gave the denizens of the area a sense of independence, which Anna could now see had resulted in a certain ignorance about how to behave around the well-born.

In truth, she herself knew very little about such manners except what her mother had taught her. But instinct kept her from addressing her new employer, who stood with arms crossed, tapping her foot on the colorful woven carpet that lay in front of the gleaming white marble hearth. Within minutes, a woman of perhaps fifty years entered the room, her footfalls making no sound on the wooden floor.

"Yes, Lady Greystone?" The woman wore a simple black woolen dress, and her greying brown hair was pulled severely into a bun at the nape of her neck. Her posture was rigid, her face an expressionless mask.

"This is Mrs. Dobbins, my housekeeper." Lady Greystone

glanced at Anna. "Mrs. Dobbins, this is Newfield, my new companion. You will give her Peel's room."

"Yes, my lady." Mrs. Dobbins beckoned to Anna. "If you please, miss." Her slight nod to Mrs. Brown was an order to follow her, as well.

Following the housekeeper, Anna wondered if she should offer some parting words of gratitude to Lady Greystone, but a glance over her shoulder revealed the viscountess making her own exit through a different door, which had been opened by a blue uniformed footman Anna had mistaken for a statue.

In the manor house's front entryway, Mrs. Dobbins's rigid posture relaxed considerably even as she retained a dignified carriage. So even the most powerful servant in the house feared Lady Greystone. Anna would not try to guess what challenges lay ahead. She prayed only that she would not disappoint Major Grenville and that his kindness to her would not cause a problem between him and his mother.

"Oh, Anna dear." Mrs. Brown gazed around the large, dimly lit chamber. "Such a grand house, but there don't seem to be much happiness here."

"If you please." Mrs. Dobbins gave Mrs. Brown a scorching look. "Servants do not speak unless addressed."

"I ain't no servant—"

Anna set a hand on her friend's arm. "Thank you, Mrs. Dobbins. I am certain we have much to learn."

"Just so, miss." The woman began her ascent up the gracefully curved marble staircase. Her gnarled hands gripped the dark oak banister, and she pulled herself up each step.

Anna's heart went out to the woman. It appeared her knees gave her much pain, as Father's had toward the end of his life. Had Major Grenville experienced as much difficulty climbing this staircase with his wounded leg? Perhaps both would benefit from willow bark.

At the top of the stairs, Mrs. Dobbins indicated a long hallway on the right. "Do not enter that wing. Lord Greystone's chambers are there, as are his brothers'. Follow me." She marched stiffly down another hall, stopping at a wide white door. "This is Lady Greystone's suite. You must not enter unless summoned." Continuing on, she came to a smaller door across the hall. "Here is your room, miss."

She led them inside where Anna gazed around in wonder. The chamber was half again larger than her old room at the vicarage. The furnishings were elegant but not lavish, with everything she would require to be comfortable: a four-poster bed covered with a green counterpane, a mahogany wardrobe and a wingchair. In addition, a tall window—or perhaps it was a door—promised sunny mornings, for she guessed it to be on the east side of the house. What more could she ask for?

"I will have your baggage brought up," Mrs. Dobbins said. "If Lady Greystone wishes you to dine with the family tonight, she will send word. I shall send up supper if she does not ask for you." She listed more rules of the house and imparted other essential information, while Anna wondered how she would remember it all.

After a tearful embrace, Anna said goodbye to Mrs. Brown. The dear lady would depart by early post the next morning, leaving Anna bereft of all she had ever known.

No, not bereft. In the scriptures, the Lord said He would never leave her nor forsake her. She would rest in that promise. And perhaps if she could see Major Grenville's friendly smile from time to time, it would give her the strength to carry on in her new life.

Chapter Five

Edmond awoke to the midday sun streaming through the double glass doors leading to his balcony. He had slept long and well for the first time in years. No narrow army cots in tents that failed to keep out wind and rain. No ships' berths on rolling seas. No lumpy mattresses in wayside inns. Amazing what one night of good rest could do for a man.

Across the room Matthews dozed in a chair, his uniform in surprisingly tidy condition. Had he risen early and made himself presentable in anticipation of Edmond's needs?

As if his thoughts had sent out a signal, Matthews jerked awake and rubbed his eyes. "'Morning, sir." He stood, tugged at his red jacket and lifted his eyebrows expectantly. "Good sleep?"

"Good, indeed." Edmond stretched and yawned. "I suppose Greystone's already had his morning ride." He still was not certain he could ride, but he would attempt it to spend time with his brother away from the house.

Matthews chuckled. "Aye, sir. Twice."

"Huh?" Edmond threw his legs over the side of the bed and snatched up his dressing gown. "What do you mean?"

A few odd aches reminded him of his injuries, but not nearly as painfully as on the long trip home.

"You've slept since we arrived evening before last, sir."

"What?" Edmond surrendered to the news by plopping back on the bed with a hearty laugh. Just as quickly, he shot to his feet, swaying a bit as he regained his balance. "What news of Miss Newfield?" More precisely, how had Mother treated her?

"Not much, sir. Below stairs says Lady Greystone hasn't summoned her yet, so she's kept to her room."

"Uh-oh. Not good." Edmond ran his hands over his face. "Let's get me presentable so I can go find out what's what."

While Matthews called for water and laid out fresh clothing, Edmond opened the doors and stepped out onto the narrow balcony. The familiar meadows and distant woods dappled with autumn colors sent a vague pang of longing through him. He inhaled a deep breath of the crisp October air to bring his thoughts more into focus. Despite Mother's sternness, she was not a beast. Nor was she forgetful. So why would she leave Miss Newfield in her room all this time? Old Miss Peel had been permitted to wander the house and grounds at will when Mother had no need of her companionship. Perhaps the young lady did not understand her privileges. Edmond slapped his forehead. He had indeed failed her by not informing her of what would be expected.

His gaze strayed toward the east wing of the L-shaped manor house, and something jolted in his chest. There stood Miss Newfield on her balcony, her black mourning weeds blowing about her in the mild wind. Across the distance he could not quite make out the expression on her fair face, but her straight posture gave no indication of misery. Considering what he had witnessed of her character so far, he should have had more faith in her ability to cope, no matter what the circumstances.

She turned his way and lifted a hand to wave at him. Now he could make out a smile, and he waved back. Admiration and satisfaction filled him. She was faring well in spite of her solitude. He could ask for nothing more.

Anna wondered whether she had erred by waving first, but in her happiness at seeing Major Grenville, her hand seemed to lift of its own accord. Apparently he did not find her greeting inappropriate, for his broad smile reflected her own. Then, noticing that his dark red clothing was not his uniform but a dressing gown, heat rushed to her cheeks. Perhaps aristocrats had different customs regarding what was appropriate to wear out of doors. She offered a tentative parting wave and returned to her bedchamber.

Her foolishness struck her immediately, for her balcony seemed an extension of this room. No doubt the major felt the same way about his childhood quarters, so of course he would step outside upon waking. Had she not done the same thing these two mornings? She prayed his smile was an indicator that his health was already improving.

Taking a seat in the upholstered wingchair beside the bed, she picked up *Papá*'s Bible and resumed a search she had begun the day before. Surely some scriptural example could help her discover how to be useful in this household, but until she understood her employer, she could not be certain her actions would be appropriate. Lady Greystone had not sent for her, and Mrs. Dobbins had made it clear she was not to leave until summoned. Thus she had remained in the room, reading her Bible and praying for Lady Greystone, Lord Greystone, kind Major Grenville and all of the dear people she had left behind. And of course Peter, healing somewhere in the vast wilderness called America.

"Miss Newfield?" The call through her door was followed by a scratch, and she set aside her Bible to cross the chamber and open the door.

"Good morning, Johnson." Anna gave the butler a welcoming smile. Other than the little chambermaid who brought hot water each morning, he was the only person she had seen, and only when he brought her meals. But this time he brought no tray, and Anna's stomach rumbled a quiet protest.

"Lady Greystone requires your presence in the breakfast room." The man's formal facade never wavered. "If you would follow me, please."

"Oh, yes." Excitement, gratitude…and a hint of fear… swept through Anna. At last she would learn about her duties. "Thank you." She felt a mad impulse to ask the butler whether her appearance was acceptable, but refrained.

Johnson started down the hallway, but uncertainty drew Anna to the long mirror on her wardrobe door for a quick inspection. She touched the high collar of her black bombazine gown and checked the tidiness of her hair, which was pulled into a soft bun a little less severe than Mrs. Dobbins's. *Mamá*'s silver and sapphire pin was her only adornment, but at the last moment she removed it and stored it in the drawer of her dressing table, lest it be considered improper for mourning.

She hurried out of her room, but the butler had vanished. Walking in the direction he had gone, she hoped memory served correctly and she would find the front stairway around the corner. Her weariness two nights ago had prevented her from making sufficient mental notes about her surroundings, which would be humorous under other circumstances. But she certainly did not wish to get lost in this great house.

She turned the corner and entered a broad space that indeed led to the stairs. Relieved, she strode across the patterned runner, hoping to see the butler descending the staircase.

"Miss Newfield."

The call came from her left. She turned to see Major Grenville walking slowly toward her, cane in hand and Matthews at his side. The major's color had greatly improved, as had his posture. His uniform of a red jacket and white breeches appeared spotless. Morning light shone through tall windows across from the landing and glinted off his black boots, which were polished to a brilliant sheen. As he came near, she was reminded of his height, and her awe increased. What a fine-looking soldier. With some difficulty, she tamped down the giddiness stirring within her as he approached.

"Major Grenville, how well you look."

"As do you." His smile gladdened her heart. "What do you think of the Lodge? Has anyone taken you out to see the gardens and the park yet?"

"I, um…" As they walked side by side to the wide staircase and began their descent, Anna searched for a response that would not cast aspersions on his mother. "Lady Greystone has just now sent for me and—"

"So it's true?" He stopped suddenly and seemed about to pitch forward.

"Easy, sir." Matthews was beside him, ready to assist.

Anna stopped, too, and heat rushed to her cheeks. But what else could she have said?

The major leaned toward her, frowning. "I heard you haven't been summoned from your room since we arrived."

Standing two steps above her, he seemed even more formidable. "That's outrageous."

Under his scrutiny, Anna drew in a bracing breath and somehow managed a light laugh. "I am certain Lady Greystone understood my need to recover from the journey. You cannot imagine how I appreciated the opportunity to rest."

He relaxed a bit and his frown slowly faded, replaced by a sad smile. "You would say that, wouldn't you?" He resumed his descent and she fell in beside him. "In fact, I've slept these two days myself."

"Ah. Then you do feel better?"

By the time they reached the ground floor, their conversation had shifted to the safe topic of weather and hopes of spending time outside in the sunshine before winter closed in.

"Perhaps you can begin your riding lessons." The major's firm, well-formed lips quirked up on one side, and one eyebrow lifted. He was teasing her, just as Peter used to do, and her heart skipped.

In response, she shuddered comically. "And perhaps not."

His laughter echoed throughout the hall just as they reached a door a footman held open for them. Anna surmised it was the breakfast room, for the aromas of coffee, sausages, eggs and freshly baked bread greeted her senses in the most pleasant way. Her stomach registered its request for satisfaction, and she hoped no one could hear. As she, the major and Matthews entered, the inhabitants seated at the dining table turned as one. Two gentlemen stood and offered enthusiastic greetings to the major.

"Here comes the hero." The man at the head of the table, surely the viscount, strode toward them. As tall as the major and equally well-proportioned, he might have been a twin save for his sky-blue eyes.

"Brother." The second man, almost a triplet except for his lighter brown hair, also approached him. "Welcome home." Anna assumed this gentleman was the cleric Major Grenville had spoke of during their journey.

Lady Greystone, seated at the foot of the table, regarded them through her quizzing glass. "It is past time you put in an appearance, Edmond." Her stare landed briefly on Anna, and her lips curled up with distaste before she turned back to her youngest son. "What, pray tell, did you find so humorous before you entered the room?"

Edmond ignored Mother's question, choosing instead to plunge into the embrace of his two older brothers. "Greystone. Richard." Much backslapping and many endearing insults ensued while the brothers reestablished the bond that had been their lifeline since they were boys. Separated by mere fourteen-month intervals, they now appeared very near the same age, or so it seemed to Edmond.

"So, Greystone, what news from Parliament? Have you saved the country from the French yet?"

The viscount waved away the question. "You first. You must tell us about the war in America."

"Only after I congratulate Richard for his ordination." With the hope that no one would ask him about the war again, at least not in Miss Newfield's company, Edmond clapped a hand on his middle brother's shoulder. "Do you have a living yet?"

Richard glanced in Mother's direction. "Um, well—"

"Never mind," Edmond murmured. No doubt Mother was directing Richard's appointments as she did his own. "You can tell me later."

"Yes, well." Greystone gripped Edmond's arm. "Richard, you must present our baby brother to our new sister."

"Ah, I'd heard that you married." Edmond followed Richard to the table, where a pretty and very expectant young lady stood, a light blush coloring her pale cheeks. "Mary, may I present my brother Edmond of His Majesty's Royal Dragoons."

"Mrs. Grenville." Edmond bent over her offered hand, while she dipped an unsteady curtsey and then leaned against Richard. The tender look that passed between them sent a strange longing through Edmond, even as he rejoiced in his brother's happiness. "What a lovely addition to our family. Welcome."

"Thank you, Major. You must call me Mary."

"And I am Edmond." He glanced at Mother, who sat observing the melee with her usual imperious facade. Was she pleased at the prospect of her first grandchild? He walked around the table and kissed her cheek. "Good morning, madam."

"Humph." While she did not rebuff him, she also did not return his kiss. "Sit down and eat. The sooner you regain your strength, the sooner you can return to duty."

Not if he could sell his commission and resume his study of law. "Yes, madam." As he moved toward his assigned seat where he had eaten many a meal while growing up, he noticed Miss Newfield still standing by the door. Remembering Mother's neglect, he started to invite the young lady to the table.

"Come, come, Newfield." Mother whipped her hand in the air, summoning her and indicating her place adjacent to the foot of the table in one gesture. "Here beside me."

"Yes, my lady." Miss Newfield's voice was strong and confident. With a grace worthy of an aristocrat, she sat in the chair pulled out by the footman. Once again Edmond experienced no shame for bringing the lady to his mother, for she had not cowered in the midst of the family chaos. Seated beside her, he offered a smile, to which she responded in kind.

When a footman brought serving dishes, Edmond saw the hesitation in the lady's eyes. Directing the man with a tilt of his head, he demonstrated how to serve his own plate. She followed suit, smiling her appreciation of the silent lesson. During their journey he had learned of her limited experience with servants, so he must look for opportunities to inform her of how to accept their service.

"This is my new companion," Mother said amidst the flurry of breakfast being distributed around the table. "Her name is Newfield." She took a sip of coffee. "Now, today I should like—"

The door opened and Johnson brought in the mail on a silver tray. He paused and glanced between Mother and Greystone, then carried the tray to the viscount. Edmond guessed the senior servants were often confused when Greystone was in residence, for Mother had ruled the house since Father had died some twenty-three years ago. When Greystone reached his majority six years ago, other than his entering Parliament, nothing changed. But then, Edmond's eldest brother had always been an agreeable fellow, taking Mother's dominance in stride.

When Johnson delivered the tray to Greystone, Edmond experienced a hint of satisfaction. Then a hint of shame. Scripture instructed a man to honor his parents, but it was rarely an easy task with Mother.

"Ah, good news." Greystone held up a letter. "Uncle Grenville is coming for a visit. Should arrive the first week in November."

"What?" Mother set down her coffee cup with a clink. "How dare he invite himself—"

"Not at all." Greystone raised a hand to stop her. "I invited him."

"You invited him?" Mother breathed out an angry sigh. "Well, then, I suppose I have no say in the matter."

Edmond seized a bite of bread to keep from cheering. Perhaps Greystone was at last taking his rightful place as head of the family.

Greystone did not respond, but Richard, ever the peacemaker, leaned toward Mother. "You began to tell us your plans for the day. Is there any way Mary and I may help?"

Mother answered with one of her impatient "harrumphs," and everyone fell to eating with no further comments.

Edmond's thoughts darted here and there with unreasoning emotion not far behind. Perhaps Uncle Grenville's visit was an answered prayer, if one could call a man's fervent hopes a prayer. Father's younger brother was a London barrister, Edmond's desired profession. He had begun his law studies at Oxford until Mother insisted upon his joining the dragoons. How little she knew about her youngest son, for he would far rather face courtroom battles than the military sort. But the prospect of gaining his uncle's patronage sent hope bubbling up in Edmond's chest, and he coughed to clear his throat rather than choke on a bite of sausage.

Eyebrows lifted, Miss Newfield glanced his way as if trying to discern his distress. He returned a small shrug to dismiss her concern, adding a slight grin to show his appreciation. In every way this young woman exuded kindness, and he prayed Mother would not destroy her gentle spirit.

"Newfield." Lady Greystone's sharp tone cut into the silence that had descended upon the breakfast table. "Your mourning attire is incomplete."

Anna glanced down at her dull black bombazine gown, but resisted touching her hair to see if any strands had escaped their pins. "Forgive me, my lady. I will be happy to—"

"Your black bonnet will do for out of doors, but when you are indoors you must wear a black lace or crepe scarf." Lady Greystone eyed her briefly before returning to her eggs. "I shall have Hudson find something for you."

Anna had yet to meet Hudson, but she knew her to be Lady Greystone's lady's maid. "I thank you—"

"This afternoon we will make our rounds of the village. Wear your walking shoes." Her perpetual frown deepened. "You do have walking shoes?"

"Yes, my lady." Anna's heart lifted. Perhaps she would find people to whom she could minister in the village, as she had in Blandon.

"Edmond, you will accompany us." The viscountess eyed her son as if daring him to decline.

The major did not respond immediately, but at last said, "It will be my pleasure."

Relief and concern vied to dominate Anna's thoughts. How good it would be to have the major along, but only if he could manage the walk. A quick glance in his direction revealed a clenched jaw, thinned lips and eyes focused on his nearly empty plate. In her short acquaintance with him, she had noticed this response when a situation met his disapproval. Surely his mother would be sympathetic to his pain, should the outing prove too arduous.

"If you please, madam." Seated across the table from Anna, Mary Grenville gave Lady Greystone a hopeful smile. "May I accompany you as well?"

Anna could see the longing in the young woman's eyes. Was she a kindred spirit with a desire to minister to the less fortunate?

"Nonsense." Lady Greystone spread a thin layer of strawberry preserves on a piece of bread. "Over that rocky terrain in your condition? I'll not lose my grandson to your whimsy."

Disappointment clouded Mary's face. Richard reached over to squeeze his wife's hand. "Never mind, my darling. We'll take a turn or two around the gallery after breakfast."

At the other end of the table Lord Greystone and Major Grenville talked in low tones. Yet without any effort, Anna heard the major say "Newfield," "saber" and "no doubt killed."

"What are you discussing?" Frowning, Lady Greystone eyed her sons.

The two men exchanged a look Anna could not discern. Then Lord Greystone glanced at Anna before he addressed his mother. "Edmond was just telling me about the gallant officer who saved his life and, um, was—" He cleared his throat. "Miss Newfield's brother."

"Hmm. Oh, yes." Lady Greystone dabbed her lips with a napkin. "I believe you mentioned that the other evening." She, too, glanced at Anna. "Clearly the man knew his duty."

Tears threatened, so Anna pulled in a deep, quiet breath, even managing a nod toward the viscountess. But she studiously avoided the sympathy she'd seen emanating from Major Grenville's handsome face, for his kindness could prove her undoing.

Chapter Six

The mid-October breeze was brisk and biting, but nothing like the North Atlantic winds that had buffeted the ship bringing Edmond home to England. With his cape drawn close around him and his hat firmly in place, he fended off the chills that had plagued him during the voyage. But he did lean heavily on his cane and Matthews's arm while trying to avoid dips in the uneven ground, all the while endeavoring not to grunt with every painful step.

Ahead, basket in hand, Mother marched along the woodland path with Miss Newfield striding along behind her like a good soldier, another basket over her arm. The young lady possessed a carriage much like her brother's, yet in every way feminine, an elegant posture devoid of arrogance, her chin held high, as if she was looking forward to reaching her destination. Occasionally she glanced back and smiled, although her eyes expressed her concern for Edmond.

Under her kind scrutiny, he refused to falter. Instead, by force of will, he gazed at the pale blue sky and the brilliantly hued trees showing off their autumn colors. The leafy, musty scents of the forest filled his senses, reminding him of childhood games with his brothers. Mother had never permitted her sons to fight or even wrestle, but hidden from her and their tutor among these trees, they could wrestle as much as they liked. And it was here they imagined many adventures to come. Yet how differently each of their lives had turned out.

The little village had not changed. From the farrier's cluttered stable to the shopkeeper's tidy window displays, not a horseshoe or bonnet seemed to have moved. Only the children appeared different. The lads who'd once chased each other about the rutted street were no doubt in school or working in the fields beside their fathers, and their youngest brothers now stirred up the lane with their dusty games. The sameness of Greystone Village, which used to bore Edmond, now awoke a longing within his heart. Despite their unremarkable lives, these country folk had a certain security which seemed to define their character. They grew up knowing where they belonged and what they would do with their lives, whereas uncertainty had plagued Edmond since he first realized he would have to find his own way in the world.

Not until he began his law studies at Oxford had he discovered his true passion. But Mother had decided law was an inferior profession for the youngest brother of a viscount. When she learned that Arthur Wellesley, an earl's fourth son, had received his own title, political prestige and a vast fortune during his service in India, she declared that Edmond must obtain an officer's commission in the army. She paid for it herself, less a generous gesture than simply another means of controlling one of her sons. He'd had two choices: accept her offer or become dependent upon his eldest brother's charity.

Of course Edmond rebelled, but after a misspent Season in London for which he still felt much guilt and had many regrets, his godly middle brother had brokered a truce. A surrender, actually, for Edmond had capitulated to all of Mother's demands. But although he had managed to pay off his gambling debts, his service in America had brought neither fortune nor prestige, only wounds that matched the scars on his soul.

"What a charming village." Miss Newfield gazed about the scene as if surveying some grand garden. "So like Blandon in every way."

"What?" Mother stopped her march and turned to glare at her.

Edmond caught up in time to see a slight blush touch the young lady's cheeks. "Indeed? I suppose most English villages boast the same quaint scenery." He hoped his cheerful tone would diminish her discomfort.

"We are not here to chitchat." Mother resumed her march, not stopping until she reached a tiny redbrick house where smoke curled from the chimney. "Humph. A fire at midday in October? Such a waste."

Edmond gritted his teeth. He would not be able to remain silent if she scolded the dear old pensioner who lived here, the woman who had been nurse to him and his brothers, supplying the love lacking from their only parent. While Richard had been the old woman's favorite and no doubt the reason for his penchant for spiritual matters, Edmond and Greystone had adored her, too. If Mother refused to supply wood for her hearth, he would find a way to do it himself.

Cheered by Major Grenville's pleasant rejoinder, Anna shrugged off her dismay over Lady Greystone's reproach. Clearly she must not comment on anything unless asked. But, oh, how hard that would be when so many things sparked her interest, from the squirrels gathering acorns in the woods to the children playing outside the wood frame houses. Still, if she wished to be the best possible companion to the lady, performing her duties heartily as unto the Lord, then she must learn to remain silent.

Lady Greystone stopped at a singular brick house amongst the wooden ones and ordered the major to knock. Curiosity seized Anna. Who lived here, and why did they deserve such a superior, albeit small dwelling? She gave the major a questioning glance and was startled to see anger in his eyes. He looked her way and the anger disappeared, replaced by a wry grin and accompanied by a shrug.

The door was opened by an elderly, black-clad gentleman. The light in his pale blue eyes reminded Anna of *Papá*. In fact, his entire facade and bearing resembled a man of God.

Lady Greystone stepped back. "Mr. Partridge." She peered beyond him into the dimly lit room. "Has Mrs. Winters—"

"No, no, madam." The gentleman emitted a scratchy chuckle. "She is well enough for her many years."

The major leaned toward Anna to mouth "the vicar."

A bittersweet pang tore through her, but she forced a smile. Her intuition had been correct. But did he live here? Was this humble dwelling the vicarage? The church stood at the far end of the village, whereas her father's church had been next door to their home. And she could not think a wealthy peer such as Lord Greystone would house his clergyman so meanly.

"Well," Lady Greystone huffed. "Will you grant me entrance or not?"

"Of course, madam." The vicar gave her a slight bow. The warmth in his eyes as he moved back revealed a respect uncluttered by trepidation.

The party moved into the room, except for Matthews, who waited outside.

"Now, Winters." Lady Greystone approached a grey-haired woman hunched into an upholstered armchair. "What's all this? Have you called the vicar for last rites?"

Anna could detect no kindness in Lady Greystone's tone, but like the vicar, the old woman smiled without fear. Anna deposited the observation in her memory to consider later.

"No, my lady. Just holy communion. I cannot travel the distance to the church, so he brings it to me."

Once again Anna felt a sweet pang of remembrance. *Papá* used to offer the same service to his elderly parishioners. Perhaps her emotions showed on her face, for Major Grenville gently squeezed her elbow as if he understood.

"Of course. Just as he should." Lady Greystone sat in the straight-backed chair next to the old woman and set her basket on a battered side table. "Now, I have brought you some of Cook's apple tarts, bread and lamb stew, along with a bit of tea and some cream."

"All of that and cream, too? Oh, my lady, how grand." Mrs. Winters's eyes glistened. "Thank you."

"Nonsense." Lady Greystone clicked her tongue and her hawk-like features sharpened. "It is your due for faithful service, and my duty to provide it."

"Yes, my lady." Mrs. Winters adjusted her spectacles. "Is this my Edmond?" She reached out to the major. "Oh, dear boy, come close so I may see you." Now her tears slipped down her wrinkled cheeks.

The major knelt by her chair. "Hello, my dear Winnie." He kissed her cheek, and she patted his.

Watching the encounter, Anna's heart performed a dozen somersaults. Not only was she touched by the major's gentle gesture, but she also longed to know more about this old woman, more about the vicar. These were gentle souls, people to whom God had brought her that she might minister to them. Her grateful prayer was cut short when the old nurse's gaze fell on her.

"And who is this lovely creature you have brought to me? Edmond, is this your bride?"

Laughter bubbled up inside of Anna over such a silly assumption, but the major jolted to attention, and shock covered his handsome countenance. "Why, no—"

Lady Greystone uttered a mild, unladylike epithet. "She is nothing of the sort. Nothing at all, really. My new companion, if she pleases me."

The woman's expression grew sober, except for her eyes, which danced merrily. "As you say, my lady."

The major swallowed noisily next to Anna while his mother opened her basket. "As you already have an unseasonable fire burning, shall we have tea?"

"Ah." Mrs. Winters turned her attention to that offer. "How lovely. Mr. Partridge, will you put on the kettle?"

"Nonsense." Lady Greystone waved the vicar back to his chair. "Newfield, see to it."

Grateful to be useful at last, Anna hurried to the small hearth where she dipped fresh water from a crock into a battered tin kettle, hung the kettle on the iron arm and swung the arm over the amber coals. A gentle stir with a poker ignited the flames, and soon steam wafted from the kettle spout. She hesitated before measuring tea leaves into the porcelain teapot. Did Lady Greystone like weak or strong tea? She glanced behind her to see the viscountess inspecting Mrs. Winters's knitting project.

"You waste too much dye on your wool," Lady Greystone said. "A pale scarf is as warm as a dark one for these village children. They'll turn them dark soon enough in their games."

Economy seemed to be the lady's watchword, so Anna measured two scant spoonfuls of tea leaves into the pot and poured in boiling water. Once it had steeped she served the others, and to her relief, no one complained about the weakness of the beverage.

"Will you not have a cup, my dear?" Mrs. Winters gazed at Anna as if she were an old friend.

"Why—" Anna glanced at the major for direction, but quickly shifted her gaze to Lady Greystone. The lady's eyebrows quirked briefly in what seemed to be assent. "Thank you, ma'am." She chose a cup and saucer from the mismatched china on the mantelpiece and savored the warmth of the tea against the chill of the room. Truly, it was not too soon for old Mrs. Winters to have a fire, but Anna could hardly admonish her employer.

While Lady Greystone conversed in low tones with the old woman and the vicar, Anna stood by the hearth and studied the cozy but sparsely furnished parlor. Dark green drapes were drawn aside from two small windows, permitting sunlight to brighten the room. The plaster walls were painted pale green, and wrought iron sconces hung above the faded settee where Major Grenville sat looking a bit sour.

Was he still dismayed over the old woman's erroneous assumption about their relationship? If so, he really should learn to laugh a bit more at such ridiculous conjectures. After all, she was clearly in mourning, and her black lace cap bespoke a spinster not seeking a husband. He was an aristocrat not likely to marry someone of her station.

Never mind. People would soon understand it all. While the gentleman would make a fine husband for some fortunate lady, Anna would not be the one. The thought generated a modicum of sadness, but she refused to give place to such nonsensical feelings. After all, scripture taught that a merry heart doeth good, like medicine. Through many experiences she had seen that laughter was the best remedy for any unhappiness, the wisest contradiction for any false speculations.

Perhaps she should teach him how to play "What's the worst thing?" as her family used to do.

Edmond could hardly keep from squirming on the settee, not just because of its lumpy seat or his aching leg, but because dear Winnie had created an awkward situation. If Miss Newfield sat beside him or if he stood and offered her his place, the old nurse would tease again, and Mother might begin to view the girl as a threat and cast her out. While her sons' occupations held first place in her machinations, not far behind was her determination that they should marry well to someone of their own class. More times than he could count, she had railed against aristocrats who married members of the gentry. Such unions not only tainted the blood, she claimed, but they created disorder by lifting unworthy souls above their God-given place on the Great Chain of Being. Thus these marriages were nothing short of sin.

Edmond had always accepted her reasoning, for every aristocrat he knew held that view. Of late, however, he had begun to reconsider, particularly after a superior man named Peter Newfield died in his stead. And as each hour and day passed, Edmond grew more and more determined that Newfield's sister must never want for security.

For the present, however, the only safe course for both Miss Newfield and himself was to effect polite indifference toward each other. Which would be decidedly difficult for him if the young lady continued to view the world so agreeably with those merry green eyes.

Chapter Seven

During her first evening with the family, Anna sat on a straight-backed chair by the drawing room door while Lady Greystone supervised the after-supper activities. Anna imagined that their customs were similar to her own family's, with every member expected to contribute to the entertainment. A finely polished maple card table had been unfolded and matching chairs set around it, so perhaps they would play whist or another card game. Anna hoped she would not be called upon to join in, for cards required a quick memory and she always found her mind wandering during the game. If asked, she could play the pianoforte without embarrassing herself, but Lady Greystone had just assigned that particular duty to her daughter-in-law.

Although she had to lumber to the instrument, Mrs. Grenville appeared eager and her nimble fingers moved over the keys with a respectable musical skill. After her brief concert, the gentlemen discussed politics and news, with Lady Greystone glancing up from her needlework to comment from time to time. No games seemed to be planned, which left Anna to revise her speculations. Did they truly just talk in the evenings? No charades? No word games? She could barely keep from yawning.

After more than an hour, she decided she had been forgotten. Major Grenville offered a glance or two her way, but he gave her no smile. Perhaps he was still offended by his former nurse's comment that afternoon, but Anna could hardly be faulted for it. Despite his previous courtesies, he had seemed almost to avoid her on the walk back to the manor house and throughout supper. Still, he had done more than enough by bringing her here. She should expect nothing beyond that. Instead, she sat on the edge of her chair to remain alert and cheered herself by deciding this was preferable to sitting on the edge of a highway with no place to go. From here she could observe the family and pray for them.

"Newfield!" Lady Greystone's sharp voice jolted Anna, and she realized she had been near to dozing after all.

"Yes, my lady." Face burning, she rose, crossed the room and stood near the settee where her employer sat with her eldest son.

"You will begin your riding lessons tomorrow." The viscountess barely glanced at Anna and continued her needlework.

Anna knew she must acknowledge the order, but her throat closed. How she had hoped Lady Greystone would forget this frightening project.

"Edmond," the lady said, "you will teach her. If this *gel* you have brought to me is to be an acceptable companion, she must ride. Peel always disappointed me in her fear of horses. Why, the woman trembled so much she made the beasts skittish. Such nonsense."

Major Grenville's jaw dropped, and he, too, seemed at a loss for words. Anna could think of no way to rescue either of them.

Hidden behind a newspaper, the viscount coughed, but Anna could not decide whether it was an attempt to cover a laugh or a symptom of an illness. When the major glared in his brother's direction, Anna was both relieved and dismayed. Of course she would not wish the viscount to be ill, but she could find no humor in the situation. And while she would enjoy the major's company under any circumstances, she had never managed to overcome her fear of horses. Only one escape seemed possible.

"Forgive me, my lady, but I have nothing proper to wear for riding."

The viscountess gave her a sharp look, then eyed her up and down through her quizzing glass. "Hmm. Easily solved. You will wear Peel's habit."

"But, Mother Greystone—" Mrs. Grenville had moved from the pianoforte to a chair beside her husband "—Miss Peel was tall and thin as a reed." While she did not look at Anna, her remark was nonetheless appreciated.

"Also easily solved," the viscountess said. "You sew, do you not, Newfield?"

Anna swallowed, and her heart sank. "Yes, my lady."

"Then go at once and find Hudson. She will direct you to the garment and the sewing supplies."

After offering a quick curtsey, Anna fled the room, praying tears would not overtake her. Upstairs she found the viscountess's lady's maid and soon had the project in hand. While no one could call Anna stout, she hoped the thin woman's gown would not have enough material to enlarge it. Alas, the side seams were more than wide enough. After letting it out, Anna enlisted Mrs. Hudson's help in measuring how much to increase the hem. That done, the maid declared the project a success and retired for the night.

Anna knelt beside her bed and offered up an urgent plea that somehow the Lord would deliver her from tomorrow's trial. Not only must she face a large, fearsome beast the likes of which she had rarely come near, but she must also face Major Grenville, who should not be riding yet and who clearly did not wish to teach her.

She fell asleep trying very hard to play "What's the worst thing?" to cheer herself. But the game only generated dreams of being thrown to the ground while her four-legged adversary whinnied its triumph above her.

"Really, Mother." Edmond scowled at his parent while ignoring Greystone's smirk. "I hardly feel ready to ride, much less ready to teach someone else how to do it." He despised sounding weak in front of his brothers, but better that than to announce his true reason for disliking this assignment. As much as he would enjoy the young lady's company, it would not be proper for them to venture out alone and still keep her reputation intact.

"And may I add—" Richard's slender face wore an uncharacteristic frown "—it would hardly be proper for the young lady, spinster or not, to be out with Edmond without a chaperone."

Edmond exhaled a sigh of relief. His brother the cleric would be an ally in this matter.

"Nonsense." Mother rose from the settee. Everyone else stood as well. "They will have the groom with them." She moved toward the door, then turned back to face Edmond. "As we walked back from the village today, you leaned upon your man less and less. All you require for complete recovery is additional exercise and a return to your riding. Furthermore, you need something to do. This will be good for you." She sniffed, as she often did when displeased. "And why must I repeat myself? If this *gel* is to be my companion, she must ride." She strode out of the room, head held high like a general marching away victorious from a battlefield.

"I say, Edmond." Greystone stretched and yawned. "I should think you would enjoy the company of a young woman after all your military duties."

Edmond laughed without mirth, hating what he was about to say. "Preferably someone of our class, not a servant." As he said the words, a sick feeling churned in his belly. Miss Newfield was the gentlest, kindest Christian lady he had ever met. He had no right to claim superiority over her.

"Well," Richard said, "strictly speaking, a companion is not a servant." As if looking for agreement he gazed down at Mary, who sat tucked under his arm now that Mother was not in the room.

Mary returned a beatific smile. "If you say so, my darling."

Edmond felt his heart lighten just observing their mutual devotion. How grand it would be to have a wife of his own to cherish. "No, I suppose not. But you know what I mean."

"No, I don't." His eldest brother continued to smirk.

"Stubble it, Greystone. If Mother thinks I admire the poor girl, she'll boot her out." He walked toward the door.

Greystone followed a few feet behind him. "And of course you do not admire her." His teasing tone held a world of good humor.

Edmond stopped and turned so quickly his brother almost collided with him. "Listen to me. This woman's brother died in my place. I have a duty to make certain she is not misused or abandoned. That is all."

"Of course." Greystone's lopsided grin contradicted his assertion. "Why do you insist upon thinking I am suggesting anything else?"

Too tired to argue, Edmond limped from the room and headed toward the staircase. With each step, he was forced to admit Mother was right. Today's exercise had helped work out some of his discomfort from having been laid up for so long. But he could not envision getting back on a horse tomorrow morning. Nor could he envision working for hours with the lovely Miss Newfield without coming to admire her entirely too much.

Anna endeavored not to tremble as she descended the wide front staircase. The Lord had not answered her prayers as she wished. Nor had He given her peace about the upcoming trial. But scripture said He would never leave her nor forsake her. Anna could cling to that promise far more easily than she would be able to cling to a saddle. If an injury was in her future, so be it. She would try to bear it as bravely as Major Grenville bore his wounds.

When she reached the bottom of the steps she inhaled a deep breath and blew it out, then squared her shoulders and walked through the wide front door held open by the liveried footman. A cold breeze smacked her face, bringing with it the strong smell of horseflesh. Against her lingering hopes, the major stood talking with another man, most likely the groom, for he held the reins of a brown horse. The creature eyed Anna with a look of boredom. Or was that a challenge in those large black eyes?

Still using his cane, Major Grenville stepped over to greet her. "Good morning, Miss Newfield." He took her hand but offered no smile, which only added to her trepidation…and disappointment. "Ah, you're trembling," he whispered. "Don't be frightened. She's the gentlest horse in my brother's stable."

A nervous laugh bubbled out before Anna could stop it. "Oh, doubtless, she is." But she could not keep doubt from her voice.

He pulled her around in front of him, gripped her upper

arms and captured her gaze. "Miss Newfield, you may count on me." The firm, warm touch of his hands set her heart to fluttering uncontrollably. "I will not allow you to be harmed." The intensity in his eyes held the gentle rebuke of a friend, and his masculine presence nearly took her breath away.

She swallowed and looked down, struggling to regain some semblance of dignity. "I thank you, Major Grenville." Her eyes stung, but she forbade tears to fall. "You have shown me nothing but kindness. I do trust you." She inhaled yet another bracing breath and looked up at him again, this time with a teasing smile. "Shall we begin? After all, what's the worst that can happen?"

Releasing his grip on her arms, he stepped back and chuckled, then laughed out loud, a most welcome sound. "Your brother told me about your family's game. But let's not play it, at least not today." He took her elbow and led her to the horse's head. "Miss Newfield, may I present Bella." He ran a hand down the creature's nose. "Bella, this is Miss Newfield," he murmured as he took Anna's gloved hand and guided it down the creature's nose. "Unlike poor Miss Peel, she is not the least bit nervous."

"You should not lie to her." Anna's voice wavered, but whether it was from the touch of the major's hand on hers or his deep, soothing tone, she could not tell.

Again he chuckled, and a shiver, not at all displeasing, swept over her. She mentally shook it off. Why should this man's presence have such a disconcerting effect on her? Why did his smiles mean so much to her? She must dismiss all these thoughts, including her sympathies for Lady Greystone's late companion, and remember Peter's fearless determination to ride so he could become a dragoon.

Setting aside his cane, Major Grenville gripped Anna at the waist and lifted her into the saddle. With every care for propriety's sake, he settled her left shoe into the stirrup and helped her drape her right knee over the pommel. Pressing her foot into the stirrup, she rose slightly to adjust her seating, and the saddle dipped on that side. Anna dropped back with a gasp.

"It's all right," the major said. "The girth is firmly cinched. It won't slip." He gave her a reassuring smile such as one might give a child, then nodded to the groom.

The man clicked his tongue and tugged on the bridle. Bella lurched forward. Or so it seemed to Anna. She grabbed for the front edge of the saddle.

"Easy." The major walked along beside her, cane in one hand and his other hand stretched out toward her, should she need it. "If you must hold on, you can grip her mane. Try to sit straight and balance your spine over hers. Keep your eyes straight ahead."

Anna followed his instructions and soon was able to sit without holding on for a few seconds at a time. They walked around the circle drive in front of the manor house, and she found herself moving comfortably with Bella's walking gait. Her confidence grew, probably because of Major Grenville's presence. Well into the second time around, she ventured a sidelong glance at him.

"Have you taught many people how to ride?"

"A few young dragoons who'd not had the advantage of learning at home." He grimaced, and she guessed his injured leg was giving him pain. Yet he made no complaint. "You're doing very well."

Pleased at his compliment, she relaxed into the saddle. "If that is so, it is your doing."

"Nonsense." He used his mother's favorite word, but without the sharpness the viscountess employed. "Riding is in your blood. Newfield was the best rider of all my officers, some of whom had ridden all their lives."

"Peter has always been fearless." Anna refused to speak of her brother as though he were dead, despite the shadow that passed over the major's handsome face.

"Indeed. Fearless describes him well."

They fell silent as they continued their walk, and Anna grew more and more comfortable on Bella's back. She lost count of how many times they circled the great fountain in the center of the drive. She imagined the structure would be quite lovely in the spring and summer, when water flowed from the marble pitchers held by four dainty Grecian maidens in marble gowns. She prayed she would still reside at Greystone Lodge to see it. And although she wished the major a speedy recovery, she hoped he would still be here then, too. Like her father and brother, he made her believe she could do something that frightened her beyond reason. And he was right.

After spending the morning with Miss Newfield, Edmond experienced a satisfaction unlike any he could recall. She was nothing like the young ladies he had observed in London, the girls who simpered and giggled and posed in their pretty frocks while trying to ensnare some unattached peer or heir. The same young misses had turned their backs when he approached because he was a younger son lacking both title and fortune. He could not imagine any of those giddy girls facing a challenge as admirably as Miss Newfield. Although she had been afraid, she had not only faced her fears but done it with good humor, just as her heroic brother might have done. Her insistence upon giving him the credit for their successful lesson soothed a hidden wound in his soul.

To his relief, he observed that Miss Newfield did not wilt under Mother's scorching rule, which had been his concern from the moment he invited her to Greystone

Lodge. Thus he could not regret bringing her here, for he felt certain she would do only good for the entire household. Still, he must remain on his guard against any display of admiration, especially in the presence of his mother and his bothersome eldest brother. While Mother seemed oblivious to Miss Newfield's beauty, Greystone took entirely too much delight in teasing Edmond as if they were still boys and his joking could create no lasting damage.

But indeed, it could utterly destroy a kind and innocent soul, should Mother decide the young lady had set her cap for him.

Chapter Eight

Anna had no illusions that her good experience with the first riding lesson indicated she would become a skilled rider, for Major Grenville had kept Bella at a walk the entire time. Horses also trotted and galloped. What would the mare have done if the groom had released the halter? If something had startled her into a run? Anna prayed she would develop both aptitude and proficiency very soon. And a much better attitude would not hurt. So when Lord Greystone met Anna and the major in the front entry and asked her how the lesson went, she put on her best face.

"Major Grenville is a remarkable instructor. I am certain I shall become competent enough on horseback to please Lady Greystone." She ended in a rush, for this was the first time she had addressed the viscount. Or any peer.

"Ah, yes, I have no doubt my brother is an excellent riding teacher." Lord Greystone chuckled and nudged the major, who scowled at him. "And if you manage to please my mother, madam, you will have accomplished something no mortal has yet been able to do these past seven and forty years." He sauntered away, still laughing, but not before he cast a smirk in the major's direction.

Still scowling, the major stiffened. He stalked away, but

then turned and strode back to her. "Miss Newfield, it has been a pleasure." He bowed over her hand without smiling, then left her.

Anna stood in the center of the marble-floored entryway trying to guess what this little scene meant. She had no doubt the brothers cared deeply for one another and probably teased each other just as she and Peter always did. But the moment they encountered the viscount, the major became defensive. Perhaps they had quarreled. With a sigh, she climbed the marble stairway, resolving to pray for the brothers, that they might dwell together in unity.

As she passed the door to Lady Greystone's suite, Mrs. Hudson emerged and curtseyed. "Did the habit suit you, miss?"

"Yes, thank you." How odd to have this older woman treat her with such deference. "I could not have altered it without your help."

Mrs. Hudson's pale blue eyes brightened. "Why, thank you, miss. You're kind to say so."

Her genuine surprise at the compliment gave Anna pause. She had much to learn about the complex social levels among the servants.

"Mrs. Hudson, perhaps you can advise me about something."

Again, shock registered across the woman's pale, wrinkled features. "I'd be honored to help, miss. What is it?"

"Well, you see, I am not certain what my duties are as a companion. How is my job different from yours?"

Mrs. Hudson drew back. "Such a question, miss."

For a moment, Anna thought she might walk away. Instead, she straightened her shoulders and lifted her chin. "I have the privilege of seeing to all of Lady Greystone's personal matters regarding clothing and hair. She is a most meticulous lady and knows exactly what she wants. My job is to be in or near her chambers at all times in case she requires my services, and to make certain she is dressed fit to meet the most august personage, even the Queen."

"Ah, yes. I noticed her perfection the moment I first saw her. And you are the one who's responsible." She did not intend to flatter the woman, but her words sparked a blush of pleasure.

"I do try." Mrs. Hudson continued to beam. "As to your duties, miss, you're to be at the ready, as well, but you are privileged to accompany Her Ladyship wherever she goes. That is, wherever she wants you to go. She may have you read to her or fetch a fan or deliver a message to a servant or perform any other such errand. Sometimes she will want you simply to be with her."

"I see." Now Anna understood the viscountess's comment about youthful energy, for this job would certainly require that. "Should I wait to be sent for at mealtime?" She had not gone down to the breakfast room this morning and was beginning to feel the effects of that omission.

"Unless Lady Greystone or His Lordship has a guest, you may assume you should be present at every meal." Mrs. Hudson wrinkled her forehead. "And of course, it depends upon who the guest is."

"Very good. Thank you so much, Mrs. Hudson." While this conversation did not give her a complete picture of her duties, it was a start. Further, Mrs. Hudson promised to warn Anna if she was about to do something wrong or wear an inappropriate gown. Not that she had many to choose from.

With a new friend and a new sense of purpose, Anna felt comforted in her lingering grief over *Papá*'s death and Peter's absence. Now if she could just discover what caused the problem between Major Grenville and his eldest brother, perhaps she could urge them to reconcile. But then, that was hardly her place—and might be just enough to see her dismissed.

* * *

To Anna's great joy, on Sunday morning everyone in the household walked through the woodlands to the village church. Lord Greystone led the way with his mother, Richard and Mary followed, and Anna strolled beside Major Grenville. Behind them stretched a group of some twenty or so servants, all dressed in their best clothes, hats and bonnets. Anna had plundered poor Miss Peel's leftovers and found a warm woolen cape that proved black enough to receive Lady Greystone's approval for a mourning garment.

The days seemed colder than usual for late October, but with numerous villagers and members of the local gentry filling the church, no healthy person could complain of a chill. Anna sat with the family in a place of prominence, much as she had at home, except that here she was at the outside end of the front pew. As the service commenced, she had no need for her prayer book, for the order of events was printed on her mind. During the aged vicar's sermon on faith, she glanced up at Major Grenville and noticed with satisfaction that he seemed to be enjoying the service as much as she. On the journey to the church, she had also been pleased to see an easy camaraderie amongst the three brothers. Perhaps the mysterious offense of a few days ago had been dealt with.

In spite of the brisk wind, after the service many people lingered outside the church to visit. Anna watched Lady Greystone and her sons chat with various parishioners, but she was unsure of what to do. Since *Mamá*'s death, she had acted as her father's hostess and often invited church members to the vicarage for an afternoon meal. She'd had no difficulty talking with the people of Blandon, but no one here knew her. Without an introduction, she could not approach anyone, even a villager.

As often before, Major Grenville glanced her way but made no move to approach her, nor did he offer a smile. But he was speaking first with the vicar and then with old friends, so why should he acknowledge his mother's companion or introduce her to the neighbors?

"Miss Newfield?" The vicar approached her, his black cassock and white hair whipping about in the wind. "How nice to see you this morning. I do hope you enjoyed the service."

Her heart lifted by his kindness, Anna curtseyed. "I did, Mr. Partridge. The text you read from Hebrews is one of my favorites."

"Indeed?" His bushy grey eyebrows rose. "Are you a student of scripture, then?"

She laughed softly. "Oh, yes. One does not grow up a vicar's daughter without developing an appreciation for God's Word."

"Ah, I had no idea." Now his face shone with a paternal glow, much like *Papá*'s. "Newfield. I seem to recall that a William Newfield was the vicar of Blandon. Is he your father?"

"Yes. Did you know him?" Tears threatened to erupt, along with a world of emotion she had held in these past many days.

"I knew of him. A man of irreproachable reputation, as I recall." The vicar touched her shoulder and gazed into her eyes. "May I assume he is—"

"In the presence of the Lord…and with my mother." Anna forced her emotions into obedience and briefly apprised him of the circumstances that had brought her to Greystone Village.

"Ah, yes, your brother." Mr. Partridge glanced toward the dwindling crowds. "Major Grenville just told me of his courageous actions. Now that I know more of your situation, perhaps that is why he asked me to speak to you."

Surprised, Anna gazed across the churchyard. The major caught her look and ducked away, but not before she saw his slight grin. His kindness swept over her like a warm blanket, once again causing tears to form.

The vicar squeezed her shoulder as *Papá* used to do. "Miss Newfield, if Lady Greystone permits, may I call upon you? Sometimes we are helped in our grieving when we have a friend to talk with."

Anna could do no more than nod and offer a trembling smile. And lift a silent prayer of thanks for both the vicar and the major, two gentlemen whose compassion for her was clearly God's consolation in her grief.

Edmond gratefully watched Mr. Partridge visit with Miss Newfield, but discomfort replaced approval when she seemed about to cry. Then like a gallant dragoon, she visibly reined in her emotions, easing his concern. Mother would not have a weeping woman for a companion and would doubtless send the young woman away, should she be given to tears. Most mornings in the breakfast room, her eyes were rimmed with red, and an ache to comfort her formed in Edmond's chest. Yet she soldiered on through the day with a pleasant countenance.

He could not help but wonder what deep thoughts dwelt behind those intelligent green eyes, which seemed to miss nothing and more often than not exuded a selfless interest in others. Then again, he could not watch her too much or Greystone would begin his teasing once more. If he did, Edmond would be sorely tempted to thrash his brother, title notwithstanding. He'd never been a cruel fellow, but he seemed oblivious to the danger he put Miss Newfield in with his unfounded innuendos.

Edmond held no more rancor toward Greystone than he did toward Richard, who was far more circumspect in all matters. But Greystone had never had a care in the world. With wealth and power at his disposal, his future was assured. He could participate in politics as much or as little as he wished and even avoid too much involvement in Parliament without loss.

Yet in only one way did Edmond envy Greystone: he alone had any memories of their father, who died when Edmond was only three. Did his brothers wonder, as he often did, how their lives might have been different if Father had survived the influenza that struck Greystone Village in 1789? Would Mother have been a softer woman, more kindly and generous, instead of a woman to be feared by those whose lives she controlled? But neither Mother nor Greystone spoke of the fourth Lord Greystone, either for good or for ill, leaving only unanswered questions. Even his portrait was hung at the end of the family's portrait gallery where no daylight illuminated it.

As the family fell into line behind his parent and eldest brother to begin their journey home, Edmond offered his arm to Miss Newfield. Surely Mother could not object to this simple courtesy. For his part, the young lady's pretty smile lightened the weight in his chest caused by his dark musings and replaced it with an unexpected surge of joy. In the presence of her refreshing optimism, he found himself believing she would bring good things to his family. But as she set her delicate, gloved hand on his arm, he found it exceedingly difficult to watch the scenery when he would much prefer to study her fair face, a regard that could cause them both some serious difficulty.

Chapter Nine

Early the next week, Lady Greystone announced at breakfast that she would spend the afternoon at the village school. After her talk with Mrs. Hudson, Anna need not ask whether she would be accompanying her employer. In fact, the excursion sounded more than a little appealing.

"Edmond." Lady Greystone stared down the table at her youngest son. "You will go with me." Her words carried a commanding tone.

"Of course." Major Grenville sounded bored as he toyed with his eggs, but his eyes betrayed an awareness that incited Anna's curiosity. As if sensing her gaze, he turned to her. "Miss Newfield, you may be interested to know that Mother subscribes to Hannah More's view that all English children, whatever their social status, should be taught to read the Bible. She established the school for that purpose."

"How wonderful." Anna's opinion of her employer improved significantly on the spot. "I will enjoy observing the teaching methods utilized by the teachers."

"Humph." Lady Greystone sipped her coffee. "The National Society for Promoting Education for the Poor should have reached every corner of England and Wales by now. Have they no school in Brandon?"

"No, my lady." Anna refrained from reminding her that the village was called Blandon. "Unlike Mrs. More and the Society, Squire Beamish holds the view that farmers' offspring do not need to read, write or cipher, which my father found lamentable. To rectify the situation, he established his own Sunday morning school, but also taught classes two days a week."

"And did you help him?" The major's eyes lit with approval.

Anna felt heat rising in her cheeks. Why did his attention cause her such emotion? "I did, sir, but I had no training for the work."

"But the children did learn?"

"Oh, yes. They were very bright and were eager to read for themselves."

"Very commendable, Miss Newfield." Lord Greystone lifted his coffee cup in a salute to her. "Do you not agree, Edmond?"

The major scowled at his brother and started to speak, but Mr. Grenville dropped his cup into its saucer with a loud clink, and liquid sloshed onto the damask table cloth.

"Why, something should be done about your Squire Beamish." Although the cleric surely meant to address Anna, his eyes were focused on the major. "Mother, perhaps you should write to Mrs. More and incite her to reform that gentleman's thinking."

All eyes now aimed toward the viscountess. "Indeed," she huffed. "Am I to suppose you think that woman's word would carry more influence than mine?"

As if she had rebuked them all, the table grew quiet except for the clatter of utensils on plates and the sounds of footmen removing dishes and refilling cups. Anna could sense a return of that odd tension between the major and the viscount, as well as their brother's subtle peacemaking, but she could discern no reason for it. What undercurrents of discord flowed here? And why did these Christian gentlemen not resolve their differences? How Anna longed for *Papá*'s godly intervention.

Edmond chided himself for bringing attention to Miss Newfield, but she offered him such a gentle, inquiring look that he felt compelled to say something. And of course Greystone took advantage of the situation. At least Edmond had Richard on his side, even though it earned him Mother's rebuke. As Edmond saw it, he had two choices. He must speak to Greystone in a manner that brooked no argument, or he must begin to treat Miss Newfield with utter disregard, as if she were a servant. That would be impossible, for he still must continue in her company and would never wish to cause her pain. The only solution was to accost Greystone after the trip to the village school.

The day was cold, and the wind cut through Edmond's cloak like a knife as he followed along behind the ladies, his injured leg aching with every step. Miss Newfield, however, walked behind Mother at a pace he could only describe as lively. Her eagerness to reach their destination spread to him, easing his struggle. He never ceased to marvel at her optimism in the face of her own tragedies and challenges. She had grown more confident in their riding lessons, and soon he would increase Bella's gait to a trot. Perhaps the time had come for him to get back on a horse so he could help her. But then, Mother might regard that as an indication he was ready to go back to war, a dreadful prospect.

The school was located in a thatched-roofed house a half block from the village center and boasted a loft above its single room that served as the teacher's living quarters. With harvest completed, every village child between the ages of six and twelve was expected to come for daily lessons. Edmond suspected Mother would demand a roll call.

She approached the house and waved Edmond forward. "You will announce me."

He opened the door and stepped inside to see a dozen or so children seated or standing around a greying, middle-aged woman, each child taking a turn reading from a prayer book. In a tone that would have made their butler proud, he announced, "Lady Greystone."

Every eye swung in their direction as Mother sailed into the room. The teacher stood and ordered the children up. "Lady Greystone." Her breathless tone revealed surprise and a modicum of awe. "Welcome. Children, what do we say?"

"Welcome, Lady Greystone," rang the chorus. While the girls dipped perfect curtseys, the boys executed excellent bows, each tugging a forelock to demonstrate their tenant status.

Mother's chin lifted slightly. She then favored them all with a condescending nod. Edmond could discern neither approval nor disapproval in her posture or expression.

"Good afternoon, Mrs. Billings, children." Mother pulled her quizzing glass from her reticule and scanned the room. "Carry on. I have come only to observe."

Mrs. Billings directed two older boys to bring chairs for the ladies, then resumed her lessons. Edmond noted with satisfaction that Miss Newfield watched the class with genuine interest. Were the post of teacher not taken, she might fill it admirably. Mother's interest centered on the behavior of the boys, who despite her august presence could not keep from mischief. Several seemed bent on slyly pinching another behind their teacher's back. Or perhaps they were testing her, something Edmond and his brothers had often done. To protect the lads from a scolding, he straightened to his full height and narrowed his eyes as he did to insubordinate soldiers. The tomfoolery ceased immediately.

When the major put the boys in their places with only a severe look, Anna had to suck in her cheeks to keep from laughing. These children misbehaved just like the students in Blandon. All they required was a firm hand to bring them to order. While one would think Lady Greystone's presence would incite flawless decorum, it was Major Grenville, ever resplendent in his crimson uniform, who put a stop to their naughtiness. And, of course, all the little girls sent admiring glances his way while pretending to be engrossed in their lesson. Anna did not blame them, for the major was indeed a handsome gentleman whose presence she always found pleasant and comforting.

Shocked by this thought, she doubled her efforts to pay attention to the little girl who now stood before them reciting a psalm. But her mind would not be still. She must not form an attachment to this gentleman. Even in the small, remote village of Blandon, she had learned that sons of the peerage could destroy their futures should they marry beneath their station. No matter what the laws of God were regarding the equality of all his children, human society had relegated every person to a particular rank. And woe to those who dared to seek a higher position or who married a person considered inferior. Thus, she must guard her heart, more for Major Grenville's sake than her own.

But then, all of these thoughts were utter nonsense. The major had been kind to her, but he had never shown the least interest in her other than brotherly concern. And if her foolish heart insisted upon attaching itself to him, then it deserved any pain that resulted.

* * *

While Mother gave instructions to Mrs. Billings, Edmond watched Miss Newfield take a small, timid child on her lap to play cat's cradle. The chosen girl gazed adoringly at the lady, perhaps unused to being singled out. He had his own admirers, for every boy in the room swarmed around him asking questions. While offering a few battle anecdotes of the milder sort, he let each lad try on his tall black hat and touch his sword. To a man, each one declared himself ready to fight for England. In return, Edmond expressed confidence in their ability to defend their homeland when they reached manhood. When Mother announced the visit was over, their little party left behind a schoolroom full of cheerful souls, if their well-pleased expressions were any indication.

The late afternoon wind cut into them even more sharply than on their trip to the village. At the sight of Miss Newfield shivering in her wrap, Edmond experienced a strong impulse to enfold her in his heavier woolen cape. But, as always, she forged gamely onward in Mother's footsteps along the narrow path. Perhaps a little conversation would take their minds off the cold.

"I say, Miss Newfield, you seem to have made some friends among the girls." Edmond ignored the sharp look Mother sent over her shoulder. How could she object to a simple chat?

Miss Newfield glanced at Mother, then graced him with one of her exquisite smiles. "I would say the same for you, Major. The boys were clearly enthralled by the grandeur of your uniform." Was that a smirk on those perfect lips? A hint of teasing in her tone?

Edmond's heart skipped. As always, Miss Newfield was nothing short of a delight.

When they reached the Lodge, even Mother camped

beside the hearth in the small back parlor and called for tea.

"I think I'll find Greystone," Edmond said when he had recovered from his chill. He would not put off any longer the much-needed discussion about Miss Newfield. "Johnson, do you know where His Lordship is?"

A fresh tea tray in hand, the butler crossed the room and set it on the occasional table. "Yes, sir. He asked me to inform Lady Greystone that he's ridden over to Shrewsbury for a few days."

"What?" Mother scowled at the news, then shook her head. "Well, after all, he is no longer required to answer to me."

Edmond's displeasure could not be shaken off so easily. True, Greystone did not have to tell the family where he was going, but courtesy should have required it. Furthermore, Edmond would now be forced to cool his heels for who knew how long before taking his eldest brother to task for his thoughtless insinuations.

Chapter Ten

"Good morning, Miss Newfield." Major Grenville gave Anna a jovial smile, one that lacked the caution he displayed in the presence of his family. He stood beside Bella, but behind him the slender young groom held two more horses. "Are you ready to ride out into the countryside?"

While her heart did a nervous tumble, she tried to match his cheeriness. "Yes, by all means. I was beginning to think we would continue to circle this fountain all winter. Lovely as it is, I should like to see more of the countryside before the autumn colors fade." She stopped abruptly, wondering why so many words seemed to roll off her tongue unbidden.

But the major laughed in a rather carefree manner. "Well, come along, then. I have a bit of instruction for you before we go out."

He lifted her into the saddle with his usual ease, but today his grip on her waist sent a shiver up her spine. Or maybe it was the brisk breeze. Either way, she must hasten to dismiss the sensation so she could concentrate on his instructions.

"Thus far, you have kept an excellent seat, but we've

only walked." He adjusted her left foot in the stirrup and helped her drape her right knee over the pommel.

Anna forced away the pleasant sensation his touch created. After all, she was not one of those giddy schoolgirls who had eyed him so adoringly yesterday. And last night she had prayed she might grasp the reins of her emotions just as securely as she now grasped Bella's reins and take charge of her feelings. She must not mistake the gentleman's kindness for anything more than a performance of his duties.

"We won't try anything faster than a trot," the major was saying. "But it is perhaps the most challenging of the gaits to become accustomed to."

Anna emitted an involuntary and altogether too squeaky laugh, and her face heated despite the cutting breeze. "Oh, dear. I shall do my best."

"You'll do splendidly." Major Grenville lifted one hand as if he were about to pat her knee. But his eyes widened. He withdrew the hand and cleared his throat. "Be sure to stay in the center of the saddle. You've done well at that for walking, but now you'll need to concentrate. Remember to keep your left heel down, look ahead and let your seat move with Bella."

"So much to remember." Anna blew out a deep breath. "But I'm ready."

"You can do it." The major grimaced. "I fear I am a poor teacher. Before you begin to trot, I must tell you how to slow or stop your horse."

Another nervous giggle escaped her. "Yes, I suppose that would help."

"This is important. You must sit back and pull gently on the reins. Not too hard, or you'll hurt her mouth." He grinned. "Got all of that?"

She snorted in a most unladylike way. "Oh, of course

I do." She was becoming entirely too comfortable in the major's presence.

"That's the spirit. Let's give it a try. You can take a turn or two around the fountain." The major waved the groom forward.

The man secured the other horses to a post and came to stand beside Bella's head.

"You'll forgive me if I don't—" The major's cheeks appeared slightly pinched, as if he were suddenly embarrassed.

"Of course." Anna's heart went out to him. These exercises could not be easy on his injured leg. "George, shall we do it?" She bolstered her courage with yet another deep breath and gave the groom a nod.

"Aye, miss, that we shall." The groom clicked his tongue and off they went.

At first they walked. Then George picked up his pace, keeping a grip on Bella's bridle. Soon he was loping, the mare trotting, and Anna bouncing hard against the saddle, trying with all her might not to cry out.

"Keep to the center of the saddle," the major called. "Sit tall. Press your left leg against the girth to steady yourself."

Determined not to fail him, Anna forced herself to work with Bella's bouncing gait. After all, what other young woman in her situation had the opportunity to learn from one of His Majesty's cavalry officers? And what was the worst that could happen?

Before she could answer her own foolish attempt at humor, the major cried out.

"Huzzah, Miss Newfield! I do believe you've got it."

Indeed, she did. No longer bouncing against the saddle, she was moving in unison with dear little Bella. And laughing with the sheer joy of it. Most important, she had won. She had conquered her fear. At least for today.

"Shall we ride out?" The major untied his horse and, with the groom's assistance, mounted the fine black beast, which he called Brutus. "Are you ready?"

He reined Brutus toward the long drive that led to the main road. Anna urged Bella up beside him. To her relief, they walked along the lane at a leisurely pace. From time to time one of the horses would nicker or blow out a breath, and the other would answer. Behind them the groom hummed a merry tune.

As long as they walked, she settled into the saddle and surveyed the scenery. The air held a hint of smoke, no doubt from breakfast fires in the distant cottages. In the fields, farmers raked the grey earth to prepare it for winter. A wind swept across the terrain, blowing leaves from the trees to form showers of red, orange and yellow to blanket the land.

This landscape looked so much like the area around Blandon that a melancholy ache began to throb in Anna's chest. Oh, for those autumn days when she and Peter played with the village children in the haystacks or drove the dog cart to the apple orchard for harvest. But she doubted she would ever see Blandon again. Or Peter.

No. She would not think it. Peter was alive and well and recovering from his wounds somewhere in America. She must believe that. She must.

"A fine day, is it not, Miss Newfield?" Edmond noticed the moment her cheerful expression disappeared, but he could detect no cause for it.

She cleared her throat as though dismissing the emotion that had gripped her, and gave him a genuine smile, which suddenly made this pleasant day even brighter. "Oh, it is indeed. But does the weather seem a bit cold to you for this time of year?"

"Yes, I've noticed that as well." He ran a hand down his steed's neck. "As the days get shorter, the horses' coats grow denser. This year I am convinced they're thickening earlier in preparation for a bitter winter."

"How interesting." Miss Newfield copied his gesture, bending forward to caress Bella's neck. She seemed to be growing more comfortable in the saddle, but only when she was distracted.

"Look." He pointed to a wooded area as they passed it. "Were I a betting man, I'd wager not an acorn was left under the oak trees after the squirrels and nuthatches laid in their winter stores." Not the most intelligent observation, but he wanted to keep her mind off her riding.

"Were I a betting woman, I would not take that wager."

The lilt in her voice brought a chuckle from Edmond. For a simple country vicar's daughter, she had a delightful wit. But then, her brother had kept the regiment entertained with his humor. As often before, he thought how grand it must have been to grow up in such an agreeable family.

"Major, why does Lady Greystone want me to ride? I have not observed her riding."

Edmond hesitated, but decided she must know the truth. "No, she does not often ride. However, I believe she will want you to go along with her for the foxhunts."

"Oh, my!" At her cry, Bella skittered to the side, causing Miss Newfield to gasp and stiffen as she tried not to fall.

"Easy, Bella." Edmond bent forward to grasp the bridle and steady the mare. "It's best not to startle your horse, madam."

Her face pale, she nodded and adjusted her seating. "Forgive me, Major. I am not given to alarm." She gave him a weak smile. "Most of the time."

He reached across and patted her shoulder. "So I have

noticed. But what is it about foxhunting that alarms you? It is a necessary sport. The foxes eat the game birds and rabbits. They attack the geese and chickens even in a well-protected farmyard." He would not tell her that sometimes small children were attacked by those pests. "They must be exterminated as surely as we exterminate rats."

"I do understand that." The fear remained in her eyes. "But, you see, Squire Beamish orders annual foxhunts. The riders tear about the countryside, jumping hedges and fences and—" Her voice trailed off and her posture stiffened again. "I shall never be able—"

Edmond searched his thoughts for some way to encourage her. "Ah, well, perhaps you can cry off. As far as I know, Miss Peel never accompanied Mother on the hunts."

"Yes, I know." The young lady gave a wry shrug. "Perhaps that is why Lady Greystone insists that I must." She leaned toward him, her eyes pleading. "I do so wish to be the best of companions to your mother, but—"

"No need to say 'but.'" He straightened his posture and held up his hand to silence her. He must not let her falter, but could she take a bit of prodding, as he might goad a reluctant dragoon? "Come now, Miss Newfield, you can do this. We will urge our mounts to a trot. The first one back to the Lodge can claim victory."

"Oh—"

"Come along. That's a good soldier." He reined Brutus around and was pleased to see her copy his actions. In the corner of his eye he could see George trying to hide a grin, as if the groom approved Edmond's methods.

He clicked his tongue and gently dug his heels into his horse's sides. After all his hesitation, he truly felt alive on this magnificent beast. Brutus had been restless to begin with and doubtless would prefer a full-out gallop, as would Edmond. But that would serve only to ruin the lesson. As much as he reveled in being on horseback again, he and the gelding would have to settle for a brisk trot. "Come along, Miss Newfield," Edmond called over his shoulder. "We should make it back to the Lodge in time for our midday meal." Another glance revealed a startled look, then narrowed eyes as determination took over her face.

"Go, Bella. Hurry up."

Impatience resounded from Miss Newfield's voice, to no avail. Bella had made up her mind to wander to the side of the road where some tufts of still-green grass beckoned, and no amount of kicking would deter her.

"Whoa." Edmond pulled Brutus around. He'd neglected to tell her that horses sometimes liked to take advantage of a timid rider. Trading a look with the groom, he gave the lad a nod.

"Come now, missy." George leaned out of the saddle and grasped Bella's bridle. "Time to show the lady what you're made of." He tugged the mare along and urged his own horse to a trot.

"Let's go, silly girl." Miss Newfield's voice wavered, but resolve was written across her face.

What a good soldier. What a gallant soul! Edmond felt his heart edging ever closer to a sincere attachment to the young lady, and he seemed to have no power to stop it.

Anna bounced in the saddle, sometimes with Bella's gait and sometimes against it. She would be sore tonight, but it would be worth it for the lark she'd had this day. Still, she hoped Lady Greystone did not want to go to the village this afternoon for her usual Thursday visit, for Anna would enjoy a nice lie-down much more than a walk.

She arrived at the Lodge just a few lengths behind the major, but only because he was a gentleman. Oh, how she would like to ride well enough to actually have a race with him. What fun that would be. And no doubt very inappropriate. She permitted herself to admire him as a very fine, handsome soldier, but letting her sentiments go any further would be foolish. Still, when he lifted her down from Bella, she had to work hard to dismiss the giddy feelings in her chest and the pleasant shivers sliding down her arm.

"Congratulations on a job well done, Miss Newfield." He swept off his black, plumed dragoon hat and bowed gallantly. "You will be riding to the hounds in no time."

"Or perhaps I'll have a bit of luck and break my leg." She gave him a teasing grin, as she would to Peter, and he laughed.

"No, my dear lady, trust me when I say you do not want to break your leg."

He offered an arm and they walked together through the wide front door of the Lodge. As if ordered by a silent command, they both stopped abruptly. For Lady Greystone stood in the entryway, arms crossed and a scowl sharpening her hawkish features. "Where have you been, Edmond? The vicar has been waiting in the drawing room to see Newfield for over an hour."

Chapter Eleven

"To see me?" Anna had forgotten that Mr. Partridge had asked to call upon her.

"Is that not what I said?" Lady Greystone waved an arm toward the stairway. "Do not keep him waiting any longer. Go and change."

Anna curtseyed and then dashed up the stairs like a mouse in the rafters. As she hurried down the hallway toward her room, she realized she had not taken her leave of Major Grenville. But surely the gentleman would forgive her under the circumstances.

In her room she found her black bombazine gown freshened and laid out on the bed. But she had not left it there.

Mrs. Hudson appeared at the door. "I took the liberty, miss."

"I thank you, dear lady." Anna snatched off her bonnet, leaving her hair ripped from its pins. "Oh, dear."

"Permit me?" Mrs. Hudson helped her make a quick change and then deftly arranged her hair in a tidy bun and affixed the black mourning lace over it. "There. Quite presentable."

"Mrs. Hudson, you are a jewel." Tears stinging her eyes, Anna placed a quick kiss on the woman's cheek.

She gasped. "Here now. None of that. 'Twas just a little thing." But her eyes also filled. "Now, be off with you."

Despite her words, they clung to each other for the briefest moment. Then, heart pounding, Anna did as she was told and hastened down the front stairs, taking a moment to catch her breath before nodding to the smiling footman to open the door. How good of the household servants to make her feel so much at home here at the Lodge.

"Mr. Partridge, how good of you to call." Anna crossed the room to the grouping of chairs where the vicar waited with Lady Greystone. She hid her disappointment that Major Grenville was not present as well.

"My dear Miss Newfield." When he stood, the clergyman's tall, slender form was accentuated by his somber black suit, making him look like a friendly, grey-haired scarecrow.

After curtseys and bows and greetings were exchanged, they sat in the matching blue brocade chairs.

"Newfield, you will pour." Lady Greystone nodded to the silver tea service on the occasional table.

Both she and the vicar watched as Anna poured steaming tea into china cups, although Mr. Partridge's expression was measurably kinder. Still, Anna had poured many a tea for *Papá*'s guests and did not falter now. Of course, they had not owned a silver service, but she had never felt the need to apologize for the quality of their tea. Like his books, *Papá* valued good tea.

Asking each about their preferences for sugar and cream, Anna adroitly completed her assigned task. In addition to tea the tray held cucumber sandwiches, which the viscountess passed around as they chatted about the weather. Hungry from her ride, Anna endeavored not to devour the tasty treats, even as she waited for the vicar to address her. It seemed quite strange that Lady Greystone lingered, for when *Papá* had visited parishioners, no chaperone was required. But then, so little here at Greystone Lodge compared to her old life in Blandon.

"And so, Vicar," Lady Greystone said, "you will not permit the village children to engage in any of that wicked All Hallows' Eve mischief." It was a clear command.

"Why, no, madam." Mr. Partridge's eyebrows rose, but a merry twinkle lit his eyes. "I believe the good people of Greystone Village are far too pious to engage in such activities, especially with the thirty-first occurring this Sunday. But of course we will hold services for All Saints' Day and All Souls' Day as usual."

"As it should be." Lady Greystone's response sounded very near to approval. "Well, then, I shall leave you to your discussion." She gave him a knowing nod as if they shared a secret, then rose and glided from the room.

Straightaway, the atmosphere in the room seemed to lighten, but Anna felt a twinge of guilt for such an unkind thought about her employer.

"Miss Newfield, when we spoke the other day you seemed burdened by your grief, which is entirely understandable." He took a sip of tea and she refreshed his cup, remembering his preference for two lumps of sugar and a tiny splash of cream. "As I said then, I would be pleased to counsel with you, if you like."

"I thank you, Vicar. So often we are told to hide our sorrows, but I believe we have a duty to help our fellow Christians to shoulder their burdens."

"Such a wise sentiment from one so young." His wrinkled face beamed approval. "But I cannot help but notice that today your face bears a certain, shall I say, *radiance*." He leaned toward her with a gentle smile. "May I ask the cause?"

Anna touched her cheek. By now it should have warmed

from the effects of the biting wind. "Why, I have no idea." She had enjoyed the ride with Major Grenville, but why would that cause a heightened complexion? As if to answer, warmth crept up her neck.

The vicar chuckled, a paternal sound so much like *Papá*'s. A familiar ache tugged at her heart. Perhaps she had not dealt with her grief so well, after all. So she shared with Mr. Partridge a few memories of *Papá, Mamá* and Peter, making sure to emphasize her expectation of hearing from her brother one day soon.

"I am convinced he survived. Otherwise they would have found his…remains." That last word did not come easily.

"Yes, Major Grenville told me of your sentiments in that regard." The vicar idly stirred his tea and tapped his spoon on the edge of the cup. "Tell me, my dear, do you like your living arrangements here?"

The shift in topic jarred her for a moment. "Why, I—" She waved a hand to take in the whole room. "Only an ingrate would fail to appreciate this lovely house." And a certain gentleman's encouraging presence. But she could hardly tell the vicar about her fondness for and dependence upon the major.

"Ah, yes, it is truly elegant. But would you not like a home of your own?"

A longing for that very thing teased at the door of Anna's mind, but she refused it entry. "Why, Mr. Partridge, I am convinced God has willed for me to be a spinster. I am content with that."

"Hmm, hardly a spinster, my dear. When a man reaches my age, he views his twenties as barely out of childhood."

Anna laughed. "I cannot agree, sir. Consider the gentlemen in this house, all in their twenties. Lord Greystone serves in Parliament. Major Grenville has fought for England. And of course, Mr. Grenville's ordination—"

"Yes, of course." A hint of dismay shot across his pale blue eyes as he stood and walked to the nearby window.

Did he suspect he would soon be replaced by Lady Greystone's middle son? What a dreadful way to live, not unlike her own uncertain situation.

He stared out through the hazy glass. "Miss Newfield, I will be blunt, but I hope not offensive. My beloved wife died eight years ago, and we were not blessed with offspring. Of late, I have been lonely. It has occurred to me that a young lady in your situation, without family or funds, could do worse than marry a humble country vicar."

Shock tore through Anna. His offer was entirely unexpected.

The vicar still did not look her way. "I do realize you are in mourning, but perhaps you will forgive me if I am overstepping. And of course you need not respond immediately. You see, with your unique training in your father's home, you would be a blessing to both me and my parishioners. And you may be assured that my pension will be yours when I die." He still did not turn to face her, perhaps fearing her response. "I assure you, I will not expect—"

"Mr. Partridge." She could not let him continue. "You cannot imagine how honored I am." She sent up a quick prayer for wisdom. But surely the vicar had prayed about this, too. Would she be thwarting God's will to decline?

He turned to face her, his eyes wide, his lips parted as if he would speak. But he remained silent, the question written across his weathered features.

Anna could not speak either, but only continue to plead with God for a clear answer. Did Lady Greystone know he was going to propose? Did that mean her employer was displeased and wished to be rid of her? Or was this some sort of a test? And if so, why? When no answer to these questions came to mind, Anna could think of only one way to avert disaster.

"Sir, I believe God has called me to be Lady Greystone's companion. Until He or the viscountess releases me from this position, I must follow His leading."

Was that relief softening the vicar's expression? "I would never advise someone of your spiritual sensitivity to disobey God's leading." His gentle smile once again became paternal. "But if you ever find this situation untenable, I—"

Anna crossed the small gap between them and gripped his hand. "My dear Mr. Partridge, you are a true friend. How you honor me with your kindness."

He patted her gloved hand. "We'll say no more about it." He offered her his arm, she accepted, and they walked toward the door. Just as the footman opened it for them, a shout sounded on the other side.

"You what?" Major Grenville's voice echoed throughout the entryway. "Mother, what are you thinking?" He swung his gaze toward Anna and the vicar, his eyes lighting on her hand resting on the clergyman's arm.

Anna resisted the urge to jump away from Mr. Partridge. There was nothing improper about their contact. But the major must have thought so, for he spun away and stalked up the staircase.

Edmond could not get to his room fast enough. Pain shot up his leg, but he stomped all the harder with each step on the hallway runner as if to punish himself for the position in which he had put poor Miss Newfield. He had brought her here to protect her, but Mother had sold her as a lamb for slaughter.

He slammed his door and flung himself into a velvet

wingchair, despising its soft cushions, despising the opulence of this entire estate and all it represented. If Uncle Grenville did not come soon, Edmond would find a way to go to London to visit him, with or without Mother's permission.

He could not fault Miss Newfield for grasping for a life of security or seeking to escape Mother's unpleasant temperament. The vicar was a kind, godly man who would treat her well. But the idea of their marriage caused Edmond's belly to rumble like a volcano preparing to erupt. There had to be a different solution to her dilemma.

Perhaps he could investigate what went wrong with the inheritance her father had arranged. An annual income of fifty pounds was nothing to dismiss, and he now knew her well enough to realize she would not have misunderstood her father's promises. If Edmond could solve that situation before she married, she might change her mind. He could not believe Mr. Partridge had fallen in love with a girl less than half his age. The vicar was not an old fool. Edmond would visit him and explain how responsible he felt for the sister of the man who saved him, perhaps convince him to withdraw his offer before the banns were cried.

Worn out from the morning ride and the pain in his leg, not to mention his emotional struggle, he scrubbed his hand down his face and laid his head back into the chair wing, surrendering to his blackest thoughts. Oh, for the day when his strength returned and he could resume normal living.

"Feeling poorly, sir?" Matthews stepped into the room with Edmond's freshly done laundry.

"A bit." He could always be truthful with his batman. The lad had a proper fondness for Miss Newfield. Maybe he had an idea about what to do.

"Do you mind a bit of gossip from below stairs, sir?" Matthews lifted one eyebrow.

At this point, any diversion would do. "You know the parameters." He wouldn't permit cruel or salacious rumors.

"Aw, it's just a bit of a chuckle. No harm to it." Matthews placed the shirts, stocking and breeches into the mahogany wardrobe, making sure each item was evenly stacked with similar garments.

Edmond longed for the day when he could don civilian clothing again, but he suspected Mother took pride in being seen with him in uniform. "Go ahead."

"Seems the good old vicar just offered for Miss New-field." Matthews chuckled. "Can you beat that?"

Edmond eyed him. Did no protective bone dwell in this man's body?

"John the footman said he'd never seen such a gracious rejection in his life. Though I doubt the lad's seen all that many."

Edmond bolted up in the chair. "Rejection?"

Matthews chuckled. "O'course. You don't think our bonnie Miss Newfield would marry an old codger like the vicar, do you?" He winked, as only a close servant would dare. "Meaning no disrespect to 'im, sir."

Laughing uncontrollably, Edmond leaned back in the chair again, unable to account for the utter joy that surged through his chest and radiated to every part of his being.

Chapter Twelve

Not knowing whether to leave the front entry or go to her room, Anna watched as Lady Greystone conferred privately with Mr. Partridge. At last the vicar gave the viscountess a final bow and left.

Lady Greystone seemed to have forgotten Anna, for when she saw her, she raised her eyebrows and stared at her up and down. "Well." Nothing in her expression revealed her thoughts, either approving or disapproving. "We go to the village this afternoon. No doubt you require a rest after this morning's ride, so I will have your midday meal sent to your room."

Understanding she had been dismissed, Anna curtseyed and began her ascent up the staircase. With each step her body ached from the bruising ride, but she forced herself to keep climbing in case Lady Greystone was watching her.

In the upper hallway she met Major Grenville, whose well-formed features were all the more handsome for the bright smile he gave her. "Did you have a pleasant visit with the vicar?" His dark brown eyes seemed to ask much more than his simple question.

"Yes." Her throat closed with unexpected emotion. Had

she accepted Mr. Partridge's proposal, she might never again enjoy the major's company, at least not in the same way. "I thank you for asking."

"You're welcome." He continued to gaze at her, and she could not break the contact. Nor did she wish to.

But she must, so with some effort, she dismissed the foolish rush of feeling created by his presence. "If you will excuse me, Major, Lady Greystone sent me to my room."

"What?" Now he frowned, but even so, his face was pleasing to her.

"I mean, she suggested that I should rest. We're going to the village this afternoon."

"Ah." He breathed out a long sigh. "I thought perhaps... but never mind." His smile returned. "Then go rest, dear lady. I did put you through your paces this morning, didn't I?"

Anna gave him a playful smirk. "I continue to hope for that broken leg."

His jolly laughter rang throughout the hallway, and he patted her shoulder as he walked past her on his way to the stairs. "And I intend to have you jumping within a fortnight."

She could not help but laugh, too, despite the trepidation his warning generated.

In her room she searched for her woolen shawl to use as a cover. If she turned the bed down for her rest, the upstairs maid would have to come and make it again, and the poor girl had enough to do.

"Miss Newfield?" Mrs. Hudson tapped on the door and opened it slightly.

"Do come in." Back in Blandon Anna would have offered her tea, but now she had no means of extending hospitality. "I thank you for your help earlier. I felt quite presentable after your ministrations."

Unlike her previous visit not an hour ago, the woman wore a considerably brighter expression, almost a smile. "It was my pleasure, miss. Did you have a pleasant visit with the vicar?"

Anna stared at her. Why was everyone asking this? "Why, yes. Thank you."

"How nice." Mrs. Hudson's eyes glistened. "Everyone's so glad it turned out as it did."

"But—" Anna dismissed her questions, for it all became clear. The footman inside the drawing room might look like a statue, but he most certainly was not one. He must have quickly spread the word about her conversation with Mr. Partridge. And to think that everyone who had heard about the proposal was pleased to know she had turned the dear man down. A funny little tickle in her chest bubbled up into a laugh. Undoubtedly Major Grenville knew all about it as well. From his merry mood, she could only assume he was also pleased. Such a happy thought made it impossible for her to fall asleep, no matter how much she needed the rest.

Edmond didn't know whether to be glad or sorry to see Greystone return from his visit to Shrewsbury. He longed to spend time with his eldest brother and reestablish the close bond they had shared in childhood. But he must address the issue of Greystone's prodding him about Miss Newfield once and for all. She had graciously dodged the cannonball of marriage while maintaining her employment, but Mother's apparent complicity in the proposal revealed her awareness that the young lady was much more marriageable than her previous companion. Perhaps it had been a test to see if it was safe to keep her here with two unmarried sons, to see if she would set her cap for someone above her station. That thought brought him up short.

In his view, Miss Newfield was every bit as worthy as any peer or aristocrat he'd ever known.

Greystone arrived in time to miss All Souls' Day but not Guy Fawkes Day, one of the few annual celebrations during which he reveled in his lordly status with his tenants. In spite of a nasty cough, he ordered the requisite effigy to be constructed, candies to be made and fireworks to be prepared. The entire household welcomed him home and Mother ordered a supper of roast lamb, Greystone's favorite, which he nibbled at without much comment. After the meal, he declined to gather with the family in the drawing room and instead took to his bed.

Mother's concern was evident in the deepening lines of her face, but she conducted the evening's activities without commenting on his uncharacteristic conduct. She even chose whist over a poetry reading or one of Mary's pleasant but unremarkable recitals on the pianoforte. But her strategy at the game lacked its usual cunning, with only Miss Newfield playing a worse game. Finally, Mother announced she would visit Greystone and then retire, but left permission for the rest to entertain each other as long as they wished.

"Oh, dear." Mary, as always, had eyes only for Richard. "Poor Lord Greystone. If Lady Greystone is worried, his illness cannot be insignificant."

Seated beside her on the settee, Richard patted her hand. "Do not fret, my darling. It cannot be good for our son." He shot a glance at Miss Newfield and Edmond, and his color heightened.

Edmond could not fault him for his concern and even envied him a little for the devotion they shared. He and Richard had managed to have a few conversations without Mother's interference, but Richard was often preoccupied with making certain Mary was not overtaxed. Perhaps this small gathering was fortuitous. Although Miss Newfield had been in the house for over two weeks, he had yet to see Mary speak to her. But then, as the niece of a baron, she might feel it beneath her station to befriend an employed gentlewoman, even though they were both daughters of clergymen. The idea burned in Edmond's chest like a hot stone, not against Mary, but against the entire social system that refused to value a person not born of the aristocracy. He would hate to see Richard become the kind of minister who deferred to the wealthy and spurned the poor, something clearly forbidden in scripture. A plan formed in his mind to search out his brother's convictions in the matter. He hoped Mary and Miss Newfield would join in the conversation.

"Well, then, how shall we amuse ourselves?" Edmond eyed each of his companions. "Another game of whist? Mary, you can take Mother's place."

Her eyes widened with alarm. "Gracious, no. I have no talent for cards of any kind."

"Ah." Edmond had hoped for a casual discussion around the card table, but now he would have to open the topic a little more bluntly. "Then perhaps we are left with conversation to pass the time. Tell me, Richard, in your studies of scripture, what say you about the passage in chapter two of James in regard to respect of persons?"

Richard blinked and one eyebrow quirked upward. "Do you study scripture yourself, Edmond? Will you enter the ministry, then?" His expression softened. "Or did your battle injuries persuade you of your mortality and drive you at last to seek God?"

Irritation grated through Edmond. Richard had always been the conscience for his brothers and had been grieved by Edmond's disastrous youthful escapades. But then, as the youngest of the three, Edmond was often the recipient of unwanted advice, as though he did not possess a brain to figure things out or learn from his mistakes. He started to deflect Richard's intrusive question with a self-protective barb, but that would not help Miss Newfield. Instead, he gave his brother a rueful grin.

"No. My quest for the Almighty began when I met a remarkable young lieutenant named Newfield. His faith set an example for the entire regiment." He had not intended to say that, but from the sweet smile on Miss Newfield's face and the shock on Mary's, he knew it was right.

Richard shot an uneasy glance at Miss Newfield. "The same man who—"

"Saved my life. Yes, one and the same." Edmond must keep the conversation from speculation about Newfield's demise, lest it distress the young lady. "But about the passage in James. Does it not say that we are not to regard one person as more important than another, no matter their position in life or the clothing they wear?"

"Yes, of course." Caution colored Richard's tone.

"Then how do we justify the teaching of the Great Chain of Being, which values kings and nobles as closer to God than the rest of us? Or aristocrats such as you and me as more valuable in His sight than a courageous lieutenant who was born to the gentry?" Once again, he found himself returning to Miss Newfield's brother.

Richard stared off for a moment. At last he returned his gaze to Edmond. "Perhaps you are confusing the positions in which we are born with our value to God."

"But that's my point exactly. Saint Paul tells us in Galatians that we are all one in Christ. How does a Christian society dare to value one man more than another when the Lord clearly does not?" Edmond ran a hand through his hair. From Mary's pinched expression, he could see he had offended her.

"You almost sound like an anarchist." Richard chuckled. "Or an American, what with their rebellion last century and this ridiculous war over British deserters."

"All of this talk wearies me, my love." Mary shifted uncomfortably on the settee. "May we retire?"

Edmond ground his teeth but forced a smile. "Forgive me, sister. Such conversation is not fit for a lady in your condition."

With Richard and Mary leaving the room, Edmond had no choice but to retire as well. Even with the footman at the door, it would not be proper to spend the evening alone with Miss Newfield. Discouraged by his failure to persuade his brother, Edmond trudged up the stairs beside her, trying to think of something pleasant to say before they went their separate ways.

At the top of the staircase she touched his arm, and an agreeable warmth ran up to his shoulder. "Major Grenville, I appreciate your kind words about Peter." She peered around him toward Richard and Mary, who were halfway down the west hallway. "I believe we both can recognize the value of a man as God sees him, but we live in a fallen world in which things are seldom as they should be. Thus we must abide by society's prevailing ideas and find a way to serve God where He has placed us."

He took her hand and gazed down into her lovely green eyes, which tonight had a weary grey cast to them. "Ah, dear lady, but those misbegotten ideas lead to wars in which good men die and nothing ever changes."

A shadow passed over her fair face, and he wanted to kick himself for that cruel allusion to Newfield's death. Then she smiled and leaned toward him with a confidential air.

"But things do change. I will confide in you that I admire the Americans for winning their freedom from the

Crown. Although I am thankful to be an Englishwoman, God made it abundantly clear that He wished to create a new country with a new form of government." She gasped softly and stepped back, her eyes wide. "Do I sound like a traitor?"

He gave her a crooked grin. "Prodigiously so. I shall have you arrested on Friday."

"Friday?" She laughed. "Why then?"

"Because it's Guy Fawkes Day, the day when all traitors must learn how we deal with them."

She made a snickering sound that, coming from her, was entirely ladylike. "Then I must get my rest before I am carted off to the Tower of London." After a playful curtsey, she took a step toward the east wing.

Before he could stop himself, he gently grasped her arm and turned her back around. He had meant to make a jest, asking her preference between the beheading and hanging, but when he gazed again into those shadowed eyes the question seemed out of place. Instead, he took her hand and kissed her fingertips.

"Good night, dear lady." Surprised by the emotion in his voice, he cleared his throat.

"Oh, Major, I pray you are not succumbing to Lord Greystone's illness."

To his shame, in his eagerness to forge a friendship between Miss Newfield and his sister-in-law, he had forgotten his eldest brother was sick. Even now Greystone's violent cough could be heard down the west hall. As always, Miss Newfield thought of others instead of herself, and in doing so, set an example for Edmond. In fact, she excelled in every way, from her agreeable association with the schoolchildren to her kindly rejection of the poor vicar's proposal. Would that they could breach Society's walls and spend an eternity inspiring each other to good deeds. The thought brought him up short. Yet, at this moment, he could find no fault in his desire to see it come true.

Chapter Thirteen

"His Lordship coughed all night, miss." The girl who brought Anna a pitcher of hot water each morning, along with the latest household news, worked at the small hearth to revive the fire. "Lady Greystone's been with him the whole time."

"I'm sorry to hear that, Betty." As Anna splashed water over her face and neck, she tried to think of how she might help her employer. When she had heard the viscount coughing the day before, echoing *Papá*'s final illness, it concerned her more than a little. Learning he had not rested increased her alarm.

"Aye, and Major Grenville rode out at dawn to fetch the physician." The girl stirred the coals into a flame around a small log.

"Oh, my." Poor Major Grenville, having to ride today when yesterday's excursion had caused him pain. Although he had not complained, she had seen him wince as he walked last evening. An unexpected warmth infused her chest as she remembered the tender way he had kissed her hand, no doubt as reassurance that he had not considered her comment about the Americans seditious. How pleasant to have someone with whom she could banter over the absurdities of life. In truth, she enjoyed every minute in Major Grenville's presence.

"Will there by anything else I can do for you, miss?"

"No, Betty. Thank you." Eager to be of use to Lady Greystone, Anna dressed and hurried out of her room. She tapped on her employer's door, seeking Mrs. Hudson.

The lady's maid appeared straightaway. "Any news, miss?"

"No. I was hoping you knew something. What do you suppose I should do to help? What would Miss Peel have done?"

Mrs. Hudson snorted. "That one? She'd cower in her room and pray not to catch the sickness."

"Oh." Anna could think of no response, but sympathy for the late companion was never far from her thoughts. "Should I go to Lord Greystone's room to help?"

Mrs. Hudson wrung her hands. "I wouldn't like for Her Ladyship to be displeased with you."

Anna almost blurted out that she had never actually pleased their employer, but bit back the uncharitable thought. "I cannot sit by and do nothing."

"No, I suppose not." Mrs. Hudson squeezed Anna's hand. "And it's more your place than mine to offer help."

Anna nodded, even though she failed to understand the division of duties in this household. Why couldn't everyone just do what was necessary? With no one to answer her questions, she hurried down the hall and made her first foray into the west wing.

Long before she reached Lord Greystone's room, she could hear his deep, harsh cough even through the heavy white door. She knocked softly, yet the sound caused her stomach to do a turn. She prayed she was not making a mistake. But after six months in *Papá's* sickroom, she would not shy away from doing anything required to help the viscount.

Gilly, the viscount's valet, peered out, his usually tidy appearance utterly rumpled. "Yes, miss?" The middle-aged man's eyes were bloodshot, his pale features haggard.

"Good morning, Gilly. Would you please ask Lady Greystone how I may help her?"

"That's most kind of you, miss." He offered a weak smile. "I shall inquire." Leaving her there, he closed the door. In a few moments, he returned. "Her Ladyship says you're to come in."

Anna gripped her emotions and walked quietly across the red-and-gold carpet, resisting the urge to wave away the smell of sickness that assaulted her nose. The curtains of the canopied bed were closed. Lady Greystone sat in a red brocade wingchair, resting her head in one hand.

"How may I help you, my lady?" Anna whispered.

Lady Greystone looked up and her eyes widened in surprise. "Newfield. Ah, yes. Sit." She indicated a wooden chair nearby. The lines on her face had deepened overnight, and like Gilly's, her eyes were red from lack of sleep. "You tended your father in his illness, did you not?"

"Yes, my lady." Anna wished she could grasp the lady's hand to comfort her, but feared her employer might find the gesture offensive. "And many a villager through the years."

"I see." She inhaled a deep breath and let it out with a soft hiss. "I will depend upon you to sit with Lord Greystone when I must rest. Of course Gilly will be here, as well. Edmond should return with the physician soon."

A dry, barking cough sounded from behind the curtain, followed by a groan.

Lady Greystone stood and pulled aside the curtain to reveal the viscount thrashing about in the bed and gasping between each cough. "Wring out the cloth and give it to me."

Anna located a bowl on the bedside table and obeyed. Lady Greystone pressed the cool cloth to the viscount's neck and forehead. He settled back down to an uneasy sleep.

"We've not had much sickness in this family. My boys are a hardy lot." Lady Greystone appeared to talk to herself as she resumed her place in the wingchair, so Anna did not respond.

After a while, her stomach rumbled softly, and she pressed a hand against it. Not appearing to notice, Lady Greystone let her head loll against the chair wing.

"My lady." Anna touched the chair arm. "May I have breakfast sent up for you?"

The viscountess rolled her head in her direction. "Yes."

With no further directions forthcoming, Anna hurried to complete the task. She also made quick work of her own breakfast. It would not do for her to falter in her duties because of hunger. After eating, she made her way to the front staircase where she met Major Grenville just in from his errand.

"Is the physician with you?" A foolish question, for the front door was closed and only a footman stood by it.

The major touched her shoulder, worry clouding his brown eyes. "The man has taken to his own sickbed."

Anna gasped. "Does he suspect an epidemic?"

The major shook his head. "No. He is suffering from fatigue and a severe pain in his chest."

"Poor man. We must pray for him."

He gave her a weary smile, but his gaze had turned intense. "Always thinking of others, aren't you?"

"Am I?" Her heart fluttered under his scrutiny. She

swallowed before speaking. "We must inform Lady Greystone."

In the sickroom the major whispered the bad news to his mother.

"This is untenable." She clenched her fists and her nostrils flared. "If he is not ill, he must come."

The major shook his head. "The man could barely lift his head. He is having difficulty breathing, and he complains his entire left side is numb."

"But he must come and bleed Greystone."

At her words, Anna cringed. "My lady, forgive me, but my father's illness was very similar to Lord Greystone's. Each time the surgeon bled him, he grew weaker. It did not help at all."

"Nonsense," Lady Greystone huffed. "Everyone knows bleeding releases the evil humors." But a hint of doubt colored her tone.

Anna decided to press the issue. "My lady, does the scripture not say that the life of the flesh is in the blood? Why then do we take from the sick person the very thing that can heal him?" She saw Major Grenville's eyebrows arch in surprise. Somehow she must encourage him to be her ally in this matter, so she gave him a quick nod.

"What?" Lady Greystone glowered at her. "Where does it say such a thing?" She paced back and forth across the carpet. "Never mind. I will ask Mr. Partridge."

Anna wondered why she would not inquire of her son, who had studied the scriptures and resided right across the hall. But with the physician unavailable to do the bleeding, the matter was not urgent. Perhaps Lady Greystone would accept other suggestions.

"There were certain treatments that relieved my father's suffering. Perhaps we could apply them to Lord Greystone."

Lady Greystone ceased her pacing and glared at her accusingly. "But your father died."

"Mother." Major Grenville's scolding tone did not change the woman's cross expression.

Anna appreciated his taking her part, but she was becoming used to the viscountess's disposition. "Yes, he did, but he was much older, and I believe the bleedings hastened his death. I also believe Lord Greystone's lifelong good health will help him overcome this."

The viscountess pondered her words for several moments. "What do you advise?"

Anna thought of the various treatments she had administered to *Papá.* "If he can bear it, he should rest against pillows rather than recline. This will help him breathe more easily in spite of the congestion." She tapped her chin, recalling her actions. "Then apply a plaster and give him clear broth, preferably chicken." These actions might not have saved *Papá,* but they had alleviated his suffering and that of many villagers who had suffered violent coughs. "A potion of willow bark helps with the pain and fever."

Once again, the viscountess appeared to ponder the suggestions. At last, she nodded. "Very well." She strode across the wide room to the bedside. "Edmond, Gilly, help me with the pillows. Newfield, prepare the plaster and willow bark and order Cook to bring a broth."

Over the next hours they administered the treatments Anna had prescribed. Each time Lord Greystone suffered another coughing spell, activity swirled around him. When he slept quietly against the propped pillows, everyone found a place to rest so they might be ready for the next attack. Lady Greystone refused to leave the bedside, but slept in the wingchair while Anna and the major took turns sitting nearby.

From time to time the viscountess would speak softly

to the sleeping viscount, and Anna could not help but hear her words. "You must not die, Greystone, for Richard's pliable nature makes him unsuitable for the responsibilities of a peer." From her detached tone, one would think she was talking about some mundane matter instead of her eldest son's life. "Do your duty and fight this illness. When we go to London for the Season, I will find you a suitable wife. Then you will have your own son for an heir instead of your brother."

If the viscount's illness were not so serious, Anna would have laughed at this little speech. How like Lady Greystone to insist that her son rise up from his sickbed for duty's sake. But should God, in His unfailing wisdom, choose to take Lord Greystone from their midst, Anna had no doubt Richard Grenville could rise to the occasion.

Late in the afternoon, with the haze of a light slumber infusing her mind, Anna recalled a steam treatment one mother in Blandon had applied to her coughing infant. The child had survived. But while one could hold a baby near enough to a boiling teakettle to breathe the steam, how would one administer the cure to a grown man in his bed? Tiptoeing across the room to where Major Grenville rested in an overstuffed chair, she knelt down and posed the question to him.

"If I am not mistaken," she added, "the mother put crushed peppermint leaves in the teakettle to create a fragrant mist that broke through the congestion."

The major gathered Anna's hands in his. "Dear lady, you have been a blessing and a lifesaver. I will see to it." He grimaced as he drew in his stretched-out legs to stand.

"Sit still, Major." Anna rose and patted his shoulder, as he often did hers. But was the gesture too familiar? From his gentle smile, she guessed not, and it pleased her very much. "I will tend to it. I know there are peppermint plants in the conservatory, but how can we bring a constant flow of steam close to him?"

Eyeing the room's large hearth, he wrinkled his forehead in thought. "We should not move him, but we can set a small brazier on the side table, if we take care not to damage the surface."

"Of course. I should have thought of that." Anna experienced a flash of camaraderie with the major, almost as if they were comrades-in-arms in their battle for his brother's life.

Within the half hour, they had aromatic steam pouring into the enclosed bed. By nightfall the viscount was sleeping comfortably.

Edmond jolted awake at a sound he could not quickly identify. Was it one of Greystone's hounds growling beside his brother's bed? In the blackened room, the light of a single candle floated in the darkness, illuminating Mother's profile as she stood over Greystone. The sound came again, and Edmond realized his brother was attempting to laugh. *Laugh.* What grand news that was. In a thrice he joined Mother beside the bed.

"Say, old man, you shouldn't frighten our poor mother this way." Edmond had to force the last words out on a rushed breath to hide the emotions behind them. "Time to get back to work, whatever work it is that you do."

Mother huffed out a cross sound but didn't scold him.

Greystone chuckled, a horrible croak that nonetheless revealed a cheerful humor. "I'd be pleased to get to work, brother, but I fear you'll have to take my place this year."

"What are you talking about? Shall I go down to Parliament and tell them how to defeat Napoleon?"

A soft laugh sounded behind Edmond. He turned to

see Miss Newfield's radiant smile and merry eyes. At her beauty, his heart seemed to leap into his throat.

"No, foolish boy." Greystone croaked out the words on a cough. "This is Guy Fawkes Day. As I am still in my sickbed and your Miss Newfield prescribes continued bed rest, you must lead the festivities."

Edmond stared at Mother, mouth agape, expecting her to quash the plan.

Instead, she gave him one of her imperious nods. "It is our duty to oversee the celebration."

"But why not Richard?" Edmond had never coveted his eldest brother's position, nor would he supplant Greystone's heir presumptive.

Mother blew out a cross breath. "He refuses to leave Mary's side."

Nor should he, of course. "Very well. I will do my best." Pleased at the prospect of enjoying some much-needed gaiety, he turned to leave.

"And, Edmond—" Greystone coughed again, but it sounded like his congestion had broken up, a good sign that he was mending "—unless Mother requires Miss Newfield's presence, you must take her along with you to help distribute the candy to the children."

The smirk on his haggard face doused a large portion of Edmond's enthusiasm and goodwill. Greystone's earlier "your Miss Newfield" had not escaped his notice. At the first opportunity, he would advise his brother in no uncertain terms that he must stop these misbegotten jests. Why could Greystone not comprehend the threat to Miss Newfield, should Mother actually *hear* those jests and decide there was some truth behind them? Why, she would not have the slightest compunction against tossing the dear girl out in the snow. In the dead of night. Without a farthing.

At all costs, Edmond must not permit that to happen.

Chapter Fourteen

In the fading twilight Anna walked beside Major Grenville toward the village, following a footman who carried a lantern to light the path. Anna savored the aroma of the treacle sweetmeats and gingerbread in the basket on her arm. In the distance she could see the villagers piling dry branches on the pyre in the square. Behind her the hushed, hurried voices of two other footmen revealed their excitement over the coming revels. Or perhaps they were eager to taste the cakes in the boxes they carried.

"You must instruct me in my duties, Major. I have little experience with Guy Fawkes Day." Anna's pulse pounded in cautious anticipation. "*Papá* disapproved of the celebration, although as a churchman he did appreciate the sentiments behind it."

"So there were no festivities in Blandon?" A basket on one arm, he used the opposite hand to grip his cane. His halting gait suggested he found each step a struggle, but he did not complain.

If he could ignore his pain, Anna would follow suit, but how she wished he was resting after their vigil with Lord Greystone instead of making this journey. "Oh, yes. Squire Beamish would have nothing to do with the day, but the villagers made much of it. Unfortunately, without supervision, the young men often engaged in riotous actions beyond burning Guy Fawkes in effigy."

"I can imagine." The major gave her a knowing nod. "That's just the sort of thing the first Viscount Greystone hoped to prevent by organizing these celebrations. Each subsequent Lord Greystone has also given his people a holiday so they won't see any need to burn the manor house down."

Anna drew in a sharp breath. "Oh, dear. Would they do that?"

"One would hope not." He chuckled. "I would not alarm you, but with the riots up north and the Luddites' mischief, even Mother has seen the wisdom of continuing the revels. With Halloween given no sanction in Greystone Village, people need some sort of excitement after harvest and before winter sets in. This event seems to appease our villagers."

"Ah. I see." In truth, she did not see. Like *Papá,* she had never experienced the restlessness that afflicted many people. If Peter had not been so restless, he might still be close by her instead of a world away. Instead of—but she would not permit the thought to go further. "So now you must tell me what to do when we arrive at the bonfire." With only some fifty yards to go, she hoped his instructions would not be complicated.

"Very simply, you must take Mother's accustomed place and hand out the sweets." He stumbled briefly as the path dipped, but recovered his balance before she could comment. "Actually, I must first report to the people on Greystone's condition and offer his apologies. Then the effigy will be brought forth, I will read His Lordship's customary speech about the significance of the day, the effigy goes over the pyre, and the fire is set. Dancing and revelry ensue." He gave her a sidelong glance. "Of course we could set the sweets out for children to help themselves, but that would invite nothing short of chaos." His face creased comically, and he rolled his eyes in an expression all the more clownish in the flickering lantern light.

Anna laughed to ward off her unaccountably giddy feelings. Like her brother, this man was handsome even in his absurdity. "I do believe I can manage the task." Memories of her visit to the classroom assured her that these children were not entirely untamed. It was more than she could say for her heart, which was now wildly tripping over itself.

In the glow of the lantern Edmond could see the merry sparkle in Miss Newfield's eyes, and his heart lifted considerably. With her by his side, he could face the villagers and say all the proper things on his brother's behalf. In fact, with her encouragement, he sensed he could accomplish anything he set his mind to. If they had a private moment with no gossiping footmen nearby, he would ask her opinion of his ambitions to sell his commission and become a barrister. Until Uncle Grenville arrived, he longed for a confidante. He could think of no one who would listen as impartially as Miss Newfield.

They arrived at the torch-lit village square to much acclaim and cheering. It was the uniform, of course. At his every appearance among these good people, they made much ado, calling him a hero and pushing forward to greet him. Nothing he could say diminished their praise.

Wending his way through the lively crowd, he led Miss Newfield to the small platform prepared for Greystone and Mother, then helped her up the single step and onto the bench provided for them. In the back of the mob he noticed several youths consorting together, so he quietly ordered his footmen to make certain they planned no mischief. Their disappointment obvious, the footmen set down their treasured boxes and mingled with the throng, but not before Edmond promised to save them a goodly portion of the cakes as a reward for their efforts.

Surrendering his basket to Miss Newfield, he stood and raised his hands. The villagers and farmers, dressed in their finest clothes, grew quiet, and all eyes were on him and his companion. A few people gave them knowing glances and nudged each other, sending misgivings threading through him. Did the sight of him and Miss Newfield together hint at impropriety? Edmond renewed his vow to treat the young lady circumspectly so no suspicion would taint her name.

"Good people of Greystone, I bring you a happy report of His Lordship. He is resting well and sends his apologies for missing his favorite celebration."

A hearty cheer arose for several moments.

"Now let us begin. Bring out the villain!"

Cheering of a different sort rose up to echo throughout the village square and no doubt beyond it as the people surrendered to their merriment. If the denizens of Greystone Lodge could not hear the din, they were surely deaf. Two hardy farmers strode in with the effigy held high on a pole. They hung it on the flimsy scaffold above the pyre.

Edmond pulled a vellum sheet from his inside jacket pocket and unfolded it. Parents shushed their children and everyone listened attentively as he read the story with his best theatrical flair. By the time he reached the end, he felt a burst of English pride equal to that of any man in the crowd. "And when Guy Fawkes was discovered guarding the explosives beneath the House of Lords, our good King James I was delivered from certain death by the hand of Divine Providence. The Gunpowder Plot had failed."

Another cheer burst forth from the crowd, along with

cries of "Death to Guy Fawkes," "Death to the plotters" and "God save the king." Torches were taken from their stands and tossed into the pyre. Soon flames roared up and lapped at the figure's tattered linen gown.

In spite of the noise, Edmond heard a gasp beside him and turned to see dismay written across Miss Newfield's lovely face. She stared at him wide-eyed, then quickly looked down at her folded hands.

Edmond sat beside her and touched her shoulder, resisting the sudden urge to embrace her. "What is it, dear lady?"

She shook her head. "Please, pay no attention to me."

Before he could insist upon an answer, fireworks began to explode on the far side of the square. Rockets shot up into the sky, bursting into showers of red and yellow stars that rained back down to the earth. Edmond hadn't had time to inspect the safety of the fireworks, but Greystone had assured him that the blacksmith was competent. For several minutes, the crowd shouted their approval and celebratory songs rang out. Then, from his vantage point on the platform, Edmond watched with horror as a thin grey thread of smoke rose from the thatched roof of the schoolhouse down the lane.

"Fire!" His experience in the heat of battle triumphed over his alarm. "Form a bucket line."

The chaotic scene of a moment before quickly transformed into an organized brigade. The farmers who had been in their cups snapped out of their merriment to form a line to the well. Mothers whisked their frightened children away from the area, while the youths who had seemed up to no good now became men.

"John!" Edmond called to one of the footmen, who hurried to the platform. "Take Miss Newfield to the manor house."

"Aye, sir."

Assured she was in good hands, Edmond thrust aside his cane and took his place in the bucket line. To ward off the crippling effects of his pain, he marked the leaders among the villagers, heroes all, who knew how to combat the fire. He must inform Greystone of his tenants' courage.

In a surprisingly short time the schoolhouse was saved from destruction and order restored. The men called for the women and children to return to the square. And called again. But not one woman, girl or male below the age of twelve put in an appearance.

Anna ached with exhaustion but she forced her fingers over the keys of the small church organ. With the help of Mrs. Billings and John the footman, she had gathered the women and children into the church to pray for the men fighting the fire. When the smallest children began to cry, Anna offered to play so they could sing. Brave Mrs. Billings led the songs, even though her house was in danger of being destroyed.

Even as she played, she still shuddered at the memory of the burning effigy. Or, rather, the frayed linen gown that burned so quickly, for it brought back a tragic scene. A dear woman in Blandon had burned to death after her chemise caught fire as she stirred a pot over her hearth. Anna had to help prepare the body for burial while *Papá* tried to comfort the grief-stricken husband and child. To imagine someone dying by fire brought her no pleasure, no matter how wicked Guy Fawkes and his fellow conspirators had been to plot the king's murder.

The church door flew open and a gust of cold wind blew into the stone sanctuary. A soot-covered Major Grenville marched in, followed by Mr. Partridge and all the men of the village. Anna ceased her playing and unbidden emotion welled up within her. As though it were a Sunday morning service, the men found their families and filed into their customary pews. The major moved into the front row where his family always sat. When his gaze met hers, he sent her a warm smile, and heat rose up in her face to rival the earlier conflagration at the schoolhouse.

After Mr. Partridge informed a much-relieved Mrs. Billings that her home was saved, he took his place behind the pulpit, but not before he gave Anna an approving nod. To her relief, nothing in his demeanor indicated any feeling toward her beyond his position as her pastor.

"Thank you, Miss Newfield, Mrs. Billings, for helping these mothers keep the children out of danger and happily occupied. The fire is out, and Will Thatcher says the roof can be easily repaired. We have much to be thankful for. Let us pray."

Uncertain about what she should do, Anna remained on the organ bench with head bowed while the vicar offered up thanks. After his "amen," he dismissed the congregation, and she hurried to embrace Mrs. Billings. To her surprise, Mr. Partridge then claimed the teacher's attention. From his tender expression, it appeared the lady would be the next object of his interest.

"You did not obey orders, Miss Newfield." Major Grenville leaned on his cane and loomed over her. "You were to go to the manor house with John the footman, whom I must also charge with disobeying orders." His obvious effort to look menacing was thoroughly ruined by the twinkle in his eyes and the grin he could not hide.

"Ah, but you gave no order to me, Major." She crossed her arms and glowered up at him. "As for John, he still can escort me back to the Lodge now that I am prepared to go." A mischievous smile tugged at her lips. She could no more keep her own joy at bay than he could. They gazed at each other for a space of time she could not measure until each seemed to recall they were not alone. Anna inhaled a deep breath, filling her lungs with cold, refreshing air. "God is merciful and kind."

"Indeed He is." The humor in his expression faded into tranquillity. "Shall we go?"

"But I have not yet discharged my duty." Anna nodded toward the boxes and baskets at the front of the church.

The major chuckled. "That would be the cause of much disappointment amongst the children."

"And no doubt among the adults as well."

After a word to Mr. Partridge about their plans, they moved to the door of the church and dispensed the sweet-meats and gingerbread as the parishioners left the building.

By the time every man, woman and child had received a tasty treat, weariness had drawn deep lines around the major's eyes. Anna imagined her own face must appear just as weary. As if comprehending her longing for rest, he summoned the three footmen, and they began their walk back to the manor. She noticed the severity of his limp and longed to offer her shoulder as support. But even if such contact were not improper, she feared her offer might injure his pride.

At last they arrived at the Lodge, where the silence and dimly lit interior suggested everyone had gone to bed. The footmen dismissed, Anna and the major trudged up the front stairs to the landing.

"Get some sleep, dear lady." He grasped her hand and kissed it. "You have done well this night."

"And you performed heroically, sir." *In spite of your pain.* Anna wondered how he could remain on his feet.

Once again, they gazed at each other without speaking for uncounted seconds, or perhaps minutes.

The sound of coughing came from the direction of Lord Greystone's room, and they both stepped back.

"He sounds better." Anna felt warm in spite of the hallway draft.

Still gazing at her with a look she could not decipher, the major nodded. "No longer a barking mastiff."

"Tsk." She shook her head. "Good night, Major Grenville."

"Good night, Miss Newfield."

Somehow she sensed he was watching as she walked away, so when she reached the turn in the hallway, she glanced back. Still soot covered, still leaning on his cane, still appearing wearier than she had ever seen him, he bowed to her.

And no matter how much she prayed or tried to reason away her unruly feelings, her pounding pulse kept her awake far into the night.

Chapter Fifteen

When Edmond could barely rise from his bed the morning after the fire, Matthews urged him to plead sick and get a few days' rest. He managed to abide by his batman's advice for several hours until concern for Greystone's health obliged him to visit the suite across the hall. Mother was there, of course, looking older than her years. But despite her somber mourning clothes, Miss Newfield's serene presence brightened the room.

Greystone had suffered a relapse in the early morning hours and even now coughed sporadically. His pallor concerned Edmond but it did not alarm him. As one who had seen as many deaths by disease among his fellow soldiers as he had battlefield fatalities, he felt confident his eldest brother would not succumb to this illness. For that reason alone, he hoped for a moment alone with Greystone so he could convince him that the jests about Miss Newfield must cease.

But Greystone remained ill throughout the weekend. Mother of course rarely left his bedside, even when Edmond and the others attended church on Sunday. Already an unfashionably thin woman, she had lost weight, and her face had become gaunt. At last on Tuesday evening, Miss Newfield prevailed upon her to sleep in her own bed rather than the wingchair.

"I will watch him, my lady. You may depend upon it." Compassion shone from her eyes, although Mother had never spoken a kind word to her.

After glaring at the young lady as if she'd been insulted, Mother grunted. "Very well." She rose wearily and stepped over to the bed. She lifted one hand as if she would touch his face, but then dropped it to her side and strode from the room.

Edmond patted Miss Newfield's shoulder. "You rest, too, dear lady."

A raspy chuckle came from the bed, followed by a short bout of coughing. "And leave me to your rough ministrations, Edmond? No, the lady must stay, and you as well." Greystone's blue eyes, red-rimmed though they were, glinted with good humor.

Hands fisted at his waist, Edmond cast a wilting glare at him, which only brought forth more coughing laughter. "Should you not save your voice, *milord?*"

Miss Newfield looked from one to the other, settling her fair gaze at last on Edmond. "Major, I am well rested from my afternoon lie-down. You are the one who needs a good night of sleep."

Fatigue taunted Edmond, daring him to surrender, but he fought it off. He had found nothing as healing as Miss Newfield's company, and he would not leave her alone to deal with Greystone, even with Gilly hovering in the shadows. "I am hardier than I appear."

"If you say so." She moved to the bedside table to check the brazier and crush more peppermint into the teakettle. "My lord, would you care for more cough tonic?"

Greystone answered with a cough that sounded genuine. "I do find it helpful, not to mention tasty." He accepted the golden liquid she poured in a spoon. "Edmond, you should try it. Its healing qualities are enhanced when administered by a lovely young lady."

Even in the dimly lit room Edmond could see the blush coloring Miss Newfield's cheeks, and he felt his own flush of anger. "Listen, brother—"

"My lord—"

The lady and Edmond spoke at the same time. Both stopped. He nodded to her. "Please continue." Whatever she had to say would be better than his addressing the troubling issue with Greystone in her presence.

"I thank you, sir." She returned the nod. "Shall I read to you, my lord?"

"Ah, 'twill be like hearing a song from on high." Greystone looked at Edmond as he spoke.

"Oh, much better than that." Miss Newfield found her Bible beside the brazier and sat in the wingchair, adjusting the small candelabra so its light illuminated the page. "'Tis the word of God Himself. I thought you would enjoy hearing the passage Mr. Partridge preached on this Sunday past…Psalm 1."

Greystone's face creased with comical confusion, and Edmond had to clench his jaw to keep from laughing. He doubted the lady had any idea of His Lordship's spiritual condition, but Edmond had never observed in his eldest brother the same propensity for the scriptures Richard enjoyed.

"Why, uh, of course." Greystone looked anything but pleased, yet he did not dismiss her offer. "Please proceed."

As she opened the holy book, a gentle glow lit her face that had nothing to do with the candlelight. "Psalm 1. 'Blessed is the man that walketh not in the counsel of the ungodly, nor standeth in the way of sinners, nor sitteth in the seat of the scornful. But his delight is in the law of the Lord; and in his law doth he meditate day and night.'"

While she continued to read, a strange feeling settled in Edmond's chest. Peace. Assurance. Joy. A sense that he could do all things through Christ, whatever He bid him to do. Only once before had he felt this way. The night before the battle in which he had been wounded, New-field had read this same Psalm to him and urged him to accept Christ's salvation. After further discussion, the words of scripture Edmond had known all his life finally made sense. Newfield guided him in an earnest prayer, and Edmond felt the hand of God touch his soul with the assurance of eternal life.

Did Greystone have that same assurance? Or did his lifelong confidence, which often bordered on arrogance, come from his title and wealth and power? For the first time in his life, Edmond prayed for his brother's salvation. Perhaps God would have him address that issue rather than the teasing so dangerous to Miss Newfield.

"'For the Lord knoweth the way of the righteous: but the way of the ungodly shall perish.'" Miss Newfield completed the psalm and closed her Bible.

The room went silent for several moments.

"Good words to ponder, Miss Newfield." Greystone gave her a weary smile. "I thank you for reading. Now, you and my brother must retire. Gilly can attend me."

"Yes, my lord." Miss Newfield rose and touched the back of her hand to his forehead. "I believe you will rest well tonight." She glided past Edmond. "Good night, Major."

He glanced at Greystone. This would be the perfect time to talk to him, but his eyes were closed and his breathing quieter than it had been in many days. After a moment of indecision, Edmond's stronger urge to speak with Miss

Newfield propelled him after her. Once outside the door, he whispered her name.

"May I tell you something?"

She turned back and, as always, smiled. "Yes, Major, of course."

"Like the man in the psalm, your brother was that tree planted by the rivers of water. I am just one of the many fruits of salvation the Lord brought forth—" he had meant to sound poetic, but emotion choked his words "—in the season of his godly life."

In the dim candlelight shining from a wall sconce, he could see tears streaming down her cheeks. "I thank you, Major. Your words bring me much joy for two reasons. Peter was…has always been a faithful servant of God. And I rejoice to know of your salvation. Without the Lord, how can we live?"

"And yet, sadly, many people do." Without meaning to, Edmond glanced toward Greystone's door.

"Ah, but it is not too late. Let us agree to pray for him and—" She looked down.

"My mother?"

She gave a little shrug. "Again, good night, sir."

Edmond watched her go, amazed but not surprised by her elegant carriage that belied her many wearying hours of vigil at Greystone's bedside. He had noticed her slip, speaking of her brother in the past tense, then quickly correcting herself. So she did doubt Newfield still lived. It grieved Edmond to see her face this reality. He grieved even more that he could do nothing to help her, as she so often helped him.

Rising early the next morning, Anna dressed and went to Lady Greystone's room, where Mrs. Hudson informed her their employer was still sleeping. They agreed she should not be awakened. Anna's next stop was Lord Greystone's room, where Gilly reported His Lordship was still sleeping and had slept well all night.

With this good news, she made her way downstairs to the breakfast room. The footman welcomed her as the first one down and set a steaming plate of eggs and sausages before her. She had barely tasted the delicious fare when Mr. and Mrs. Grenville entered the room. The clergyman greeted her with a nod and a slight smile, but as always, his wife ignored her. Anna sighed to herself. How nice it would be to have a friend to chat with. But clearly this woman found her insignificant. Major Grenville had told her Mrs. Grenville's uncle was Lord Egmont, a baron whose title bore an ancient patent. Anna supposed that gave her some claim to pride, but it was all beyond her understanding. To ward off the hurt trying to worm its way into her heart, she prayed Mrs. Grenville would have an easy delivery. The event must surely be imminent.

Major Grenville arrived moments later looking refreshed and handsome in his uniform. His hearty "good morning" rang throughout the room, causing even the footman to smile. "Another very fine, very cold day." He waved away the footman and helped himself to the breakfast buffet, greeting his brother and sister-in-law as he sat beside Anna at the table.

"Well, Miss Newfield, shall we ride today?"

Anna almost choked on her sausage but managed to swallow. "I would think it's too cold for the horses to be out and about."

He traded a look with his brother, and they both chuckled. "Not at all. That's why they grow those shaggy coats… to keep them warm in the winter. I know Brutus appreciates a good gallop in this weather."

Anna swallowed hard. "Gallop?" Her appetite fled, and her heart raced at more than a gallop.

Mr. Grenville snickered. "Well, now you've done it, Edmond. You have frightened the poor girl out of her wits."

Anna could see the sour expression on Mrs. Grenville's face but could comprehend no reason for it. Had she stepped out of her place as Lady Greystone's companion by responding to the gentleman? Was the lady cross because her husband had noticed Anna's alarm? How did one go about sorting these things out?

At the first opportunity, she must ask the major more about her duties. In the three weeks she had been in this house, she had yet to receive any real instructions. It was frustrating not knowing what to do when it seemed she had been very much needed in more than one instance.

"Never fear, Miss Newfield." The major reclaimed her attention. "I will have George give Bella a good run before our riding lesson. Then she'll be ready to settle down for a nice trot."

"I thank you, sir." Although she looked forward to being out with him, her body ached when she recalled her last jarring ride. Nonetheless, she drank another cup of steaming coffee before excusing herself to go upstairs and change into her riding habit. Before she could reach into her wardrobe for the garment, she looked out her window and her heart lilted happily. Surely the major would not insist they go riding in the snow flurries now swirling over the landscape. Perhaps they could find something to do indoors.

A tap on her door interrupted her thoughts and she opened it to find the major outside, resplendent in his crimson uniform and dashing black cape. Suddenly, a ride in the snow seemed just the thing. "Oh, dear. Please give me another moment to change."

"We will postpone our lesson, Miss Newfield." His eyes seemed to reflect the disappointment she now felt. "The horses must be exercised, but I would not wish for you to catch a chill."

"But, I—" At that moment, the warmth of his company seemed sufficient to keep her from that danger.

"Please trust me in this." He squeezed her forearm. "We'll have another day to ride."

"Yes, of course." As she watched him depart, Anna felt an icy draft down her back. Perhaps he was right. It would be foolish to risk illness.

With no orders from Lady Greystone, she snuggled into her woolen shawl and spent the afternoon reading, then dozing and dreaming of a gallant dragoon on horseback with his cape swirling behind him in the wind. Someone was screaming for his help. Screeching, really. The sound echoed in Anna's ears and filled her with alarm.

Shaking off sleep, throwing off her shawl, she dashed into the hallway to find Lady Greystone emerging from her chambers. Wordlessly, they hurried toward the west wing where they met Mr. Grenville, whose eyes were wide with alarm.

"The child is coming!"

Chapter Sixteen

Another scream split the air. Mr. Grenville cringed.

"Really, Richard." Lady Greystone scowled toward his room. "Can she not bear it with more fortitude? Her screeching will hinder Greystone's recovery."

Anna had no fear of that, for the viscount, though still weak, continued to improve. But of course she could not correct her employer.

Mr. Grenville sighed. "Madam, if you can quiet her, you will be working a wonder."

As if to punctuate his claim, Mrs. Grenville screamed for him to return immediately.

He ran a hand through his unkempt hair and looked at Anna. "Do you know where Major Grenville is?"

"He is exercising the horses."

"Richard, see to your wife. Newfield." Lady Greystone glared at Anna in her customary way. "Send a footman to find Major Grenville. Have him fetch the village midwife."

"Yes, my lady." Anna hurried toward the stairway to complete the task.

"Newfield."

Anna stopped so quickly she almost tripped over the edge of the carpet runner. "Yes, my lady?"

"Have you attended a lying-in?"

"Yes, my lady." Several years ago, when Anna realized she would spend her life as a spinster, she had begun to assist the village midwife whenever possible so that she might observe the wonder of childbirth. Each time she held a newborn infant she longed for one of her own, but doubted that would ever be. Without a dowry she could not expect any gentleman to seek her hand.

"Then hurry back and see if you can quiet Mary." Lady Greystone strode toward Lord Greystone's room.

Although Anna doubted she could accomplish that last task, she made quick work of finding a footman and sending him on his way. She asked Cook to boil water and Mrs. Hudson to bring cloths and a pair of sharp scissors. When the lady's maid brought the items, Anna tried to enlist her help.

"Oh, miss, I cannot think of doing it. I'd be useless."

Her answer shocked Anna. "Have there been no children born here? What about—"

"I've been with Lady Greystone for over twenty years." Mrs. Hudson gave her an apologetic grimace. "She had already borne her sons and…" Her words died out.

"Of course." Anna gave her a quick hug, which the woman must be getting used to, for she returned the gesture. "Then your duty will be to pray for an easy delivery."

"Thank you, miss. I will."

With a prayer that Major Grenville would make haste to complete his errand, Anna clutched her supplies and made her way to the Grenvilles' room, which she discovered was a suite similar to Lord Greystone's and Lady Greystone's. In the bedchamber Mrs. Grenville thrashed about on the bed, alternately pulling her husband closer and shoving him away. Her usually well-groomed hair lay in wet strings across the white pillow.

"What is she doing here?" The lady ground out the question between groans and glared at Anna much as Lady Greystone did.

"Shh, my darling." Mr. Grenville brushed wet strands of hair from his wife's forehead with a damp cloth. "She is here to help."

The lady shot a poisonous look at Anna, then emitted another scream. "Then get over here and help me."

Anna obeyed, but had no idea what to do at this point. Her previous experience had been limited to watching the event and washing the newborn and—a memory interrupted her silent excuses. "Mr. Grenville, please go outside and fetch a large bowl of freshly fallen snow."

The poor man seemed happy to escape, for he did not even grab a coat before dashing out the door. His wife cried after him to no avail.

Anna searched her memories for other helpful ideas. Even though the lady seemed to despise her, she must find a way to assist.

"I am dying." The last word hung in the air like a cry of defeat.

Anna moved to the bedside and grasped her hand. "You will not die, Mrs. Grenville. Babies have been born since Eve's first son."

"You know nothing about it." She snatched her hand back. "You are a spinster."

"That is true, madam." Try though she might, Anna could not deflect the sting of the sharp words. She had noticed a tender side of this woman, but only when she spoke with others in the Grenville family. While Anna found contentment in knowing Christ loved her, she had to admit that she missed the human affection ever present in her own family, the reassuring words that made the darkest day bright.

After many long minutes of enduring Mrs. Grenville's abuse, Anna decided that the poor women of Blandon bore their children with far fewer complaints than this aristocrat. But she dismissed the uncharitable thought. Perhaps this pampered lady had never before faced real pain.

At last Mr. Grenville returned with the snow. Anna instructed him to spoon it to his wife to slake her thirst. In time Mrs. Mullin arrived and sent Mr. Grenville out with orders not to return until called, much to Mrs. Grenville's displeasure. Anna noticed that the lady also used a harsh tone with the midwife. Oddly, it helped to salve her bruised feelings.

Just before the clocks chimed midnight the child made her entrance into the world, howling lustily in complaint. While Anna bathed and wrapped the infant, the midwife tended the exhausted mother. Holding the precious new life, Anna's heart seemed to melt within her. Surely her emotions showed on her face, for Mrs. Mullin tilted her head toward the door and grinned.

"Well, go on, girl. Show the father his new daughter."

Entrusted with the treasure, Anna walked carefully into the suite's sitting room to find Mr. Grenville pacing anxiously and Major Grenville reclining on a settee. But at her appearance the two men rushed toward her, their faces wearing identical expressions of jubilation.

"Is he all right?" Mr. Grenville's hands fluttered over the baby as if he wanted to hold her but was afraid.

His question gave Anna pause, yet she had no choice but to tell him. "Your *daughter* is perfect in every way, sir." She held the baby out to him and even moved toward him when he stepped back.

"A girl?" Major Grenville's voice and eyes filled with wonder as he inspected the infant's tiny face. "I have a niece, a beautiful niece." He clapped his brother on the shoulder. "Come now, *Papá,* don't be shy. She will think you don't like her."

Mr. Grenville chuckled nervously. "Oh, no, not at all. I fear I will be her slave. But what if I drop her?"

Anna laughed. Giggled, actually. "You won't. The biggest danger is that you will hold her so securely, you may squeeze too hard." She transferred the infant to her father and stepped back to watch them bond.

"Richard!" Mrs. Grenville's shriek was nearly as loud as before she gave birth. Her husband hurried into the bedchamber, carrying their child as if she were a crystal vase.

"Well, Miss Newfield." Major Grenville patted her shoulder. "Once again you have been the calm in the midst of chaos." His face shone with approval.

Through a haze of sudden tears she gazed up at his gentle smile, and her heart skipped. "You give me too much credit, sir."

"Not at all." His hand remained on her shoulder, which both comforted and unnerved her. "Now you must retire. Who knows when another crisis will come and you'll be called upon to rescue us from it?"

Anna rolled her eyes, but his words did much to lighten her weariness. "Should I not see if Lady Greystone needs me?"

"She has been abed these past three hours. And before you ask, Greystone is resting as well." He patted her shoulder again. "Go."

"Very well, Major." Anna managed a curtsey before walking toward the door. She could not resist another glance in his direction and found him gazing at her with that undecipherable look she had seen before. While her heart longed to grant some significance to it, she dared not.

* * *

"A girl." Mother sat at the breakfast table idly thumbing through the mail. "The first female born to a Grenville for five generations."

Disapproval colored her tone, but Edmond felt anything but disappointed. His niece had entirely enchanted him, and he would happily spend his life spoiling her.

"Now, Mother, please don't say anything to Richard when he comes down. Who can order a son or daughter at will?" Taking a bite of eggs, he glanced at Miss Newfield, who seemed to be giving her plate an unusual amount of attention. "After all, you were born a girl." He sent his mother an impish grin, hoping against all odds to lighten her mood.

"Oh, yes." Her humorless laugh carried a world of acrimony. "My father's only child and a bitter disappointment to him simply for being a girl." She clamped her mouth shut, and her eyes widened briefly. She snatched up a letter and slid a silver opener beneath its red seal. "A woman has the responsibility to provide a son to carry on her husband's name. Should Greystone fail to produce his own heir, Richard has the responsibility to do so. And Mary, of course. A daughter is a luxury. An expensive luxury."

Edmond's heart constricted. Lord Brownhall, the sole grandparent he and his brothers had known, died many years ago, but he remembered a jolly old man. Perhaps three grandsons had more than compensated him for the perceived burden of a daughter. Could his treatment of that daughter lie at the root of Mother's bitter view of the world?

"Ah, good news at last." She held up the vellum letter. "Grenville will not be coming after all. It seems the weather is a bit much for the old codger to travel in."

Once again Edmond's heart stilled. Uncle Grenville was

his only hope for escaping the army. His only hope for becoming a barrister. If his healing continued and he could ride with sufficient competence, Mother would use her considerable influence to send him back to fight in America. He remembered Miss Newfield's confession that she admired the Americans for fighting for their freedom from the Crown. Perhaps when Mother demanded his return to the army, he would find the courage to declare his independence from her. But then, it would also be the day he took his first step on the road to ruin. Mother's money and her extensive influence in London could mean he would never begin a law career.

Bitterness threaded through Edmond and he could not, would not try to stop it. Why should he pay for the mistakes his grandfather had made in raising his daughter?

Eyeing the lady beside him, he pondered how Miss Newfield might regard this revelation concerning her employer's girlhood. Without doubt, he believed she would pity the once beautiful woman whose father had treated her so meanly, unlike Mr. Newfield, whose generous upbringing of *his* daughter had created such a loving, giving servant of Christ.

Should Edmond ever be blessed with offspring, either daughters or sons, he knew which father he would attempt to emulate.

Chapter Seventeen

"Shall we visit my niece, Miss Newfield?" Major Grenville asked Anna after breakfast. "The snow is too deep for your riding lesson. And Mother will be answering her correspondence for the next hour or so."

"I would enjoy it very much, Major, but I fear Mrs. Grenville would not like—"

"Nonsense." He offered his arm. When she hesitated, he took her hand and tugged her toward the staircase. "Come along. I will manage Mary."

Anna doubted he could accomplish that task when the lady's own husband could not. "Very well. If you insist."

When the major knocked on the door of the suite, a manservant admitted them to the sitting room, where Mr. Grenville sat writing at a desk. He rose and welcomed them.

"Miss Newfield, I hardly know how to thank you for helping last night." Dark circles framed his eyes, but he wore a smile of contentment.

"It was my pleasure, sir," Anna said. "Is there anything I can do this morning?"

"Let me think." He furrowed his forehead as if in thought. "The midwife is tending to Mrs. Grenville. The wet nurse from the village has arrived and set up the nursery in the small room off the bedchamber. We have sufficient infant apparel." His face relaxed back into a smile. "I believe we have it all in hand, but I thank you for asking."

"Well, then." The major eyed the closed bedchamber door. "May we see the newcomer?"

"Yes, of course." Mr. Grenville took a step in that direction. "Let me check with Mary." He paused. "Did Mother say anything about our failure to appear at breakfast?"

The major did not meet his brother's gaze. "No, but surely you can be excused from her rituals at a time like this, especially Mary."

Mr. Grenville shrugged. "One would hope so." He proceeded to the door and knocked softly.

The midwife answered and, after asking Mrs. Grenville's permission, waved them in. Anna looked at the lady to see if she would send her away, but her eyes were on her husband. Although she appeared weary as she lay against her pillows, there was also a serenity emanating from her eyes that Anna had seen in other new mothers.

"Come in." She reached out to Mr. Grenville. "Edmond, have you seen her?"

"I have, dear sister, but it was last night. May I see her again?" The major sounded like a child on Christmas morning, and Anna's heart leapt. *Papá* and Peter had always expressed a similar interest in babies born in Blandon. One day this man would make a wonderful father.

"Of course. Ruth." Mrs. Grenville called to the wet nurse, who brought the infant to her mother without delay. "Come here, my darling." She nuzzled and cooed to the child for several moments.

Tears sprang to Anna's eyes as a multitude of emotions churned within her. Oh, how she would love a child of her own, but as Mrs. Grenville had reminded her last night, she was a spinster unlikely ever to marry.

"Here, Edmond. You must hold her." Mrs. Grenville lifted the baby into his arms.

The major's eyes shone with wonder as they had the night before. "How do you do, little one. I am your uncle Edmond, and I would be very pleased to give you the world."

Everyone chuckled. Mr. Grenville added a humorous harrumph. "You will have to vie with me for that honor." As if to confirm the challenge, he took the infant from his brother.

"What's happening in here?" Lord Greystone entered the room on the arm of his valet. Finely dressed in a blue jacket and tan breeches, he looked emaciated, but his color was much improved. "Where is my niece?"

Surprised at his appearance, Anna stepped back to watch the family scene unfold. Thus far she had found the viscount a well-mannered gentleman, but how much more admirable that he should rise from his convalescence, dress as if going out and come across the hallway to welcome the baby. Clearly the new parents were delighted by his courtesy, for they drew him into the family circle. While he declined to hold her, he grinned as broadly as his brothers and made foolish promises to spoil her in every possible way.

"What have you named her?" Major Grenville asked.

Mrs. Grenville eyed her husband.

The clergyman cleared his throat. "Um, we were hoping Mother would claim that honor."

Lord Greystone stared at him. "Has she not come to meet her granddaughter?"

The new mother studied her hands and chewed her bottom lip.

Her husband shrugged. "I am certain she's busy…"

"Busy?" Lord Greystone blew out an impatient sigh. "Of course." He clenched his jaw.

Anna saw Major Grenville mirror his expression.

"Well," the viscount went on, "you have given me just cause to hasten my recuperation, for I must not miss a moment of my niece's delightful company. And if you do not name her soon, I shall call her Queen Mab or, mayhap, Titania, for she is a tiny winged creature who has enchanted all our hearts." His words brought forth many chuckles and words of agreement. "Now, we must search the attic and bring down the rocking horse and the tin soldiers and—"

"What? Are you mad?" The major eyed him with disbelief. "She must have dolls and bonnets and gowns. And of course a tea set."

While the father and uncles argued about the appropriate toys to shower upon the baby, Anna puckered her lips to keep from laughing at the good humor filling the room. Somehow these brothers had managed to keep from their hearts the bitterness that afflicted their mother. Or at least so it seemed to her.

The baby emitted a tiny cry, and the country midwife pushed her way into the midst of the aristocratic gentlemen. "See here now." She took the child from the father and handed her to the wet nurse. "Be gone, the lot of you, and let this lady rest."

Complaining like schoolboys sent back to their books, the brothers filed out of the bedchamber and took their boasting to the sitting room. Anna started after them, planning to find Lady Greystone and see if she required anything.

"Miss Newfield," Mrs. Grenville called out.

Misgiving filled Anna, but she turned back and made her way to the bedside. "Yes, madam?"

Lying back against her pillows, the lady appeared drained of all strength. "Mr. Grenville reminded me that you were most helpful during our child's birth." Her tone sounded almost conciliatory.

"I do hope so, madam." Anna tried without success to dismiss her wariness.

The lady gave her a weary smile. "You were." Her eyes closed, and she sighed. "I am grateful."

Anna waited until it became apparent the new mother had fallen to sleep and then slipped out of the room. The Grenville brothers had dispersed, with the clergyman back at the sitting room desk. He gave her a friendly wave before she walked out.

These affirmations of her usefulness lifted Anna's spirits considerably. *Thank You, Lord.* He had given her a place to serve beyond all that she could have imagined. Assuming Lady Greystone would still be in her private office downstairs, Anna made her way toward the staircase.

"Miss Newfield." Lord Greystone emerged from his chambers as she passed his door. "A moment, please."

She stopped. "Yes, my lord." His door remained open, and Gilly stood just inside—thus propriety was satisfied.

The viscount took her hand and gazed at her. She had never noticed how blue his eyes were, but she had always found dark eyes more appealing. Still, her pulse quickened under his scrutiny because of his august rank. "My dear lady, I am eternally grateful to you."

Anna stared down at the floor and forced herself not to pull back her hand. "For what, my lord?"

As if sensing her discomfort, he stepped back but did not release her. "A man cannot face his own mortality without considering the condition of his soul. In the midst of my illness, I had thought perhaps I would face my Maker and had no idea how I would present my accounts to Him. After you read the psalm to me, I consulted with Richard, and he explained some of the deeper matters of scripture, including verses that assure a man of his salvation." He leaned toward her, his eyes burning with intensity. "I found it all a most comforting truth and the path I plan to follow."

Anna's eyes filled, and she could only nod and smile.

He straightened but continued to gently squeeze her hand. "Your presence has brought only good to this house and to every member of my family. Be assured that as long as I live, you will have a home at Greystone Lodge. That is, if you are pleased to remain here."

Anna nodded again, sniffing back her tears. "I thank you, my lord. As long as God wills it, I will remain."

"What is going on here?" Lady Greystone strode across the landing and stopped inches from Anna. "What are you saying to my son? Do you think someone of your inferior position can so easily set her cap for a nobleman and expect to win his heart?" She flung her arm out toward the staircase. "Get out, and never come back!"

Edmond heard his mother's sharp voice ringing through the hallway but could not distinguish her words. Some poor servant had no doubt upset her and was receiving a dressing-down. He sighed at the thought. Since the revelation this morning at breakfast when he last realized what had made her such a bitter woman, a myriad of thoughts had swirled through his mind, not the least of which was that he longed to break free from her control. But with Uncle Grenville canceling his visit, Edmond despaired of ever achieving it.

Where could he go? What could he do? Without her financial backing and with Greystone prone to bow to her opinions, what choice did he have but to do as she demanded? On the other hand, as Edmond held his niece he'd realized something else. Someday, preferably sooner rather than later, he wanted to marry and have children of his own. But once again, without financial backing, his choices were limited.

Miss Newfield's lovely face came to mind and his heart warmed. That gentle lady inspired him, even making him feel as if he could accomplish anything he set his mind to. At the very least, her faith was an example to him. He should not be seeking to please Mother, but instead his Heavenly Father. The idea took hold in his mind. He knelt beside his bed, ignoring the painful stiffness in his injured leg, and beseeched God to guide his path.

Chapter Eighteen

"At the outset, I thought you were trying to ensnare Edmond." Lady Greystone sneered at Anna, her hawk-like features sharpening. "But then you learned he had no money and so you set your cap for a much bigger prize. What *gel,* however lowly, can resist the opportunity to win a viscount's heart?"

"But, my lady—" Shock stalled Anna's thoughts. What possible explanation could she give? Her heart quaking, she tried to tug her hand away from Lord Greystone's grasp, but the more she pulled, the tighter he held on. She glanced up to question him, but his indifferent gaze was on his mother.

"Madam, you have done our little sparrow an injustice." With his free hand, he patted Anna's shoulder, but somehow it felt different from Major Grenville's touch, more like the way one would pat a favorite dog. "I was merely thanking her for her faithful attendance upon me during my illness."

"Sparrow indeed. Really, Greystone, you must depend upon me to sort these things out." Lady Greystone stared at their joined hands. "You know so little of the wiles of young women."

"Know so little?" The viscount laughed, but not pleasantly. "After six Seasons in London? Mother, you have no idea."

Her eyes flared, then narrowed. "Will you release this person's hand at once?" At her hawk-like glare, Anna trembled, feeling very much like a sparrow about to be devoured. "I have instructed her to leave."

He gazed down at Anna. "Miss Newfield, would you like for me to release you?"

Hot tears sprang to her eyes. "Yes, my lord. Please." To her relief, he did so. She dashed across the landing toward her room. Once behind the closed door, she hurried to the wardrobe and began pulling out her clothes, taking care not to remove anything that had belonged to poor Miss Peel. Renewed sympathy for the old companion flitted across Anna's mind. As she began to fold the clothes and tuck them into her wooden trunk, she faltered, suddenly losing all strength. How would she transport this trunk? Where would she go in the bitter cold snow? And most important, would Major Grenville believe she was innocent of any wrongdoing in regard to Lord Greystone? Try though she might, she had been unable to keep her heart from attaching itself to him. If she lost his regard, how could she bear it?

Slumping to the floor against the trunk, she burst into wracking sobs.

Edmond stood in the hallway, his jaw agape with disbelief over what he had just witnessed. Moments before, as he knelt beside his bed and prayed for God's direction, he felt an urgent nudging to seek Greystone. When he emerged from his room and saw Miss Newfield dashing away from his mother and brother, it shook him to the core. Determined to learn why the young lady was being ill-treated, he stalked toward them.

"Now, Mother." Greystone rested one hand on Mother's shoulder, a contact Edmond would never dare to make with her. But then, he had never understood the connection between them. "You promised to find me a suitable bride next Season. Why do you think I would settle for a country girl with no connections and no training to be a proper London hostess?"

Mother almost smiled. Almost. "Ah, but a clever chit can get her claws into a wealthy peer in ways other than marriage."

"Mother!" Reaching where they stood, Edmond could bear it no longer. "What has happened here? Why are you discussing Miss Newfield as if she were some...some camp follower?" It took all of his self-control not to fly into a rage. "Why, she is utterly guileless."

Greystone's posture sagged, and his face creased with fatigue. "A misunderstanding, I assure you. I was merely thanking the young lady for her part in my convalescence." He heaved out a weary sigh. "Which at this moment is far from complete. Gilly." He beckoned to his valet who stood just inside his suite, his eyes as round as teacups. "Help me to my bed, will you?"

"Here. Lean on me." Edmond slipped Greystone's arm over his own shoulder and started to walk him into his room. But his brother held back and eyed Mother.

"You must apologize to Miss Newfield."

Edmond almost laughed. Never once in his life had he heard Mother apologize for anything.

She lifted her chin for a moment, then glanced toward the east wing. She turned to stare at Edmond, and a chill he could not account for swept up his back.

"Tell her she may stay, but I shall watch her. At the first

sign that she has set her cap for either of you, she will be gone." She spun away from them, crossed the landing and descended the staircase.

Relieved beyond words, Edmond traded a look with Greystone, who appeared more than a little exhausted. "Let's get you back to bed."

"Thank you." Greystone emitted a weak laugh as they helped him into the room. "You were right all along, Edmond. Be assured that I will never again jest about anything to do with poor Miss Newfield."

"A wise idea." Edmond and Gilly helped Greystone to his bed, where the valet began to prepare his sleeping attire. "You must rest now."

"And you must find a way to inform our little sparrow that she need not fly away."

"Little sparrow?" Irritation swept through Edmond. "*Our* little sparrow?" He alone was responsible for Miss Newfield, and no matter how weak Greystone was, he must settle this once and for all.

"Never mind." As he reclined with Gilly's help, Greystone waved Edmond away. "I truly meant no harm. I shall endeavor to watch my words. Depend upon it."

"Please, sir?" With a pleading grimace, Gilly tilted his head toward the door.

Edmond expelled a sigh of frustration. "I shall hold you to that promise, Greystone." He left the suite intent upon informing Miss Newfield that she could stay. But what if she did not wish to? What if she decided to accept Mr. Partridge's proposal? And how could he even speak to her without revealing his heart?

The thought brought him up short. What did he feel for her? He could not say it was love, but in these few weeks his attachment had grown considerably beyond a sense of responsibility for his late friend's sister. After all his worries about Greystone's teasing, he himself had used humor to try to deny his increasing affection, to no avail.

All this pondering did not get the job done. He approached the east wing with some trepidation but determined to complete his duty. With only a little hesitation, he scratched at Miss Newfield's door and heard a shuffling on the other side.

"Yes?" Her muffled voice sounded deeper than usual—deeper and utterly despondent, as if she had been crying.

His heart constricted, and he prayed for some way to give her the news and still save her pride. But what a ludicrous thought. How did a man save the pride of the humblest person he had ever known? One idea came to him.

"Miss Newfield, Lady Greystone will require your assistance in planning the Christmas party we give every year for the villagers."

A soft gasp, or perhaps the rustling of her gown, sounded through the door. She opened it no more than an inch. "Are you certain?"

The sight of her red-rimmed eyes twisted a knife into his soul. Fighting the temptation to pull her into a comforting embrace, he coughed away his emotions. "Oh, yes. It's quite the affair. Decorations, Christmas trees, hired musicians, even a small gift for every person. It takes over a month to prepare. The whole household must work in the evenings to complete it all in time."

Her eyes widening in disbelief, she opened the door another inch. "But surely Lady Greystone does not wish me to help. She has ordered me…"

Edmond could not stop himself. He grasped her hand and brought it up to his lips for a gentle kiss. "My dear Miss Newfield, Lady Greystone does not apologize."

"Please, Major." She snatched her hand back and stared

down the hallway toward Mother's door, fear written across her fair face.

"Yes, of course. Forgive me." He stepped back. "As I was saying, no apologies, but she does change her mind."

She searched his eyes, but doubt filled her expression. "Perhaps you can advise me."

"Of course." He still wanted to give her a reassuring embrace, but of course that would lead to disaster.

She chewed her lip for a moment, then hope flickered in her eyes. "Should I go about my duties as if nothing happened?"

"An excellent plan." Clever girl. How quickly she had recovered from a cruel blow. Now he should go to his room or risk saying and doing something that would land her back in trouble. But he found the idea of leaving her presence most disagreeable. "If the day warms a bit this afternoon, we should have a riding lesson."

Joy blossomed on her face like a spring flower. "Oh, yes. That would be lovely. If Lady Greystone does not object—"

Edmond snickered. "Why, Miss Newfield, we will simply be obeying orders." He bent forward in an elaborate bow. "Until this afternoon."

She gave him a deep curtsey and a merry—though teary—smile that sent happiness blasting through him. "Until then."

Edmond did not remember walking back to his bedchamber, but he found himself on his balcony praying that the sun would break through the haze and warm the afternoon. Then he and his little sparrow could fly free, if only for a few hours.

For a moment after she closed her door, Anna thought she might faint from the myriad of thoughts and emotions swirling through her. This morning had been most challenging, much like riding Bella at a trot with all of its bumpy ups and downs. First, the blessing of knowing she had served God's purpose in this house. Then the horror of being misunderstood. Finally, restoration.

If it was a test from the Lord, she had failed, of course. Instead of crumpling into a weepy heap of self-pity, she should have trusted Him to take care of her even if she were cast out. Or perhaps the next time Lady Greystone set upon her so unreasonably, she should stand up to her. But that idea held no appeal and could lead to a true and irreversible dismissal. After all, God had provided her a defender when Lord Greystone explained away the innocent situation.

Anna unpacked her clothes and hung or folded them into the wardrobe. Just as with her belongings, order had been restored in her life. Yet she could not help but wonder what she could do, or not do, in the future to avoid such painful incidents. At least for now, she could look forward to an afternoon with Major Grenville. Oh, how she looked forward to their time together, for in his presence everything seemed good and right, and she did not care how cold it was or how bumpy the ride.

Chapter Nineteen

Riding beside Major Grenville on the way to the village, Anna squinted and shielded her eyes to block the bright sunlight glistening off the snow. She glanced at her companion to see how he managed the problem. The bill of his hat cast a shadow over his eyes, but her bonnet sat away from her face and afforded no such protection. A parasol would help, but Mrs. Hudson explained that not a single black one could be found in the manor house, and Lady Greystone would frown upon her using any other color.

Still, she would not wish to be any place else in the world—or with anyone else. The only movement in the woodlands was the waving tree branches, who reached their bare branches to the sky as if lifting praise to God. Behind her the groom hummed his usual tune. From time to time the horses nickered or blew out a steamy breath as they pranced along the snowy path. Anna kept her seat without too much difficulty, having learned to sense when Bella was about to change her pace. Which was more than she could say about Lady Greystone's changing moods.

Anna tried to dismiss her memories of the morning's unpleasantness by thinking of the sweet newborn baby girl and the major's kindness. But despite her efforts, her mind kept going back to her employer's misinterpretation of her chat with the viscount. She could hardly grasp how her employer could sit at the midday meal and act as if nothing had happened, while she herself had felt a peculiar twinge of guilt although she had done nothing wrong. While they ate, the major had asked his mother about the riding lesson and received her approval, along with further instructions to take a basket to the old nurse in the village. Lady Greystone gave no explanation for why she would not make her customary trip herself, but Anna had observed her rubbing her hands as if in pain. *Papá* had suffered a similar affliction.

"Just a bit farther." The major tossed her a smile that warmed her despite the bitter cold.

She tried to return a smile, but her cheeks felt frozen and her dry lips threatened to crack, so she merely nodded.

"Have you recovered from this morning?"

She gave him a shrug. A balm would help her lips. Perhaps Mrs. Hudson had something she could use next time.

The major looked away and said no more. Anna would have to offer him something conciliatory once her cheeks thawed.

Few people walked the village lanes. Those who did hurried along, bundled up in hooded cloaks and shoulders hunched against the cold. In the distance, two older boys, no doubt above school age, herded a small flock of sheep with the help of a black-and-white dog. Frozen ruts of snow crunched under the horses' hooves, while smoke curled from every chimney of the thatched-roofed houses. Anna always enjoyed the woody smell of winter air, but today inhaling the fragrance chilled her lungs.

"Here we are." At the brick cottage Major Grenville dismounted and set down the basket, then lifted Anna from the saddle. "Are you all right?"

"Oh, yes. Only freezing." How hard it was to form the words.

Before she could protest, he swept off his black woolen cape, wrapped it around her and ran his gloved hands up and down her upper arms. "Does this help?"

She looked up into his fine dark eyes and her heart danced. "A little. But I do think going inside will help even more."

He chuckled, that deep, rich sound that always warmed her soul.

The groom coughed.

The major stepped back from her. "George, you may go to the tavern for a spot of tea." He tossed him a coin. "Return in half an hour."

"Aye, sir." The man caught the coin, tugged at his cap and rode away.

"Shall we?" Major Grenville knocked on the door, then opened it to peek inside. "Mrs. Winters?"

The old nurse shuffled across the wooden floor and pulled them both inside. "Welcome, welcome, my dears. How good of you to come. Will you have tea?"

"Permit me." Anna surrendered the major's cloak to him and removed her own, then hurried to the hearth. Shivering away her chill, she added a small log and stirred the fire. Soon tea was brewing in the porcelain pot.

Mrs. Winters examined the contents of the basket and clapped her hands like a child at Christmas over the cakes, lamb stew and a new pair of knitted gloves. "Her Ladyship is too kind." She patted teary eyes with a linen handkerchief.

Anna noticed the emotion flickering in the major's eyes. "Not *too* kind, dear Winnie. Without you, my brothers and I would have…" His forehead creased, and he seemed not to know how to proceed.

"Lady Greystone knitted the gloves herself." Anna would not add that the task had occupied the viscountess's hands while she sat beside Lord Greystone's sickbed. No need to alarm this dear woman about the viscount.

Gratitude shone from the major's eyes, although Anna could not guess why.

Edmond gulped back an annoying wave of unexpected feeling. Miss Newfield to the rescue again, just when he needed her. Like her brother, she was always looking out for the interests of others. And when he thought of all that Winnie had done for him, how could he not be overwhelmed with gratitude? What different men he and his brothers would be if she had not lavished so much love upon them, as if she knew she must make up for the absence of affection from their only parent. He doubted Mother had any idea of her failure. Nor did she seem to require any affection. Everything was about duty and responsibility, as though humans were soulless machines.

On the other hand, her slip this morning at breakfast gave him a bit of understanding. Her father had been unkind to her. If she had no loving nurse to supply the affection every child needed, no wonder she had adopted a stoic, unfeeling view of life. And how easy he could find it to become just like her. But holding his beautiful newborn niece this morning had changed him forever. God had not saved his life in America so he could become a bitter man.

Edmond sat back and watched as Miss Newfield chatted with Winnie about knitting and tea and how cold it was for November. Their easy conversation revealed an openness of heart that he longed to be a part of but dared not. At least not yet.

Once again his own thoughts startled him. And cautioned him as well. He must never think to deepen his friendship with Miss Newfield unless he planned to continue it for as long as the Lord granted life to both of them.

When the time came to return to the Lodge, a stronger wind swirled through the village. Taking their leave of Winnie, Edmond and Miss Newfield plunged back out into the cold. He lifted the young lady back into the saddle and could not resist letting his hands linger at her waist.

"Do you think you can manage a faster pace going back?"

Already shivering, she nodded. "Anything to get out of this weather."

"Brave girl."

With George following close behind, they managed to lope over the three quarters of a mile from the village to the stables at the Lodge. This time, when he lifted her down, her bright eyes and flushed cheeks suggested she had enjoyed the ride as much as he. Laughing from exhilaration, they left their horses with the groom and dashed toward a back entrance of the house.

Without warning, Miss Newfield bent down, scooped up a handful of snow and tossed it squarely into his face. Then she gasped. "Oh, Major Grenville. I have no idea what came over me."

He snorted out a laugh. "Then you will admit I have the right to demand satisfaction?" He scooped up his own handful of her chosen weapon.

Her responding squeak was nothing short of delightful. "Oh, no. You must be a gentleman and forgive me. I—eek!"

His snowball had landed on her pretty little nose, right where he aimed, and she brushed it off. "There. Even." He held out his hand to shake hers, but she bent down to grab another handful. He motioned for her to stop. "Whoa. Wait. What if someone sees us?"

She inhaled a quick breath and dropped her icy weapon. She stared at the windows of the east wing, and he felt certain the rich pink color infusing her face had nothing to do with the cold. "Yes, of course."

Forcing sober expressions to their faces, they entered the back hallway near the kitchen and were set upon by servants who took possession of their wet cloaks. Edmond could not be sure, but he thought he detected a twinkle or two in the eyes of several retainers, as if they had spied the snowball fight. For one wild moment he didn't care. In the next moment he chided himself for such foolishness. But he prayed the day would come when he and this delightful lady could laugh together without fear.

Anna relished every bite of her lamb stew and hot bread. This afternoon's outing had been a most enjoyable time, leaving her hungry as a barn cat. She hoped her manners were not in keeping with her appetite.

Lord Greystone still did not come down for meals, but Mr. Grenville graced them with his presence and contributed to the conversation several times.

"Mother." The clergyman set down his cutlery and let the footman remove his plate. "Mary and I have discussed the matter of our daughter's name."

Lady Greystone stared at him, her face immobile. "And how does that concern me?"

His wince was barely noticeable. "We have decided that if you will not come to see your granddaughter and give her a name, we shall have her christened Henrietta Frances."

Lady Greystone dropped her fork onto her plate with a clank. "What?" She rose to her feet and glared at him. "Why would you choose that name?"

To their credit, Mr. Grenville and the major both stood as well.

"Well, I—"

"If you insist upon calling the child Henrietta, I shall refuse to see her." She grasped her serviette and swiped at her thin lips, then threw it down. "In fact, I shall disinherit her."

Mr. Grenville's pleasant countenance creased with rage, the first time Anna had ever observed anger in the man. Beside her, she heard the major's indignant grunt.

"We had hoped to honor my father by calling her Henrietta, for Henry, and to honor you with Frances." He seemed to struggle for calm. "Clearly, I have erred. You must not blame Mary. She would do anything to please you." His narrowed eyes, so unlike him, dared her to respond.

Lady Greystone sat down and resumed her eating as if nothing had happened. When the clergyman continued to glare at his mother, Anna traded a look with the major. He cleared his throat, catching his brother's eye, and gave a quick nod. Both men sat down.

No less than five minutes passed without a word being spoken. Anna's appetite fled, despite the delicious supper before her. She prayed this woman would somehow soften toward her family, who struggled to please her yet could not.

At last Lady Greystone seized her serviette again and dabbed her lips. "You may christen the child Elizabeth Frances Grenville." She nodded to her footman, who pulled out her chair as she rose. On her way down the table, she paused beside the major. "Edmond, we will begin our plans for the Christmas party this evening. You and Miss Newfield must assist me. Obviously, Greystone and Richard will be no help whatsoever."

The moment she sailed out the door, a collective sigh emanated from every soul in the room, even the footmen.

"Richard," Major Grenville said, "you have my sympathy."

The gentleman shook his head and gave his brother a weary smile. "Not at all, Edmond. I rather like the name Elizabeth. I am certain Mary will, too, for it is her mother's name."

The major chuckled and shook his head, then turned to Anna. "I would not distress you, madam, but the custom is that the ladies retire to the drawing room after the evening meal while the gentlemen…discuss politics."

Anna jumped up from her chair before the footman could assist her. "And you have not told me this before?"

"Forgive me." He rose, lifted his hands, palms up, and shrugged to emphasize his apology. "One never knows when Mother will follow custom and when she will devise her own."

If he were Peter, she would give his arm a playful slap on the arm for the omission. Now all she could do was hurry after Lady Greystone and hope she would not be scolded for her deficiency.

Chapter Twenty

"A barrister?" Greystone lounged back against his pillows and studied Edmond thoughtfully. "Ah, yes. I'd forgotten your youthful aspirations. But what about your military career? Your service in America was exemplary. Do you not wish to see how much you can accomplish in the army?"

"Not in the least." Edmond sat forward in the bedside chair, his arms resting across his knees. "I am proud to have fought for the Crown, but I would rather do battle before the bar."

His brother chuckled, then lifted one eyebrow. "What if I could secure a post for you under Wellington?"

Like most other Englishmen, Edmond held the Field Marshall in high esteem. But not enough to return to the battlefield, even on the Continent. "Do we not have enough officers leading the troops in the fight against Napoleon?"

"Mmm." Greystone stared unfocused across the room and sighed. "One begins to wonder whether or not any number of men can defeat that demon."

Guile scraped at the edges of Edmond's conscience for being like every other sycophant who begged favors from powerful men. How easy it was to forget that his affable brother was an important voice in Parliament, with war and politics never far from his mind. Edmond had heard he possessed great influence with the Prince Regent in spite of his mere seven and twenty years. Yet he wore his rank without arrogance.

"But such questions do not resolve your dilemma. And of course it does not help that Uncle Grenville's visit has been canceled." Greystone aimed a wry grin at him. "May I assume you have not addressed this subject with our mother?"

Edmond snorted out a laugh. "Would you, if you were in my situation?"

Greystone shrugged. "Actually, yes."

Edmond's heart sank. Would his brother abandon him to the woman? Could he not see the differences in their relationships with her? He sat back in the wingchair with a groan he had not intended to release.

"Have no fear. I will not discuss it with her." Greystone's forehead furrowed. "Ideally, I would support your residence at the Inns of Courts in the event Uncle Grenville does not accept you as his protégé…or cannot afford to. However, my discretionary funds are tied up in the war." He released a long sigh, obviously weary. "And of course you must consider Mother's hard-won influence, which could harm your aspirations, should she decide to set herself against you."

Hopelessness tried to seize Edmond, but a new sense of inspiration edged it out. If Miss Newfield could manage her disappointments with her strong faith, he would do no less. "You're tired, big brother. I'll leave so Gilly can tuck you in." He stood to make good his words.

Greystone coughed out a chuckle. "Not all that tired. If you see Richard, send him in."

"Will you offer him the Greystone living when Partridge

retires?" After the debacle over the naming of Baby Eliza, as everyone but Mother had taken to calling her, he could not imagine that his middle brother would want to place himself under Mother's influence for the rest of his life.

"Yes. I would like for him to have it."

Edmond stared at him for a long moment. Then he shrugged and left the room. He would not try to comprehend Greystone's responsibilities or his bond with their mother. As the third son, he was little more than an extra appendage to the family. An appendage with the duty never to shame the Grenville name and, more important, to make certain always to bring it honor. If Mother continued to have her way, that would be through service in the army, no matter what he desired for his own life. But now he had to decide just exactly how far he was willing to go if she blocked his aspirations or prevented him from forming alliances with other influential people who might help him.

If all of Europe were not at war with Napoleon, Edmond would consider leaving England and seeking his fortune on the Continent. If he found the opportunity, perhaps he would ask Miss Newfield what she knew about Italy…and if she had ever wished to go there.

The cozy back parlor was cluttered with half-made trappings of the holiday. Seated on the green brocade settee, Anna released a quiet sigh of contentment as she completed her last stitches, folded the garment and added it to her stack. Lady Greystone had assigned her the task of making woolen cloaks for several villagers. This last one should keep some child warm in the coming months. Now she must move on to making her share of the decorations: cutting stars from sheets of gold paper and sewing red silk flowers. In a few days servants would string greenery about the house, and these items would be tied to the garlands as ornaments.

Although Squire Beamish had no interest in observing the twelve days of Christmas, at least not in regard to the people of Blandon, Anna's parents had invited the villagers into the vicarage each year for a modest Christmastide feast to celebrate the Savior's birth. While they were by no measure wealthy, they did try to follow the customs of the season by giving small gifts to those of lesser means. Anna had always enjoyed making gifts and seeing the children's happy responses.

Here at Greystone Lodge the festivities were much more elaborate. Major Grenville had informed Anna that every Viscount Greystone had continued the time-honored practices marking the holy days. Of course the villagers expected it, but the major said Lady Greystone saw it as a way to appease any possible discontent among them. For weeks the viscountess had made lists of tasks and set her staff to work so that no child, man or woman would feel neglected. Merely her duty, the lady insisted many times, but Anna decided the woman had a tender heart hidden somewhere behind her wall of severity. Yet if she ventured to remark on the viscountess's kindness, the lady appeared insulted.

For days the Lodge had been filled with the aromas of rosemary, cinnamon, apples, pumpkins, baking bread and a host of other delightful scents. Surrounded by piles of kindling, a large Yule log lay in the stable yard behind the house, ready to be set afire on Christmas Eve, with hopes that it would blaze through all twelve days. The closer the day came, the more a sense of excitement filled the air. Upper servants appeared near to smiling as they went about their duties. Lower servants, whom Anna rarely saw unless she went below stairs on an errand for Lady Greystone, hummed and walked with a lilt in their steps.

Mrs. Grenville began to take her meals with the family once more. She seemed to have forgiven Anna for being a mere gentlewoman and often engaged her in trivial but pleasant conversation as they sat in the back parlor preparing gifts.

For her part, Anna looked forward to Christmastide with both excitement and fear. Although she did not expect any gifts, she had her own stash of handmade treasures to distribute to Mrs. Hudson, Mrs. Winters, George the groom, the upstairs maid and the little chambermaid who brought her hot water in the mornings. She also had a slender handwritten book of poetry she had copied from several books in Lord Greystone's library, books she had observed Major Grenville reading. Should the major favor her with a gift, she would be prepared to return one—though she could not imagine why she expected such a kind gesture from him. She could not be certain, but from overheard remarks, she assumed the major's resources were limited, which, in her way of thinking, almost made them equals. Of course, not sufficiently equal to marry, she hastened to remind herself. But surely at Christmas no harm could come from giving a small, impersonal gift to the man who had saved her from utter destitution.

She dismissed her foolish musings only to remember her anxieties about the days to come. The annual foxhunt would take place on Boxing Day, and she would be expected to participate at Lady Greystone's side. While her riding lessons had progressed to include small jumps over fallen logs with Major Grenville close by her side, she was fully aware of the high fences in the fields that no doubt would be part of the event course.

But then, why should she live in fear when so many

good things were about to happen? That ploy worked to cheer her thoughts…most of the time.

In the dim candlelight of the back parlor Edmond could see that Miss Newfield was brooding again. The sight saddened him. He could only assume she was grieving for her family, but he could not bear to see her melancholy in the midst of all the jolly preparations for Christmas. So often her words or simply her smile had encouraged him, had made him believe he could accomplish anything he set his mind to. Now here she sat with that stack of perfectly sewn garments ready to be presented to villagers who would thank Mother, never knowing whose loving, caring hands had stitched them.

Lord, what can I say to ease her sorrow? What can I do to cheer my little sparrow? And when had he adopted Greystone's nickname for her?

Silencing such thoughts, he decided upon the perfect topic. He set aside the wooden soldier he had just finished whittling and slipped into the chair across from the settee where she sat sewing flower ornaments.

"You have done quite well in our riding lessons, Miss Newfield." She inhaled a quick breath as she looked up, and he paused. Perhaps he had startled her. "Are you eager for the hunt on Boxing Day?"

Her jaw dropped and she blinked several times. Then she laughed. "Oh, of course. I was just thinking about how *eager* I am." Her lovely face crinkled comically and candlelight sparkled in her emerald eyes. "You have a cure for a broken neck, do you not?"

Edmond chuckled. What a dolt he was. Because she had worked so hard learning to ride, he assumed she had overcome her fears. "Perhaps we'll have a snowstorm that day to keep us indoors."

"Or perhaps the foxes will repent and gather in the stable yard to announce a change from their destructive ways." She was never so charming as when she returned these clever quips.

"Or perhaps—"

"Absolutely not." Mother stormed into the parlor with Mrs. Dobbins in her wake.

"But, madam." The housekeeper wrung her hands, an unusual display of emotion. "The servants depend upon the tradition for a bit of harmless play."

Mother stopped and spun about. The housekeeper almost ran into her. "Harmless play? More like a license for immorality."

Mrs. Dobbins stiffened. "Lady Greystone, my staff is above reproach. You may depend upon it. This is merely a bit of—"

"Yes," Mother drawled. "So you said. But there will be no mistletoe in this house at Christmas. I will not have stable boys thinking they may kiss the upstairs maids with impunity."

Edmond ground his teeth to keep from saying something he would regret. True, he had planned to lead a certain young lady under the mistletoe, but only for a chaste kiss on the cheek. But then, perhaps this was best. Sometimes Christmas celebrations grew so merry that people behaved in ways they later lamented.

"Very well, madam." Mrs. Dobbins huffed out a sigh. "This will be difficult to explain to my staff." She spun on her heel and stormed from the room.

Edmond could hardly believe the woman's audacity. Miss Newfield must feel the same way, for she ducked her head and busied herself with the silk flowers.

Mother surveyed the shadowed room through narrowed eyes, and her gaze darted between Edmond and Miss Newfield. "Where are Richard and Mary?" Suspicion colored her tone.

"Mary was tired, so Richard took her upstairs." Edmond rose from the chair and sauntered over to the desk where he had been carving. "I was just explaining the Boxing Day hunt to Miss Newfield. Will you be riding, Mother?" He held a wooden soldier up in the candlelight and brushed away wood shavings.

"Of course I shall ride. I always ride." Mother snatched up a completed soldier, taking a moment to glance at Miss Newfield before she examined it. "You must paint these."

"Of course." Edmond calculated the time this additional work would take against his other duties and realized he would not be getting much sleep in the next few days.

"Newfield." At Mother's sharp tone, the young lady jumped where she sat. "You may retire."

"Yes, my lady." She packed away her silk flowers into a basket, offered a curtsey and left.

The moment the door closed, the room felt colder to Edmond, but he managed an expectant smile for his mother. "Did you require something?"

She stared up at him through narrowed eyes. But if she expected him to falter under her scrutiny as he always had in childhood, she knew nothing of military training.

"Not at all. Good night." She spun away from him and stalked across the room.

"Good night," he said to the closing door. "And happy Christmas, Mother." Perhaps with some effort, he and his brothers would manage to make it so.

Chapter Twenty-One

The small book felt heavy in Anna's pocket, but she dared not to present it to Major Grenville. As she watched Lady Greystone instruct the butler, Johnson, to hand out the various gifts to senior staff and family, she began to worry she had been too presumptuous. None of the other staff had presented gifts to the family. Yet in her ill-defined position, how could she discern what was expected? Even last night at the lighting of the Yule log, she had felt little connection to the celebration other than helping Lady Greystone distribute presents to the grateful villagers. She gazed around the festive drawing room, appreciating the lovely decorations but longing so much for her familiar old life with *Mamá, Papá* and Peter that her heart ached.

"Miss Newfield." Johnson laid a large package in her lap. "From Lady Greystone."

"Oh!" She stopped herself mid-gasp. "I thank you, my lady." The viscountess's face was immobile as she gave Anna an imperious nod, but Anna could not withhold a smile. Her sad mood disappeared as she slipped twine and brown paper from the gift to reveal a bolt of grey cotton fabric and yardage of black piping and lace. "How beautiful." Without a word, she understood. Her employer was granting her permission to wear half-mourning in place of her all-black attire.

After the viscountess's gifts had been distributed, a much-improved Lord Greystone brought out his offerings: an exquisite gold and tourmaline necklace for Lady Greystone, jeweled cravat pins for his brothers and Wedgwood china for his sister-in-law. The doting uncle also gave Mr. and Mrs. Grenville a stack of boxes that bore Baby Eliza's name, to the amusement of all. And he surprised Anna by presenting her with a mahogany lap desk with pen, ink, wax and sheets of vellum stored inside.

"Every lady should have her own writing implements." His back to his mother, he gave Anna a teasing wink. Did he know she had borrowed writing supplies from Mrs. Dobbins? Had he seen her copying the poems in the library? Oh, how heavy the book lay in her pocket.

Once all the gifts had been distributed, everyone enjoyed a grand breakfast. Then Lady Greystone advised an afternoon of quiet before the arrival of the guests for tomorrow's Boxing Day hunt.

Anna made her way to her room, still wavering between giving the book to Major Grenville and burying it deep in her trunk. Mrs. Hudson and the others appreciated the gifts Anna gave them, but after observing the gift-giving ritual Anna was beginning to understand the hierarchy of the house. Giving a gift to someone above her could be considered a terrible breach of etiquette. Possibly sufficient for dismissal if Lady Greystone learned of it and thought Anna was setting her cap for Major Grenville. Of course he would never report her blunder. But the house had many eyes, and someone might carelessly mention it to Lady Greystone.

In the sanctuary of her room Anna found an extra, unopened package, a rather large one almost the size of the lap desk. Clearly the servants had made a mistake when they brought up the others. But a tiny tag bore her name, so she opened it with trembling hands, revealing a carved wooden box and a note. She recognized Major Grenville's hand, which made her tremble all the more.

"My dear Miss Newfield, your splendid brother once told me of your interest in watercolors. Enclosed please find all you need to enjoy this delightful pastime. Yours dutifully, E.G."

Had he noticed she left her paint set in Blandon when her trunk could not hold another item? Such kind regard overwhelmed her and she did not try to stop the tears rolling down her cheeks. The box indeed contained small embossed cakes of paint in many shades, brushes of different sizes and textures, charcoal sticks and several tiny porcelain dishes for mixing colors. The hinged lid of the box was a paper holder filled with numerous sheets just waiting to be filled with all sorts of pictures. What pleasure she would take in capturing the likenesses of the Grenville family, the servants, the horses and anything else that struck her fancy.

Brushing away her bothersome tears, she decided upon a rash action and set out to accomplish it. She left her room and hurried to the west wing, no longer forbidden because she was permitted to visit Mrs. Grenville in her sitting room. But it was the door beyond that one where she stopped. Major Grenville himself answered her knock, and his face brightened at the sight of her. He stepped into the hallway and gazed down into her eyes with a knowing grin.

"Why, Miss Newfield, to what do I owe the honor of this visit?"

Anna returned a playful smirk. "Sir, as you have commissioned your portrait to be painted, we have only to find the proper setting. Perhaps you would like for the artist to capture you seated in the library reading this." She drew the poetry book from her pocket and placed it in his hand. At his shocked expression, which continued for countless seconds, she feared she had made a grave error. To her great relief, as he examined the contents of the book, his expression warmed.

"My dear Miss Newfield, you cannot imagine how perfect this is. How did you know which poems were my favorites?"

"If you hoped to keep them a secret, you should not use bookmarks."

"Ah. I see my error." His cheerful expression faded, and he glanced down the hallway. "Shall we visit my niece?"

Understanding his meaning, Anna followed his gaze. She was safe. Not even a servant approached. "Yes, of course."

"You go. I'll come in a moment." He ducked back into his room.

Anna walked to the next door, praying she would not encounter anyone before she got there. As she lifted her hand to knock, the major reemerged from his room and approached. At that instant the door flung open.

"What is this?" Lady Greystone stood in the doorway, her eyes on Anna, then on the major. "What are you two doing?"

Honor thy mother. Edmond's scripture reading that morning had been clear and convicting. No matter how she behaved toward him or anyone else, he must do what was right and forgive her many failings. But he also had a duty to protect Miss Newfield.

"Good afternoon, Mother." He gave her a quirky smile before recalling she did not care for that particular grin.

"No doubt Miss Newfield is here to see Baby Eliza, just as I am. And what about you, madam? Have you met your grandchild at last?" He hated the almost insolent tone in his words, but he must divert her attention.

"Humph. Little you know." A brief glint sparked from her eyes but she seemed to deliberately extinguish it, as if wanting to hide any gentle sentiments. "Our guests will be here soon. Do not linger too long, no matter how much she charms you."

Edmond started to protest that Miss Newfield did not charm him in the least, but that would not only be a lie, but hurtful to the young lady. Then he realized Mother was referring to Baby Eliza. As she strode away Edmond exhaled quietly and waved a hand toward the chamber door. "After you, Miss Newfield."

"I thank you, sir."

The relief in her eyes struck deep in his soul. Her very life hung upon dodging Mother's irrational suspicions, much as Edmond's life had hung upon dodging haphazard musket shots on the battlefield. But then, perhaps those suspicions were not so irrational at all.

"Mr. Terrence Ashton-Smyth." Johnson stood in the drawing room doorway and announced the entrance of each guest.

"He is the hunt master." Mary Grenville stood beside Anna, adding a word about each person who entered. This gentleman's arrival gave Anna no little alarm, for it reminded her of tomorrow's ordeal. She tried to quiet her growing fears, but her prayers did not bring the usual serenity born of trusting God in all things.

"Mr. and Mrs. Gregory Stanhope." The butler's rich tones carried throughout the rapidly filling room. "Lord and Lady Egmont."

"Ah, my uncle and aunt decided to come," Mary whispered. "Will you excuse me?" Her light steps as she hurried across the room suggested she had fully recovered from her lying-in over a month ago. Her courtesy in excusing herself from Anna gave proof of their growing friendship.

The room was filled with the fragrances of perfumes and pomades that vied for preeminence with the scents of Christmas greenery and a roaring hearth fire. Now alone behind the pianoforte, Anna tried to overcome her anxieties by memorizing each newcomer's name. With over twenty Christmas night visitors at the Lodge, Lady Greystone had instructed her to make certain no female was left standing alone. But there was little danger of that happening. Everyone seemed to know everyone else, and all the ladies—beauties one and all—had gentlemen eager to claim their attention. Dressed in black to designate her mourning, wearing a black lace cap proclaiming her a spinster not seeking a husband, Anna received a few glances, but no gentlemen requested an introduction. Which was all well and good, for she would not know what to say to these aristocrats if they did approach her. Nor did she wish to see their disappointment when they learned her actual status.

Against her will, Anna's eyes searched out Major Grenville and found him alone beside the hearth. She could not comprehend why the pretty young heiresses who were gathered around Lord Greystone did not seek his equally handsome brother's company, especially when he looked so gallant in his crimson dragoon uniform. She could only suppose it had to do with his lack of fortune, a circumstance she well understood. Of the few unattached gentlemen who had called upon her in Blandon, not one made a second visit after learning of her meager dowry. Perhaps that was just as well, as there had been no dowry at all and her inheritance a mere twenty pounds. A very strange circumstance, for *Papá* had always managed his money well. If not for Major Grenville—

As if sensing her gaze, he looked her way and lifted his punch cup in a salute. With it, he lifted her spirits. He had promised to be at her side during the hunt, and she would do everything within her power not to embarrass him.

He tilted his head toward his eldest brother and rolled his eyes. Anna had to pucker her lips to keep from laughing. Apparently, he had similar thoughts about the pretty, simpering girls surrounding Lord Greystone, along with at least one matron pushing her daughter forward. To add to the melee, Mr. Ashton-Smyth was attempting to get the viscount's attention. And yet Lord Greystone managed to bear it all with composure and good humor. With sensible gentlemen like him in Parliament, England was in good hands. Anna considered it a singular honor to have his kind regard.

At last the hunt master caught the viscount's eye. He disengaged himself from the group and conferred with the gentleman. Anna traded another look with Major Grenville. He shrugged.

Soon the viscount raised his hands. "Ladies and gentlemen, may I have your attention?"

The room silenced immediately.

"Mr. Ashton-Smyth regrets to inform me that our hunt is off."

A groan of disappointment rose up from the guests, but Anna thought she would drop to the floor in relief. She swallowed her giddy giggles and looked at Major Grenville to see if he was disappointed. He sent her a one-shoulder shrug and droll grin so charming that she had to force her attention back to Lord Greystone.

"Due to my indisposition, I have not been out and about

for many weeks, or I would have noticed the solidly frozen ground. I am certain you will agree that it would be ill-advised for us to expect our dogs to work, for it would risk their health and lives."

Again the room buzzed with conversation, sounds of disappointment mingling with approval over the decision.

"I am as disappointed as you are, and I regret that I could not warn you off to save you a journey. However, let us be of good cheer. We can still dress out in our pinks, mount up, have a stirrup cup, perhaps have a ride through the countryside, should the day permit." The viscount looked about the room. "What say you?"

Shouts of approval now filled the air and the course was decided. Soon Johnson announced dinner. In order of precedence, the entire party removed to the dining room. With everyone else paired, it was left for Major Grenville to offer his arm to Anna, which she gladly took.

"I can only assume—" he leaned toward her, his eyes dancing with good humor "—you are dreadfully disappointed about the foxhunt."

In awe of God's mercy, Anna could only nod. The major understood her fears and, like her heavenly Father, did not condemn her.

Chapter Twenty-Two

Edmond's eyes scanned an article in the week-old newspaper, but nothing on the page registered in his mind. These winter evenings in the drawing room always dragged on endlessly for him. Winter had never been his favorite season, but this year was the worst he had ever experienced. The sun rarely broke through the hazy skies, the shorter days gave little time for outdoor activities, and the long, bitter nights ground by as if the world would never thaw. Newspapers brought word that the Thames had frozen so solidly that a Frost Fair, complete with bonfires, had taken place on the ice-packed river. Such news stirred memories of long winter months spent in battlefield tents, something Edmond prayed he would never have to repeat. But the *London Times*' dismal reports about the war with Napoleon gave little hope that he could escape returning to military service, whether on the Continent or back in America.

Across the room Miss Newfield chatted quietly with Mary, but Edmond could not hear their conversation. Still, if not for her warm presence, he would no doubt fall into a deep melancholy. How did she manage to smile every dreary day and speak a kind word to every person in the household, including Mother? And how pleasant it would be to dwell in a home where the lady of the house provided sunshine when nature did not.

Throughout these three months since Twelfth Night, he'd spent little time alone with the young lady other than during their twice-weekly rides, when it was too cold to talk. During the evening gatherings in the drawing room he rarely risked giving her any special notice lest Mother misinterpret his actions. Yet even when Miss Newfield was in another room, she was in his thoughts. Close behind came thoughts of marriage. Foolish, of course, for he could not marry until he could provide a home and security for his bride. But gone forever were his former opinions regarding social rank and the Great Chain of Being. Miss Newfield had proven far superior to any aristocratic young lady he had ever met, and none other would suit him for a wife.

But how did she regard him? Her kindness extended to every person equally, so how could he claim any special place in her affections? And would it be fair to either of them if he did?

The answer, of course, was no. When Uncle Grenville canceled his November visit, he ended Edmond's hopes of gaining an audience with him to request sponsorship at the Inns of Court. Before Greystone and his entourage traveled to London for Parliament and the Season, Mother would undoubtedly ship Edmond back to the army. He had no fear of fighting or even of dying for his country. Yet his desire to fight in the courts of law had continued to grow after Miss Newfield was treated so shabbily by the infamous but invisible Squire Beamish and his solicitor. But unless he had a grasp of the legalities of the situation, he had little chance of ever helping her regain what they had undoubtedly stolen.

"Edmond." Mother's sharp voice cut into his musings, and he jolted in his chair. "You must go to London with us."

His heart began to hammer out a drummer's battle cadence. He'd barely prayed for it—and felt little faith when he did—and yet hope beyond his wildest hope had just been granted to him. London! Uncle Grenville! But if he revealed the emotions now churning through his chest, she would be more than a little suspicious. Somehow he managed a lazy, "Must I?"

Seated on the other side of Mother, Miss Newfield had no such scruples. Her eyes brightened and a full smile flashed across her lovely lips. Just as quickly she puckered away the smile, but her eyes continued to sparkle. If he doubted her regard for him, her obvious delight put that fear to rest. Had she been dreading their approaching separation as much as he?

"Of course you must." Mother took up her quizzing glass and stared at him as she did when provoked. "How else can Greystone and I secure a position for you with Wellington?" She exhaled with impatience. "Have you no ambition? No wish to make something of yourself?"

Edmond ached to glance again at Miss Newfield, to disprove his mother's insinuations and proclaim that his greatest ambition was to make certain the young lady never wanted for anything. But again he gripped his emotions and gave Mother an indolent shrug. "I thought you wanted me to return to America."

Again she sighed irritably. "Really, Edmond. Contrary to what you may think, I do not wish for my sons to be sent off to foreign lands. But we each have a duty to the Crown. Yours is to help conquer England's foes."

"Ah, well." Edmond waved his hand lazily in the air. "America, France. 'Tis all the same to me." He slid a languid glance in Greystone's direction. "Speak to whomever you will, and I shall comply."

Greystone gave him a slight nod. But his knowing half-smile and quirked eyebrow communicated a message that lifted Edmond's hopes more than anything his brother could have said. Perhaps Greystone would speak to Uncle Grenville on his behalf. Or find another barrister to sponsor him at the Inns of Courts. And perhaps Greystone was not Mother's puppet after all.

Anna tucked her new dress into the wooden trunk and closed the lid. This time no one stood by to demand an accounting of each item she packed. And this time she was filled with excitement instead of dread over the forthcoming trip.

London. Just the city's name stirred all sorts of grand imaginings. If given the opportunity, she would paint pictures of St. Paul's Cathedral and Westminster Abbey. Perhaps Windsor Castle. The Tower. London Bridge. Perhaps her riding lessons would continue and Major Grenville would take her to Hyde Park so she could capture just the right shades of the flowers.

But then, he might be returning to duty soon. Then what would she do? He had saved her from many small offenses over these past months, and she supposed opportunities to err would increase in the city. Yet if she confessed the truth to herself, she despaired of seeing him leave at all. She could see he cared for her, perhaps even beyond his sense of duty to her as Peter's sister. In all ways he protected her from Lady Greystone's groundless suspicions that she had set her cap for him. She had not set her cap for him at all. Indeed, she had not. He was her good friend, nothing more. And if she continued to tell herself that, she might just begin to believe it.

"Miss Newfield?" Mary Grenville scratched on the half-open bedchamber door.

"Please come in." Anna hurried across the room, wishing she could give the lady a farewell embrace.

Mrs. Grenville did just that, pulling Anna into her arms and squeezing hard. "Oh, Miss Newfield, I shall miss you."

"I shall miss you, too, madam." Anna struggled against tears. "I pray God will grant you and your dear family good health and happiness."

Mrs. Grenville glanced out the door, then closed it. "Will you add to your prayers a petition that Mr. Grenville will soon find a living?"

"But does he not expect to have the Greystone Village living when Mr. Partridge retires?"

The lady shook her head so hard her brown curls bounced. "I cannot discuss it, but…"

"I understand." She did not, of course, but she could pray for God's will for this good family.

"I brought you something." Mrs. Grenville pressed a silk and ivory filigree fan into Anna's hand. "You must ask Mother Greystone whether you may use it or not. It is a bit fancy for mourning."

"Oh, my. I thank you. It is exquisite." Anna fanned it open and fluttered it before her face. "I will ask, but Lady Greystone has told me that as six months have passed since my father's death I must wear only half-mourning. She will see to my wardrobe once we arrive in London."

"Humph." Mrs. Grenville glanced again at the door, as if fearing someone might hear her. "I would guess she prefers not to be accompanied by someone in black. While grey is not exactly a jolly color—" She shrugged. "I will pray for you, Anna Newfield. You will need it."

"Why, do we all not need constant prayers?" A sense of foreboding teased at her mind.

"Yes, of course." She chewed her bottom lip, an unusual gesture for the always proper lady. "Please permit me to warn you about a matter you may not have considered. You must maintain a disinterested facade when you look upon…certain people."

"But, I—" Had her eyes revealed her heart? If so, she must make every effort to stop it. "I thank you, madam."

"Please understand. We wish you the greatest happiness, but—"

"Please." Anna would cry if she continued. "Say no more."

After another fervent embrace, the lady took her leave, and Anna called for a footman to fetch her luggage. As she descended the marble staircase, she could not help but ponder Mrs. Grenville's unspoken words. And the more she pondered, the more she worried. For the next three days she would be in a closed coach with the very man she had been warned not to regard too fondly, the very man she was forbidden to love.

Seated across from Mother in the carriage, Edmond took care to maintain a bland, ever-bored facade. But in the corner of his eye he saw Miss Newfield staring out the window as resolutely as a soldier on lookout for the enemy. Although for weeks she had expressed eagerness to go to London, for the past three days she had hardly said a word and then spoke only to Mother. Perhaps something had happened before they left the Lodge. He began to list possibilities, but then chided himself for such nonsense. This young lady had suffered tragedies beyond bearing, yet she had borne them with courage. Until he had a chance to speak privately with her, he would assume she was studying the passing landscapes with thoughts of painting the pastoral scenes once they were settled in the town house. Every painting she had completed proclaimed her an artist, but his favorite was the portrait of Baby Eliza, whose merry, toothless smile he already missed.

He noticed Mother dozing, lost in a sound sleep, if her even breathing was any indication. A spark of mischief caught fire in his chest. He reached into his jacket to retrieve one of his old calling cards. Crumpling the stiff paper into a wad, he glanced again at Mother, then lobbed it across the carriage, striking Miss Newfield harmlessly on her fair cheek.

The young lady gasped softly and swung her widened eyes in his direction. Her full lips quirked up into a lopsided grin. Greystone snorted out a quiet laugh. Mother shifted and blinked away sleep, for the briefest moment disoriented. Then her eyes focused on him and narrowed. Miss Newfield looked back out the window.

And Edmond's heart soared, his winter doldrums at last dispelled.

Chapter Twenty-Three

In the afternoon of Maundy Thursday, Lord Greystone's caravan arrived in London along with countless other conveyances bringing Society to town for the Season. Anna stared out the window—gawked, actually—at the masses of people and many carriages crowding the narrow, dusty streets. She had never seen such a beelike swarm. Varied odors poured in through the windows, but unlike the country no fresh breeze dispelled the city's unpleasant stench of sewage and unwashed bodies. She did catch the scent of honeysuckle as the carriage passed a flower vendor, but most often she held a scented handkerchief to her nose, as did her fellow travelers.

Most people went busily about their work, whether buying or selling or hawking their wares. A few well-dressed gentlemen pushed through the throng, endeavoring to clear a path for the delicately dressed ladies on their arms. Boys and their dogs created their unique forms of chaos, not unlike village children.

With the carriage's numerous turns through the streets, Anna could not keep track of their direction. Should Lady Greystone send her on an errand, she would no doubt become lost. But her concerns disappeared when the carriage rolled into a wider avenue. Soon they reached a large open square and pulled to a stop in front of a three-storey brick town house. Anna counted seven bays across the front of the edifice.

"Here at last." Lady Greystone's eyes brightened, something Anna had never before observed. "Oh, do hurry, Greystone." She waved her hand toward the door, which a footman had opened.

"At your service, madam." Lord Greystone exited the carriage and rolled his shoulders, then held out his hand to his mother. With the grace of a much younger woman, she slid past Anna and stepped out onto the cobblestone. Holding on to her tall blue bonnet, she tilted her head back as if looking toward the upper floors. Anna could not see the viscountess's expression, but she could hear the lilt in the lady's voice as she spoke to her eldest son. How grand it would be if this indicated the lady had at last found something that pleased her.

"Permit me." Major Grenville took his turn stepping out of the carriage and assisting Anna. "If you are wondering where you are, this is Hanover Square." He nodded toward the park across the street. "And this," he said as they followed the others into the town house, "is Greystone Hall."

In the large, airy vestibule, Lord Greystone passed down the row of servants who had gathered to welcome him: a housekeeper, a butler, six or seven footmen in blue livery, eight or so black-uniformed maids with starched white aprons. Lord Greystone called each by name, but Anna doubted she would remember who was who. With wigs on the men and mobcaps on the maids, they seemed to have no distinguishing features to help her remember them.

Once the greetings were completed and the servants dispersed, Lord Greystone excused himself. Lady Greystone beckoned to Anna. Before she could speak, a commotion rose up at the front door.

"Ah, here you are, my dear." A short, stout lady, wearing an orange gown with a paisley sash and a purple turban with several ostrich feathers bouncing above it, hurried in and embraced the viscountess. "At last you've arrived. I know you're not *at home* yet, but I could not wait to see you."

Anna questioned Major Grenville with one lifted eyebrow.

"Mother's oldest friend," he whispered. "She lives in the town house next door."

"Julia, dear." Lady Greystone had suffered the other woman's embrace and even appeared to return the gesture with a slight hug. "How have you weathered this dreadful winter?"

The two ladies chatted like chirping birds for several moments, then Lady Greystone beckoned Anna again.

"Julia, this is my new companion, Newfield."

"Ah, what a lovely little thing." The lady reached out to touch Anna's chin with her lace-gloved hand. "So different from poor Miss Peel. How do you do, my dear?"

"Very well, thank you, Lady—" Anna stopped in confusion. How she wished Major Grenville had supplied a name.

But the lady laughed with a merry tinkling sound. "Oh, no, dear. Not *Lady* anything, but *Mrs.* Parton. My father was a mere baron, and my husband had no title at all." She leaned toward Anna as if confiding a secret. "But they were both very, very rich." She laughed again, and the lines in her round face gave evidence of a smile permanently etched there.

"Discussing money?" Lady Greystone scowled. "Do not be vulgar, Julia."

Mrs. Parton gave another laugh so delightful Anna had to smile. She glanced at Major Grenville. His lips were pulled in a tight line as if he was blocking a chuckle.

"Major Grenville." Mrs. Parton scurried over the marble tiled floor to grip his hand. "My, my, how handsome, how heroic you look in your uniform." Her adoring maternal gaze affirmed her words. "You will delight all the ladies this Season, you may depend upon it."

"You are too kind." The major bowed gallantly, but doubt filled his eyes. Or was it another emotion Anna saw? His own mother had not made such a fuss over him when he returned home. She looked away from the scene lest her own eyes betray her.

"Now, Frances." Mrs. Parton returned to Lady Greystone's side. "I cannot wait to tell you my news. I've hired a companion, too. She will be in London in a few weeks, and I cannot wait for you to meet her."

"Indeed?" Lady Greystone sniffed. "And why should meeting a mere companion excite such interest?"

Again Mrs. Parton's merry laugh rang throughout the vestibule. "Just you wait and see."

Despite Lady Greystone's indifference to the prospect, Anna's heart skipped. The new companion would live next door. Perhaps she would become Anna's friend. They could go on errands together, perhaps with Major Grenville as their guide and protector.

"Newfield."

Anna jolted from her daydream. "Yes, my lady."

"This is Esther." She nodded to a dark-eyed maid of perhaps thirty years. "She will take you to your room and be responsible for anything you need."

"Thank you, my lady." Her own maid. What a wonder that was. Anna would miss Mrs. Hudson's kind attentions, but no doubt she would be far more occupied in attending to Lady Greystone during the Season.

After the viscountess dismissed Anna, Esther led her to a third-floor suite, which was even lovelier than her room at the Lodge. The door opened upon a small sitting area furnished with a striped purple settee, two lavender chairs and an occasional table. Anna could imagine entertaining Mrs. Parton's companion on her day off. That is, if they had the same day off.

Just inside the bedchamber stood a white writing desk. Above it a tall window faced east and would let in the morning light. The cozy bedchamber boasted cream-colored wallpaper with blue periwinkles and a white marble fireplace, while the bed's white counterpane added to the air of lightness. In all ways, this house seemed brighter and happier than the Lodge, and she vowed to enjoy every minute. At least for the time being. Once Major Grenville returned to his duties, she doubted either place would hold much happiness for her.

But for now, she would think cheerful thoughts, enjoy the time with the major and remember all that the Lord had done for her. After all, this was Eastertide, the best time of the year, when every Christian recalled Christ's death and resurrection. Anna reminded herself that she had much to be thankful for, the most important being the promise of eternal life.

The Sunday morning service at St. Paul's Cathedral was more beautiful than anything Anna had ever experienced, exceeding even *Papá*'s descriptions. Of course the liturgy was the same, but the clergy wore bright, elegant vestments, the altar held ornate furnishings, and the choir sang so beautifully she almost wept. How she longed to share the joy of this worship time with a kindred soul. Without intending to, she glanced down the pew toward Major

Grenville. What she saw made her soul sing. His gaze was fixed on the cross above the altar, and devotion was written across his strong features and beaming from his eyes, just as when they worshipped in the little Greystone Village church. They had not spoken deeply about their faith, but in his face she saw the same devotion *Papá* and Peter had displayed not only in worship but in their everyday lives. A tiny ache stung her heart. Major Grenville might be a kindred soul in matters of faith, but he was still far beyond her reach.

What an odd discrepancy. She could sit here in this grand cathedral beside the family of an important viscount and enjoy all the spiritual privileges of being a daughter of the King of Kings, and yet she was unacceptable as an aristocrat's bride. But then, such were the ways of mankind.

Edmond followed the liturgy with deepening joy. The last time he had worshipped in St. Paul's five years ago he had been filled with shame over his scandalous behavior, things he refused to bring to mind in this holy place. For now he could bask in Christ's forgiveness, bought at such a dreadful price yet given freely. But while gratitude lifted his heart in worship, he could not resist requesting two blessings from the Lord. Should God grant him Uncle Grenville's sponsorship, he would always seek to honor Him in his law career. Should God grant him the means to marry Miss Newfield, he would love, honor and keep her with lifelong devotion.

Yet as he prayed, thoughts of Christ's prayer in the Garden nudged aside the desperation in his plea. *Not my will, but Thine be done.* This was the only true prayer of faith any Christian could offer, for God alone knew what was best. This realization brought joy pouring from his heart to fill his entire being. In this moment, he knew without doubt that all would be well, whether his petitions were granted or he returned to the army. And he must credit Miss Newfield and her brother for this realization, this surge of faith.

Drawn by thoughts of her, he glanced down the pew. She was gazing toward the cross above the altar, and her exquisite features shone with a reverent glow. Clearly no petitions cluttered her worship. Following her example, Edmond turned his thoughts back to the One whose goodness and mercy had brought the gift of salvation for all who would receive it.

On Sunday afternoon Major Grenville accompanied his brother on an outing, and Anna felt his absence keenly. How she had longed to discuss the bishop's lovely Easter homily with him. But Lady Greystone had guests, which no doubt would prove diverting, especially with the merry Mrs. Parton in attendance.

"The tea tray is beautiful." In the back hallway behind the drawing room, she gave Crawford, the butler, an apologetic smile. "But Lady Greystone wishes for me to taste the cucumber sandwiches before you serve them."

"Indeed?" The elderly man lifted his chin and glared at her, one perfectly groomed grey eyebrow twitching at the apparent insult. "I have served the Grenville family since Lord Greystone's father was a young man. I have never permitted anything inferior to be set before Her Ladyship."

"No, of course not." Anna tried to think of some way to soften the offense. "But I have noticed she has developed a dislike for hothouse cucumbers after this long winter. Perhaps she is eager to have something grown out of doors."

"Ah, yes." Crawford furrowed his brow. "I understand.

But of course normal cucumber harvest is some months away." He lifted the tray. "Please taste one."

Anna took one of the tiny sandwiches and bit into it. "Delicious. No one could tell they were not picked in a field. You make them with dill, if I am not mistaken."

His eyes twinkled and he leaned toward her. "And my secret ingredient, which I hasten to say not even Cook knows about."

"Ah, aren't you the clever one?" Anna did not mean to flatter the man, but his beaming face indicated his pleasure at her compliment. "Very well, then, I shall join Lady Greystone and her guests, and you can follow in a moment with the tea."

In London Lady Greystone insisted upon a stricter form of etiquette than she had in the country, causing Anna no little concern. She missed Mary, whose friendly warnings had saved her from errors at the Lodge. Yet here her employer seemed less inclined to scold, especially when her friends came to call.

She returned to the drawing room and sat in her designated chair, wondering whether Lady Greystone would pour the tea or call upon her to do it. Crawford stood in the doorway for a moment, then brought in the silver tea service.

Mrs. Parton and Lady Blakemore, the third member of Lady Greystone's triumvirate, gave the appropriate praise for the elegant presentation and set upon the sandwiches with little ceremony. Anna did pour the tea and received compliments from the two guests for her grace. She tried to still the pleasure their kindness incited, to no avail, for it reminded her of home.

"Now, we must make plans for our Season." Mrs. Parton nibbled on her third sandwich. "Will you provide us with some entertainment, Grace?"

Lady Blakemore, a still-beautiful, golden-haired countess of perhaps fifty years, delicately sipped her tea. "As I have no one to present to Society, I shall probably have only my usual ball. And you, Frances?"

"Indeed I will." Lady Greystone's slender face, usually so dour, was now animated. "Greystone will turn eight and twenty in May. I plan to surprise him—" she glanced around the room and apparently decided the footmen were too far away to hear her "—with a ball."

"How delightful." Mrs. Parton giggled. "Now when will that boy marry?"

"More important, whom?" Lady Blakemore chuckled in a deep, alto tone.

Lady Greystone grinned as if she had just won a hand of whist. "You will be surprised to know he has given me permission to find him a bride."

"What?" Both ladies were all astonishment, while Anna swallowed a gasp. But then, Lord Greystone enjoyed a much closer relationship with his mother than Major Grenville did, a sad state of affairs, to Anna's way of thinking. Her own parents had shown no such partiality between her and Peter.

"My son would never permit me that honor," Mrs. Parton said.

"Nor mine," added Lady Blakemore. "My daughter was another matter. She was thrilled with my choice."

"Humph. What young lady would ever decline a duke's proposal?" Lady Greystone sipped her tea. "Or a viscount's." The unmistakable bitterness in her tone put Anna's instincts on alert.

"There, there, Frances." Mrs. Parton patted her hand. "God was merciful in delivering you from your husband's—" she opened her fan and fluttered it before her face "—his harsh expectations."

Lady Greystone glanced at Anna and for the briefest moment, vulnerability filled her eyes.

Anna forced all signs of emotion from her face and spoke with disinterested deference. "More tea, my lady?" She reached out to the viscountess.

Was that a hint of appreciation in the lady's eyes as she handed over her teacup? Anna tried not to place too much hope in the notion. Yet Lady Greystone seemed to be changing, at least in the presence of her friends.

"Now, Grace." Mrs. Parton folded her fan and pointed it toward Anna as if eager to change the subject. "You see this pretty young companion Frances has hired. Well, I have hired a companion who will arrive in a few weeks. When will you find someone to keep you company?"

"A companion? Ha." Lady Blakemore shook her head. "I rarely require anyone else's company other than you two dears and my husband." She rolled her eyes. "Blakemore is forever wanting me to attend this or that function with him. Balls, the opera, even sessions of Parliament."

Mrs. Parton chortled in her merry way. Anna could hardly contain her shock upon hearing Lady Greystone emit a laugh that, though sounding feminine, held a similar cadence to Major Grenville's masculine chuckle. That was twice the viscountess had laughed in less than ten minutes.

"Ah, well." Mrs. Parton said. "I miss my dear Frederick, but I cannot lie. Having my own money and making my own decisions is a wonderful freedom to possess."

"Indeed." Lady Greystone took a sip of her tea. "I could not agree more."

"Yes, well." Lady Blakemore gave a weary sigh. "You both forget how it is to have a husband." She gasped, and her gaze flew to Lady Greystone. "Oh, Frances, forgive me."

Lady Greystone shrugged. "It has been many years, Grace. The pain has healed."

Anna's eyes stung, but she dared not let her tears fall. Yet, in these few words, so many things became clear. Months ago, Lady Greystone had mentioned her father's indifference toward her. Now this revelation of a cruel husband. Having had no say in her own life as a young woman, no wonder the lady ruled her sons and her servants with a heavy hand.

As Anna had done many times since becoming a part of the viscountess's household, she thanked the Lord for her own upbringing. Her mother had been a model of gentility. *Papá* had tried to emulate their heavenly Father in every way. Now that Anna understood the deficiencies in her employer's upbringing, she would endeavor not to be hurt by her severity. She would continue to pray for her. And perhaps, if the Lord gave her the opportunity, she would tell dear Major Grenville about the causes of his mother's unhappiness. As the bishop had said just that morning in his homily, when one understands what someone else has endured, one can forgive that person many offenses.

Chapter Twenty-Four

Despite the enticing aroma of freshly baked bread, Anna hesitated in the breakfast room doorway. Only Major Grenville sat at the table, and Lady Greystone might object, should she find them without a chaperone. Still, the viscountess tended to rise later in the city, so would no doubt linger abed for another hour. Anna glanced at the footman holding the door for her. His slight nod gave her courage.

"I thank you, John." She walked to the breakfast buffet to fill her plate.

"Good morning, Miss Newfield." Major Grenville stood while she completed the task.

"Good morning, Major." She chose a chair across from him, the better to memorize his well-formed features for the miniature she was painting. He still wore a hint of the glow she'd noticed on his face during yesterday's worship service. She hoped to capture that expression, for it seemed to reveal the gentleman's heart. In fact, she could not avert her eyes.

His smile broadened. "Do I have egg on my face?"

Her cheeks warmed, but only briefly. After all, when did he speak to her without jesting? But if his intention was to prevent her from forming an attachment to him, he was using the wrong tactic. "Only a little. 'Tis the jam that concerns me."

He quickly dabbed his lips, glanced at the spotless serviette, then chuckled. "Very droll. You are learning."

"Humph." She did her best to sound like Lady Greystone. "I am a master of jests. Growing up with Peter, I had to be or suffer endless torment." Thoughts of her brother diminished her merry mood, so she must find a safer topic. "Has Parliament begun?"

"Ah, you want to know where Greystone is. Should I be jealous?" He smirked and arched his dark eyebrows.

Her heart jumped and all humor fled. "Why, I…" Now her face flamed in earnest. She stared down at her plate and cut into a juicy sausage, but could not eat it. Surely the major knew that some subjects were unsuitable.

"Forgive me." He gave her a rueful frown. "To answer your question, no, Parliament will not convene until Tuesday next."

"I see."

They ate in silence for several minutes, a silence so heavy that Anna could not resist trying to recapture the light mood they'd enjoyed moments earlier.

"Actually, I should like to introduce a bill in the House of Lords."

Major Grenville pretended to choke and coughed artificially, waving his serviette dramatically. "Why, madam, I am all astonishment. A lady interested in politics. What a wonder. May I ask what this bill concerns?"

Now she was caught. She knew nothing of London and after four days did not yet have a grievance against the city. In truth, when she was with the major she found very little to complain about. Only one matter came to mind to rescue her from her absurd statement.

"Perhaps you noticed this past winter's extreme cold."

When he shuddered in his comical way, she had difficulty not laughing. "Well, I should like to have it designated a crime against the Crown—and all English citizens, of course—to repeat such severe temperatures for at least another century."

His expression sobered. Almost. The twinkle in his eyes gave him away. "Madam, that is a brilliant idea. I shall ask Greystone to see to it as soon as Parliament reconvenes."

"A law about the weather? What utter nonsense." Lady Greystone strode into the room. "What silly babble." Taking her place at the table, she ordered a footman to bring her breakfast. "Where is my mail?" She whipped her hand in the air to summon Crawford, who stood by the door.

Anna cringed, but the feeling quickly fled. The exchange with the major had ended well, and memories of his good humor would stay with her long after he left to resume his military service.

His heart light, Edmond would have been tempted to answer Mother with an impudent retort had she not moved on to another topic. Fortunately, she had not entered the room during that uncomfortable silence. Just as fortunate that he and Miss Newfield had already mended their small rift, which of course was all his fault. He knew better than to tease Miss Newfield about such matters. Further, if that was the sum of their discord, he was once again confident they would make a happy marriage. Despite the uncertainties about his future, he could not dismiss his hopes of winning her hand.

Even after his close communion with the Almighty yesterday, he wished he could march out of the house today and solve this dilemma. Against all that Mother thought, he was a man of action and found it utterly wretched that he must wait upon others for a solution. Wait upon Greystone to speak for him. Wait upon Uncle Grenville to grant him an audience. Wait upon Mother to be out of the room so he could speak as he wished to the lady he adored. How he yearned to be the master of his own future, but alas, life simply would not comply with that longing. All the more reason to petition Uncle Grenville to see him as soon as possible.

"Good news!" Greystone burst through the door waving a broadsheet. "Napoleon has been defeated! The war has ended."

"Huzzah!" Edmond rose to his feet in exultation. "What a great day for England and all of Europe."

"Praise God," Miss Newfield whispered.

"Well, it certainly took long enough." Mother thumbed through the mail Crawford had brought her.

"But it's done at last." Greystone waved away the footman and snatched up a plate to fill. On the way to the table, he picked up a sausage and bit into it.

As Edmond returned to his seat, he noticed Mother did not correct his brother's manners, something he never escaped, even as a grown man.

"Well, Edmond." Mother's forehead creased with worry. "Now you must make all haste to return to your duties."

"Madam?" He could only imagine where her logic was leading, and his exultation over the defeat of Napoleon died away.

"Why must I explain everything to you?" She glared at him as if he were a simpleton. "When our officers return home from the Continent, they will clamor for positions in the American war. You must seize your chance to gain a place of leadership before then."

Alarm spread over Miss Newfield's fair face, confirming her regard for him. Edmond swallowed to dislodge the lump in his chest, to no avail.

"Now, Mother." Greystone's suddenly lazy tone ignited a thread of hope. "Edmond has no need to rush."

"Of course he does—"

Greystone held up one hand to silence her. To Edmond's surprise, she stopped speaking.

"I am not without influence." Greystone covered his lips as if stifling a yawn. "If there are positions to be had, I can arrange, oh, something or other." He turned to Edmond, his face exuding boredom. "I fear I've grown used to having you around. Are you all that eager to be away?"

Edmond stilled his pounding pulse. "Not so eager that I would thwart any political maneuvering that would benefit you."

Greystone's eyes flickered, another sign that he had some plan. "Yes, this is just the sort of thing one uses to gain friends."

"Well." Mother gave a sniff of indignation. "It will do no harm for me to use *my* influence in this matter." She speared Edmond with a rapier-like stare. "This afternoon, we will take a ride in Hyde Park to see who is in town. Then you must accompany me to the theater. The balls will begin as soon as Holy Week is over, and I shall take you to Almack's two weeks from Wednesday."

"As you wish, madam."

Edmond's emotions wavered between despair and hope. Mother did not seem to realize that her favorite son was battling her for control of Edmond's future. Yet when— or if—Greystone won, he would hand the reins over to Edmond, trusting him not to bring shame upon the family as he once had. Respect and affection for his eldest brother filled his chest. As Edmond had experienced in the army, this was the stuff of leadership. Perhaps Greystone would bring enough fame to the family to satisfy their mother.

He tried to recapture yesterday's attitude of surrender to God's will, but could only repeat *Not my will, but Thine be done.* When no great rapture lifted his spirits as before, he added, *Lord, I believe. Help Thou mine unbelief.*

Although the April breeze found a way to slip beneath her riding cape, Anna attributed the pleasant shivers sliding up her back to Major Grenville's hands at her waist. With little effort he lifted her into the saddle, always an exhilarating experience that left her breathless for several moments. How she would miss riding with him when he left.

"I did not expect to go on this expedition." Anna settled herself and grasped Bella's reins. "I wonder why Lady Greystone insisted."

He eyed the front door of the town house. "I have observed," he muttered, "that Mother always enjoys leading an entourage." Guilt flickered in his eyes. "Forgive me. I should not criticize her."

"You speak from your heart, sir." Anna often squelched less than charitable thoughts about her employer, trying to turn judgment into prayers for the lady's happiness. She glanced at the liveried groom who stood several yards away with Lady Greystone's mare, then bent down to whisper to the major. "Your words will go no further."

"I know. You are the soul of discretion." His gaze lingered on her and a slight smile crept over his lips.

Anna's heart warmed. She could no longer deny that her feelings for this gentleman were past redeeming. She did love him. But of course she could never hope to go beyond admiring him from a distance. Still, in these moments when he seemed also to have deep feelings for her, she permitted herself to bask in his gaze like a morning glory opening to the sunlight.

The front door swung open with a whoosh. The major stepped away from Anna and reached out to Lady Greystone as she descended the marble steps. "A fine day for riding, is it not, Mother?"

"We shall see how pleasant it is." She submitted to his assistance in mounting the chestnut mare. "It will depend upon who is in the park today."

As he walked to his own horse, Anna noticed his clenched jaw. He must be wrestling with some weighty matter, though she could not guess what. Her heart ached for him. How she longed to be the one to help him.

With Anna, the major and the groom following behind her, Lady Greystone set a leisurely pace for their westward ride to Hyde Park. The streets did not seem as crowded as when they arrived the week before, but Anna had to use all of her newly acquired skill to wend her way around carriages, carts and pedestrians. Once or twice, Major Grenville reined up beside her to lead Bella away from a fruit cart or some lady's bonnet, but Anna managed to control her most of the time.

At last they arrived at the park, or rather, the open meadow. Anna surveyed the scene. A narrow river rippled by on one side, with trees and clusters of shrubbery filling its banks. Roads meandered in all directions, leading to no apparent destination. Although Anna glimpsed a few random wildflowers, she was a little disappointed not to find formal flowerbeds blooming along the pathways. For the most part, the odors of horseflesh and leather filled her senses. But she could not wish herself any other place in the world, for there was much to see and the company was incomparable.

Numerous carriages of different shapes and sizes drove

around the park, with finely dressed occupants calling out to acquaintances as they passed. Lady Greystone acknowledged the greetings of friends, but did not stop to chat. Wearing a dark rose riding habit with a matching hat, the lady sat elegantly upon her horse. Anna could see that Major Grenville had been too kind as her teacher, for he had neglected to correct her posture. She did her best to emulate Lady Greystone's regal bearing so as not to disgrace her. Still, when the viscountess increased her pace to a trot, Anna had no difficulty following.

Behind her, the major shouted, "Good show, Miss Newfield."

His praise hit its mark, so she abandoned herself to enjoying the day. She hoped Lady Greystone was also having a pleasant time. After observing her with her friends, Anna concluded that she surely must prefer London over Greystone Lodge.

Soon the viscountess slowed her horse and beckoned to Major Grenville.

He rode around Anna, giving her a nod, and approached the lady. "Madam?"

"I see the Marchioness of Drayton's barouche across the park. Her younger son is attached to Wellington in some way or another, so that is an advantage I must press for you. I shall ride ahead to detain her. You will follow with Newfield. We must make it look like an accidental meeting."

"As you wish." His jaw clenched as it had earlier. How hard this must be for him.

Anna reined Bella to follow the viscountess, but the mare faltered briefly, then limped with each step. Alarmed for the poor beast, Anna pulled her to a stop and cried out, "My lady."

Lady Greystone pulled her horse around. "What?" Impatience resounded in her tone as she rode back to Anna.

"What is it, Miss Newfield?" The major's gentler voice softened Anna's unease.

"Bella is limping."

The groom dismounted and examined Bella for injury, coming at last to the left front hoof. "My lady, she's picked up a stone." He wore a pained expression. "As it's bleeding, may I suggest I should take her back to the mews?"

"Yes, of course," the viscountess said.

"She must not be ridden." Major Grenville dismounted and lifted Anna down.

This time no pleasant feelings resulted from his touch. Anna looked up at Lady Greystone, desperately wishing to find a way to please her employer. "I—I can walk back to the house."

The lady barked out a hard laugh. "And get lost in the process? Utter nonsense. I have invested too much in you to have you get lost in the streets of London."

Indeed, the viscountess had arranged for a modest wardrobe to be made for Anna in the coming days. While the lady's words sounded harsh, they actually reaffirmed Anna's growing sense of security regarding her position.

Major Grenville, however, frowned at his mother. "Madam, please. Miss Newfield can ride Brutus. I shall walk beside her and take her home."

"No, no, no. We must not miss this opportunity. Once the Season begins, every toady and sycophant in London will be at Lady Drayton's doorstep seeking some sort of sponsorship." Lady Greystone stared across the park, then turned back to the major with a look that Anna could only describe as wily. "I have a better plan." She waved the groom away. "Take the mare back to the mews. See that she is properly tended." Her stare landed next upon Anna.

"Oh, how I do wish you were someone significant, but this will have to do. Edmond, no one is quite so heroic as a gentleman who protects a lady in distress. This is what we will do to impress Lady Drayton. You will stay here with Newfield, as you have not yet been presented to the marchioness. I shall fetch her. That is, I shall happen upon her and ask if she would be so kind as to convey Newfield back to Greystone Hall in her carriage."

"Mother, I hardly think—"

"Indeed, you hardly ever seem to think." She blew out a cross breath. "Must I do everything to advance your prospects?"

He flinched. Anna's heart stung for him. "But Lady Drayton will see through the ruse. I could simply have Miss Newfield ride Brutus."

"Nonsense. I shall tell her that your horse is too spirited for my companion, inexperienced rider that she is." She sniffed. "Now, I must be off. That bench." She pointed her riding crop to a stone bench beneath a spreading willow tree near the river bank. "Wait there." She started to rein her horse away, but turned back. "Newfield, I don't suppose you can limp."

Before she could stop herself, Anna laughed. "Limp, my lady?"

"Humph. The *gel* hasn't the slightest bit of artifice, even when it would be useful." She reined her mare around and loped away.

Anna eyed Major Grenville. They both laughed.

"Well, dear lady, shall we *limp* over to that bench?"

"Why, Major, I cannot think of anything I would rather do." But in truth her stomach felt as if a hive of bees had taken up residence in it. She had made the mistake of admitting to herself that she loved him. Now she would be alone with him, and that would challenge every whit of her self-restraint, lest her feelings be evident in every word and every look.

Chapter Twenty-Five

Beneath a clear blue sky, a light breeze stirred the trees and shrubbery along the Serpentine River. Brutus, tethered to a nearby bush, nickered his greeting to passing horses, then returned to nibbling the tender new grass at his feet. Seated on the bench beside Miss Newfield, Edmond decided to make the most of these minutes alone with her.

"Lovely day." Hardly an intelligent beginning, but she did not seem to mind, if her pleasant smile was any indication.

"It is indeed." She seemed to be studying the traffic with the curiosity of a student. "I am surprised to see so many different shapes of carriages. Is there a different name for each?"

"Yes. For instance, that is a curricle." He pointed his riding crop toward a two-wheeled chaise drawn by two black horses. "And that four-wheeled carriage is a barouche."

"Goodness, I hope I can remember which is which." The merry twinkle in Miss Newfield's eyes belied her worried tone. Here in the shade of the tree those eyes took on a rich emerald color, while the wind blew several strands of hair from beneath her bonnet.

Edmond reached out and tucked them back in place.

Her eyes widened and color brightened her cheeks, adding a lovely glow to her fair countenance.

"There. That's better." He gave her his most officious frown, as he would to a junior officer whose uniform was not entirely in order. "I thought we should tidy you up a bit after your ordeal." He should not have touched her. But in truth he longed to kiss those delicate lips now puckered with concern, longed to tell her what was in his heart. Merely touching her hair was a minor offense. What he actually wanted to do was free those dark brown tresses of all restraints and let them blow in the wind like the fluttering new leaves on this willow tree. *Hmm.* Better put a stop to such thinking before his unruly hand surrendered to another impulse. "Mother will want to present a well-groomed companion to her friend."

"Oh, yes. Of course." She looked away and a comfortable silence settled over them for several moments. "Tell me, Major, why are no flowerbeds planted in this charming park?"

He followed her gaze. "I've no idea. Perhaps we should present a bill to Parliament demanding an immediate planting."

"Oh, yes. Another bill for Parliament." She smirked in her charming way. "Perhaps they should simply turn the management of the entire country over to us."

"Indeed." He bowed to her. "I would be pleased to reign with you." *You are already the queen of my heart.* Would that he could say those words to her. Perhaps one day.

Her eyes flared briefly as they did when she was surprised. But as always, she regained her composure and gave him her impish smile. "What would you do if you were the king?"

"Hmm." He returned a smirk, then gazed off, trying to think of some nonsensical quip. But all he could think of was his looming return to war. A mad impulse gripped him. He would tell her of his feelings. No, he could not. If—*when* he returned to America, she must be free to find someone to love and marry, in spite of Mother. He heaved a sigh, weary of the battle within him. "I would grant the Americans their demands and bring our military home."

"Are you saying you do not wish to return to the army?"

He shook his head. "In a word, no."

She tilted her head in her charming way. "All this time I have been praying for your advancement. Now I will pray that you will find a way to remain in England." She brushed away a leaf that had settled on her lap. "Do you wish to remain in the army?"

"Not at all. Were it not for Mother, I would have resigned my commission as soon as I returned last October."

"Ah." Another grin formed. "And all this time I thought you enjoyed wearing your uniform. Mrs. Parton will be quite disappointed if you do not wear it to all the parties this Season, for she found you very handsome and, what did she say, *heroic*."

Edmond gently grasped her hand. "And you, Miss Newfield, would you be disappointed, would you find me less heroic, if I put off my crimson jacket for a plain black suit?"

To his shock, her eyes reddened, and a broken laugh escaped her. "I cannot imagine anything you do would disappoint me."

The trust emanating from her pressed into his soul as nothing before in his life. How gladly he would surrender everything for her happiness.

She looked away, breaking the cord that had bound their

gazes together. But she continued to rest her hand in his grasp. "When you put on that black suit, what will you do?"

Marry you. Provide for you. Work every day for your happiness. "I should like to become a barrister."

"Major, you will make an excellent barrister." Her face crinkled into pretty confusion. "Why, then, I suppose you will be addressed as *Mr.* Grenville, will you not?"

He chuckled. "Yes, well, only if I can actually achieve my goal."

"But what is preventing you?"

"Miss Newfield, have you met my mother?"

Her wry smile exuded both agreement and a rebuke. "She cares very much for you, or she would not trouble herself." Her eyebrows arched. "What is required for you to become a barrister?"

"I must find a sponsor and take up residence in one of the Inns of Courts to study under a senior barrister. After three years, if I have proved myself, I will be tested and called to the bar." He gazed across the park, imagining himself arguing some point of law before the courts.

"Why, it seems this would be an excellent career for you. Perhaps even lucrative. Why does Lady Greystone prefer that you remain in the army?"

His pleasant daydream evaporated. "She has never explained her reasons to me. But then, Mother rarely explains anything. Perhaps because fame and riches can be had more quickly for an officer during wartime."

"I see. That would be more expedient. But just this morning she said she would not like for her sons to be sent off to foreign lands."

Edmond had wearied of talking about his intractable parent. "And what about you, Miss Newfield. What do you think I should do?"

She glanced down at their still-joined hands. "I must agree with what Lord Greystone said this morning. I've grown used to having you in the household. I am not eager to see you leave."

He pulled her hand up to this lips and placed a kiss on her fingertips. "Neither am I eager to leave you, my dear Miss Newfield."

Her eyes grew round, her lips parted. "Lady Greystone—"

Not what he had hoped to hear her say.

"—is coming."

As if they were actors in a play, each knowing his part, they moved to opposite ends of the bench to watch Mother's approach. Behind her came a grand white barouche pulled by four matching dapple-greys and bearing the crest of the Marquess of Drayton. The driver in front and two footmen at the rear wore dark green livery, completing the picture of power and position.

Beneath his carefully schooled expression of boredom, Edmond's emotions churned with dread over the uncertainties of his future.

Anna could not still the pounding of her heart. She had just as much as confessed to Major Grenville that she loved him. And if the tenderness in his eyes was any indication, her feelings for him were reciprocated. Yes, it was possible she was seeing only what she wanted to see. And her mother had warned her long ago that some men used pretty words to steal a lady's virtue. But the major had offered no pretty words. In fact, in all these months since meeting him she had never observed a single incident during which he behaved as less than a gentleman.

But then, what good were his feelings or hers when a vast chasm lay between their places in society? Still, she could not regret this brief time when they had said nothing dangerous to each other—and yet had said all. Nor did she feel the slightest whit of guilt upon seeing Lady Greystone approach. In fact, she longed to say to the woman, *I love your son.* But for his sake, how much better to say, *Why can you not permit him to do as he wishes with his life?* And of course, she could say neither.

Lady Greystone reined her horse to a stop. The barouche stopped behind her. A footman jumped from the carriage back and helped the viscountess dismount. While Anna and the major rose to meet her, she waved them over impatiently, then grasped the major's arm and tugged him forward, leaving Anna several yards away.

"Lady Drayton, may I present my son, Major Edmond Grenville, who was wounded while fighting valiantly in the American war."

Anna had never before heard a single compliment fall from Lady Greystone's lips, especially for the major, yet such praise would greatly encourage her son.

The marchioness, an ancient matron with light blue eyes, smiled and extended a bejeweled hand over the carriage side. Her purple bonnet framed tight ringlets of white hair that surrounded her pale, cherubic face. "Major Grenville."

"Lady Drayton." He stepped forward, kissed her hand and bowed. "I am honored."

"Not at all, my boy." The lady's voice carried a tone of authority not unlike Lady Greystone's, but much kinder. "It is I who am honored to meet one of our war heroes." A merry sparkle lit her eyes. "And I suppose I shall meet many more in the days to come."

"No doubt, madam," Major Grenville said. "We must thank God for the victory on the Continent."

"Indeed, we must. Now, where is my friend's little companion?" The marchioness peered around him.

Anna offered a curtsey, but had no idea what to say.

Again, Lady Greystone summoned her with an impatient wave. "Lady Drayton, this is Newfield. She is a quiet little thing, so do not expect much."

The marchioness chuckled. "But that is the work of a companion, is it not? To comfort her employer by her mere presence."

Anna hardly believed herself to be a comfort to Lady Greystone, but she tucked that idea away for future consideration.

"Come along, Miss Newfield." The marchioness summoned her footman to help Anna into the carriage. "Now, Lady Greystone, I would be most pleased if you and your son would ride with us. One of my footmen can bring the horses."

"How kind of you, madam." Lady Greystone gave her a subdued smile, but Anna heard a note of satisfaction in her voice. Her plan was working. But what would that mean for Major Grenville?

Once they were seated in the barouche, the marchioness ordered the driver to take another turn around the park. Then she eyed Lady Greystone. "You have time, do you not?"

"I do, but I cannot answer for my son. Edmond?"

From the glint in Major Grenville's eyes, Anna feared he would make some jest. She held her breath.

"Madam, I am at your disposal." He waved one hand carelessly. "The regiment will simply have to do without me for the afternoon."

Lady Greystone stiffened, but Lady Drayton laughed merrily. "Ah, I can see you are a delightful young man." She eyed Anna. "Now, Miss Newfield, you must tell me, are you related to a country vicar named William Newfield?"

Anna jolted. "Y-yes, Lady Drayton. He was my father."

"So he is deceased? Oh, my dear, I am so sorry." Genuine sympathy emanated from her countenance. "I could not imagine why Lady Greystone would dress you in this black. Now I understand. And your mother?"

Lady Greystone emitted a soft huff of displeasure. Clearly, the turn of the conversation did nothing to advance her purposes. Anna would answer briefly so the exchange could return to the major's career. "Gone, too, madam."

"Ah." The marchioness reached across the carriage and patted her hand. "Like you, she was such a pretty little thing, all the rage during her Season. Mind you, one does not remember every miss who debuts in Society, but Miss Elgin was, as they say, a diamond of the first water."

Now a gasp came from Lady Greystone. But her surprise paled when compared to Anna's. "Are you saying my mother once enjoyed a London Season?"

"Yes," Lady Drayton drawled. "Did she never tell you?"

Anna could only shake her head. Without meaning to, she glanced at the major, who sat beside the marchioness wearing a bemused smile.

"What have you been keeping from us, Newfield?" Lady Greystone's honeyed tone conveyed veiled displeasure. "Or should it be *Miss* Newfield."

"There now, Lady Greystone," Lady Drayton said. "'Tis obvious the *gel* has no idea. And why would she? Her parents would hardly brag about it. As for you, do you not recall the scandal the marriage created? The daughter of Sir Reginald Elgin rejecting an earl to marry a country vicar? Although I must hasten to say many of us found it delightfully romantic." The lady's laugh was a musical trill, but she quickly sobered. "Of course she was disowned and disinherited. And all for love." She tapped a finger on her powdered cheek. "Let me see, that would be some six and twenty years ago. Perhaps you were not in town that year?"

For the first time since Anna had met Lady Greystone, the woman seemed unable to speak. Her eyes shifted from the marchioness to Anna and back again. At last she ground out, "I believe I would have been in one of my confinements at the time."

"Ah, yes, of course." Lady Drayton nodded. "And doubtless by the time you returned to London, another scandal would have been all the rage."

"Yes," Lady Greystone said. "Doubtless." She examined Anna with a critical stare as if seeing her for the first time.

"Now." The marchioness tapped the major's knee with her folded fan. "About your future, young man. What can I do for you?"

Chapter Twenty-Six

By the time Lady Drayton's barouche stopped in front of Greystone Hall, she had thoroughly questioned Edmond—or more precisely, Mother—and promised them she would speak to Wellington or even the Prince Regent himself about an advancement.

"We must wait for the appropriate time, of course. But be assured that your exemplary service in America will put you in good light, especially when you return there to help lead our troops to victory." Her maternal smile was more than his own mother had ever given him.

"Madam, you are too kind." Edmond was well aware of her power to obtain what she wanted for her friends, whether he desired an advancement or not. At least he had days, perhaps weeks, before Wellington returned to London.

After the appropriate goodbyes, he disembarked from the carriage and handed Mother and Miss Newfield down. Then the marchioness called Mother back to the side of the carriage.

"You must bring your charming son and the lovely Miss Newfield to my ball this Friday. I would postpone it until our soldiers return, but with Parliament opening on Tuesday next, I do so want to start the Season appropriately."

"We would be honored, Lady Drayton." Mother's grim expression had not softened since she learned of Miss Newfield's history.

"Very good. I shall send around your invitation." She tapped her fan on the seat. "Home, Basil."

Once inside the town house Mother ordered Miss Newfield to follow her to the small parlor. Edmond also followed, determined to prevent his parent from browbeating the young lady.

"Your presence is not required." Mother signaled the footman to close the door, but Edmond pushed through.

"Nonsense." He used her favorite word. "As I am responsible for bringing this person into your employ, I have a right to know how she has deceived us." He hoped Miss Newfield understood his purpose in speaking so harshly. He wished he could send her a reassuring wink, but Mother was glaring directly at him.

"Really, Edmond, I would hardly call it deceit." She crossed her arms. "As Lady Drayton said, it is more than obvious Miss Newfield had no idea her mother once created a scandal. It is not the sort of thing a lady tells her children."

While he was pleased she did not mean to berate Miss Newfield, the young lady's pale face and glistening eyes stirred his protective instincts. "But why do you consider it a scandal?"

"Why, isn't it obvious?" Mother snorted. "An earl, whoever he was, offered for Miss Elgin. She rejected him. And for what? To marry an insignificant village vicar with no prospects."

Miss Newfield sank down on the settee, removed her bonnet and covered her face with both hands. Edmond prayed she would not cry, for nothing annoyed Mother more than tears.

"How irresponsible, both for herself and for her entire family. And look at the result." She waved a hand toward the object of her tirade. "Disowned, *disinherited* and a daughter forced into *working* like some common farmer's offspring. The very idea—"

"My lady, if you please." Her features heroically composed, Miss Newfield rose with a grace equal to any heiress's. "I should like to retire." She did not wait for permission, but curtseyed and hurried from the room.

Edmond had never been so proud of her. Her simple action might result in her being sacked, but if so, he would do exactly what her father had done—marry the woman he loved and care for her all his life, no matter how humbly they must live.

"Madam, I pray you will not think too harshly—"

"Hush, Edmond. I am thinking." Mother began to pace, her hard-heeled riding boots thumping against the polished oak floor. She stopped at the window and spun back to face him. "I must investigate the matter and find out who her mother's people are, who this Sir Reginald Elgin is, for I have never encountered him. It may turn to our advantage for me to introduce her into Society as my protégée rather than keeping her as my companion." She waved him away. "Go on, then. Tell the *gel* she has nothing to worry about. I have no plans to let her go, if that is her concern."

"Yes, madam." Edmond took his leave and strode from the room after Miss Newfield. Clearly Mother did not know her at all. He had no doubt her position was the least of her concerns, but rather how to sort out the revelation of her family's secret.

In her little sitting room Anna rested in her favorite wingchair, but she could take no pleasure in her pretty surroundings. Although she had not entirely surrendered to her tears, a few stray drops did manage to escape as countless questions tormented her. Why had her parents kept secret the most wonderful part of their love story? Did they fear she and Peter would somehow be ashamed rather than pleased to comprehend the depth of their love? She would never know their reasons, but if given the chance, she would follow their example. If at this moment Major Grenville appeared at her door and asked for her hand, she would gladly say yes.

A knock did sound on her door. She jumped, then laughed at her own silliness. "One moment." She wiped away her tears and opened the portal. To her surprise, it was the very gentleman who consumed her thoughts.

"Major Grenville." With her emotions so heightened, this was not a good time for him to come, especially when his ardent expression seemed to convey the same affection she felt. *Especially* when she longed to launch herself into his comforting arms. Yet she dared not assume anything. "M-may I help you?"

His warm chuckle rolled over her like a woolen blanket in winter. "May I come in?"

"Well…" She peeked out to scan the hallway.

"Mother sent me." His merry smirk further encouraged her and also settled her emotions. Despite her wild imaginings—and hopes—he had not come to propose.

"Oh. Well, then, do come in." She waved a hand toward the wingchair. "I shall ring for tea." Leaving the outer door open, she stepped into the bedchamber and tugged on the bell pull to summon Esther. She returned to sit across from the major, far enough away for propriety's sake, far enough away that he could not grasp the hand she wished so eagerly to give him. "I suppose Lady Greystone is quite displeased with me."

Again he chuckled. "Not at all. In fact, I do believe you have replaced me in her schemes."

"What?"

He shrugged and his smile disappeared. "Oh, she will not stop until I've sailed for America." The twinkle returned to his eyes. "But now she is scheming to advance you."

"Advance *me?* But, as she so clearly said this afternoon, I am not someone significant." The sting of Lady Greystone's careless words had not diminished, despite these new revelations. "More important, I own nothing—no inheritance or anything of value."

He leaned forward as if he would move closer to her, and her breath lodged in her throat. "You are indeed significant to—"

"You rang, Miss Newfield?" Esther appeared in the door and stared from Anna to the major and back again, disapproval clear in her narrowed eyes.

Disappointed that the major had not completed his thought, Anna nevertheless must prevent her lady's maid from misunderstanding the situation. "Lady Greystone sent Major Grenville to advise me on some important matters. Would you please bring us tea?" She had yet to make this woman her friend, so she offered her a warm smile.

Esther's lips formed a thin line as she stepped across the sitting room and closed the bedchamber door. "Bringing tea is not one of my duties, miss."

"Oh—" Anna recalled the many times throughout the winter when Mrs. Hudson had cheerfully fetched tea for her.

Major Grenville stood and towered over Esther. "What exactly is your duty, if not to obey the lady you have been assigned to serve?" Anna could imagine his soldiers quaking under the stern look he gave the woman.

Now a pout formed on Esther's face, which might have been charming in her younger days but now merely distorted her ordinary features. "Very well, then." She spun around and marched from the room, leaving Anna to wonder whether or not she would actually bring the tea.

"Now, where were we?" Scowling, Major Grenville reclaimed his chair.

Anna could not resist trying to lighten the tone of their conversation. "Let me see. I had just stated my lack of significance, and you were about to tell me that I am significant to—?"

"Hmm. Well." He cleared his throat. "You are the granddaughter of a gentleman addressed as 'Sir.' That in itself is significant. However, we do not know whether your grandfather was—or is—a baronet or a gentleman knighted by His Majesty for some special service. In the first case the title is inherited and then passed on to subsequent generations. In the second case it is a singular honor for the gentleman and goes no further."

"I think I understand." Anna searched her memory but could not recall any mention of her maternal grandfather by either parent. How she regretted not asking them. "As I told Lady Greystone when we met, my *father's* ancestor was knighted by Queen Anne for a special service, although I have no idea what. But even if my mother's father is a baronet, he disowned her." She grieved to think her gentle mother had suffered such a fate. But then, *Papá* had been an extraordinary gentleman, much like Major Grenville in many ways, so Anna could understand *Mamá's* choice.

The major frowned. "Hmm. In truth, I do not know whether that will make a difference. But you may be certain Mother will unearth everything." He gave her a wry grin, then stood and walked to the door. "Be prepared for a great change in your life."

"Will you not wait for tea?" Anna felt a twinge of foolish desperation in wanting him to stay.

"I would greatly enjoy tea." His dark eyes filled with a gentle look she could not discern. "But perhaps we should return to the parlor rather than provide fodder for servants' gossip."

"Of course." Anna resisted the urge to remind him of how limited their conversation would be in the parlor. "I will join you momentarily."

"Your servant, madam." He gave her one of his comically elaborate bows, then disappeared down the hallway.

Anna opened the inner door and hurried into her bedchamber to sit at the dainty vanity table and fix her hair. As she suspected, having been tucked under her bonnet all afternoon, it was awry. This time, the major had not attempted to smooth it back. A good thing, too, for it could have posed great danger to her reputation if he had done so just as Esther entered the room.

"Miss Newfield?" Coming from the outer room, the lady's maid's voice sounded like a nervous chirp.

"Here I am, Esther."

"Oh, miss!" She set down the tea tray she carried. "I just heard your news. Oh, my, such an important advancement." She bustled over to Anna and gently seized her brush. "Now, now. You must permit *me* to tend to your hair." She set about working her magic on the unruly curls. "There, now, miss. Much better." And indeed it was. "You will want to change out of your riding habit." Not waiting for Anna's approval, she set about unbuttoning the dress. "This is the day we shall debut your new gown. And of course, your new black slippers." Flitting about the room in her eagerness to complete her task, Esther seemed like a different person as she fastened the buttons up the back of the dress, a grey cotton creation with black piping and lace that Mrs. Hudson had helped her make. After a last re-touch of Anna's coiffure, the woman stood back and studied her with a critical eye. "Beautiful. Simply beautiful."

Anna willingly submitted to her ministrations and, looking in her long mirror, was more than pleased with the outcome. "Thank you, Esther. I believe it is acceptable at last for me to carry my ivory fan."

The maid brought the item from the wardrobe. "Here you are, miss. May I pour your tea?"

"Ah, I had forgotten it." Anna spied the small sand-wiches beside the porcelain tea service, and her stomach demanded satisfaction. But a far stronger appetite called out to her—to see Major Grenville. "I am having tea—" she need not explain further "—downstairs."

Esther had the grace to blush. "Yes, miss."

"But you must have this." Anna waved her hand over the inviting repast. "Invite Mrs. Hudson to join you here in my sitting room."

Esther's jaw dropped. Then she smiled and curtseyed. "Why, yes, miss, I'll do that."

Anna descended the two flights of stairs and walked toward the small parlor, where a footman met her. "Lady Greystone and Major Grenville request the honor of your presence in the drawing room, miss."

Retracing her steps up the hallway, Anna felt both ea-gerness to see the major and trepidation over meeting with Lady Greystone. She had not yet settled her emotions over today's shocking news and did not feel prepared by half to receive any further reports regarding her long-lost family.

Then another thought interrupted her musings. If Sir Reginald Elgin had not yet departed this earth, she still had living family. But then, if he had disowned *Mamá,* he would not have the slightest interest in Anna. Or Peter, she hastened to remind herself. For she could not dismiss the belief that her brother was alive and recovering from his injuries somewhere in America.

Chapter Twenty-Seven

Anna held up her index finger, a silent plea to the footman to delay opening the door. The middle-aged man, whose distinguishing features were muted by his blue livery and white wig, gave her a brief nod. She could not avoid this next scene, dare she say *confrontation,* but she needed another moment to lift her petition to the only One who could help. *Lord, please—* But she had no idea what to pray. She nodded for the footman to open the door.

On trembling legs she walked across the polished floor, then onto the red-and-gold Persian carpet to reach a grouping of chairs and settees. Her eyes instinctively sought out Major Grenville, who rose to greet her. From his bemused expression, she guessed he knew nothing more than before.

"Come here, Miss Newfield." Lady Greystone waved her to the chair beside her. Her use of "Miss" set Anna's nerves tingling. Surely it could not be a bad thing.

"Oh, my, isn't this fun?" Mrs. Parton, who sat on Lady Greystone's other side, had been hidden from Anna's view when she entered. What a welcome addition, for her cheerful disposition could brighten any room.

"Good afternoon, Mrs. Parton." Anna had no difficulty returning the merry lady's smile. "Am I to suppose you refer to Lady Drayton's astonishing revelation in regard to me?"

"Indeed I do refer to your, shall we say, revelation of elevation?" Her laughter rang throughout the large chamber.

Major Grenville chuckled, but whether he laughed over Mrs. Parton's wordplay or her jovial manner Anna could not guess. Nevertheless, his laughter cheered her.

"Humph." Lady Greystone eyed Anna critically. "We do not yet know if this is an elevation or a reason to keep your identity concealed."

"My lady?" Anna's pulse slowed.

"Mother, for goodness' sake." The major sat on the edge of his chair. "Keep us…keep Miss Newfield in suspense no longer."

Anna sent him a grateful glance, but sudden fear froze out all other emotions.

"If you please, Edmond." Lady Greystone clicked her tongue in an impatient sound. "Now, Newfield, I asked Mrs. Parton if she knew about—"

"Frances, do permit me to tell the tale." Mrs. Parton's voice conveyed no hint of what the "tale" held. Neither did the kind look she turned on Anna. "You see, my dear, like Frances, I was busy rearing children and rarely came to London during the time in question. But I do recall hearing about the…oh, let us not call it a scandal, more a bit of gossip at this point. Of the little I heard, one thing is certain. Sir Reginald was a baronet of some fortune."

"Was?" Anna's heart constricted.

"Yes. Gone these ten or so years." Mrs. Parton gazed at her with sympathetic eyes.

"I see. Did he have other children?" *Have I an uncle or aunt? Anything, Lord, that I might not be alone.*

Mrs. Parton shook her head. "Not that I am aware of, my dear."

Anna's eyes stung, but a glance at Major Grenville strengthened her resolve not to let her tears fall.

"And so you can see," said Lady Greystone, "we must use discretion in discovering what sort of man this Sir Reginald was."

"Indeed." Mrs. Parton nodded vigorously and her tight curls bounced in agreement. "You must understand, my dear. If he had influential friends, his only daughter's defiance of his wishes will not bode well for her offspring."

"But perhaps he had no such friends." Major Grenville stood and walked toward the hearth, then swung around to face the ladies. "Perhaps he was not highly regarded by the *ton*. If you have never heard of him, Mother, either good or bad, there is no reason Miss Newfield may not be accorded every respect due to the granddaughter of a baronet." His dark eyes glinted with something Anna could only describe as fervor, and her heart bounced into her throat. What a grand barrister he would make.

"Do not be hasty, Edmond." Lady Greystone also had a glint in her eye, and her lips twitched into something akin to a smile. "I shall discuss this with Greystone this evening and see if he knows anything about Sir Reginald. For now, what we have spoken about must not leave this room."

Anna glanced around at the chamber's three doors. Not a single footman stood within. "My lady, I fear it may be too late."

"What?"

Her harsh tone set Anna back for a moment. "My lady's maid seemed to know everything."

"Oh!" Lady Greystone slammed her fist on the arm of her chair. "Bothersome servants. Can't keep their mouths shut about matters that do not concern them. I should toss that one out in the street."

Major Grenville snorted out a laugh. "And have her tell every lamppost in London what she's heard?"

"Never mind, Frances." Mrs. Parton patted Lady Greystone's hand. Strangely, the viscountess permitted it. "Just have your housekeeper—she is reliable, I assume— have her explain to the entire staff what damage can be done to our dear Miss Newfield, should they gossip about this matter."

She sent Anna a kind look, once again in every way such a contrast to Lady Greystone. The young woman coming to London to be Mrs. Parton's companion could rest assured she would receive only kindness from her employer.

Edmond had been too busy thinking about Miss Newfield's matter to consider anything else. But when he returned to his quarters to find Matthews diligently tending to his several changes of uniform, his own future loomed large in his thoughts.

"Tell me, Matthews." Edmond dropped down on his reclining couch and grabbed a strawberry from a bowl on the side table. "If I were to resign my commission, would you be willing to change your title from batman to valet?" He bit into the fruit and its tangy sweetness exploded in his mouth. One could not enjoy such delights on the battlefield.

Matthews gave him a quizzical grin. "Indeed I would, sir. Me family's here in London, and I don't like to think of being so far away as America again."

"Neither do I." Edmond ate another strawberry. "Pray for me, then, that I find a sponsor at the Inns of Courts, or we will both be sailing for America soon."

Matthews lifted one of Edmond's spare boots and began to polish the already shining footwear. "So you've heard nothing from your uncle, sir?"

Edmond shook his head. "Greystone has sent letters every day, but still no answer." Such neglect seemed discourteous and even irresponsible. Perhaps Uncle Grenville would not be a worthy sponsor after all, if he treated his clients as shabbily as he treated his own nephew, a peer of no little standing in Parliament.

"I'm sure you'll hear soon, sir. Keep yer chin up." Matthews winced. "Meaning no disrespect."

Edmond chuckled. "Not at all. You may always speak your mind to me. I thank you for your encouragement."

In the next few days, Mother and Greystone continued to make discreet inquiries regarding Miss Newfield's grandfather, but discovered nothing outstanding. Greystone had expressed great delight over the possibility of her becoming Mother's protégée, for he was deeply grateful for her help during his illness. But such good deeds would not be sufficient to assure her acceptance among the *haute ton*. Perverse though it was, Edmond hoped Sir Reginald turned out to be an overbearing scoundrel, perhaps a miser, whom Society regarded as unfair to his only child, whom all had proclaimed an extraordinary miss. That would bode well for Miss Newfield.

In the interim while they awaited the news, Edmond saw little of the lady who owned his heart, for Mother had ordered her a wardrobe and fittings took much of her time. When he did see her, Mother was always present. He could tolerate such conditions were he not so concerned that he would leave soon and would have failed to declare his love for Miss Newfield. But then, perhaps this was God's way of protecting them both from broken hearts.

For surely, with Uncle Grenville ignoring him and Wellington coming to London any day, Edmond would soon be returning to a war he was no longer certain he believed in.

* * *

By Thursday Anna had suffered nearly all the fittings she could endure. Yet Lady Greystone seemed to have spared no expense to prepare her for tomorrow night's ball. Anna did not wish to seem ungrateful. But having lived in the country all her life, she had never thought much about fashion or even what made one gown fashionable and another an object of scorn. And now her employer planned a small soiree to introduce her to several friends. Perhaps this was a test to see whether she deserved to attend Lady Drayton's ball on Friday night. Throughout the week Lady Greystone had carefully observed her manners and corrected her more often than before. She also had instructed the butler to inform Anna if she made a mistake. Crawford's corrections were always gently spoken and much appreciated.

Wearing a new silk gown that was more silver than grey, Anna descended the stairs to the drawing room, where Crawford stood at the door.

"You are to go right in, miss." The elderly man gave her a slight bow. "No guests have arrived yet, but Lady Greystone and Major Grenville are there."

"I thank you, Crawford." Anna entered and quickly found the object of her interest.

As the major often had at the Lodge, he posted himself near the hearth, looking beyond handsome in his crimson jacket with its golden epaulets, his spotless white breeches and his shiny black boots. Tonight his dark brown hair framed his face in a Caesar curl, a new and charming look that added to his commanding appearance. Yet she longed to see him dressed in ordinary clothing, even a plain black suit, if that meant he could work at the occupation so dear to his heart. He caught her gaze and winked. Her heart jumped, then stilled. With him in the room, she would be able to calm her jangled nerves.

"Ah, there you are, Newfield." Lady Greystone seemed to use the form of address that suited the moment, so perhaps she was ill-humored this evening. "Come in, come in. Now, have you practiced your manners as I instructed you?"

Anna curtseyed. "Yes, madam. Crawford has been most kind to advise me."

"Very good." She paced back and forth over the Persian carpet, tapping her fan against her left hand and studying tables, chairs and other furnishings with a critical eye.

What further evidence did Anna require to comprehend that her employer was also nervous about the evening? How she wished to offer a word of comfort, but such offerings had never been appreciated.

"Mrs. Parton," Crawford announced.

The lady bustled across the room and embraced Lady Greystone. "Now, Frances, I forbid you to be nervous. Everyone will adore Miss Newfield." She scurried over to Anna and patted her cheek. "My, my, dear girl, you look lovely. This gown is divine, yet absolutely proper for half-mourning. Well chosen."

"I thank you, Mrs. Parton." Anna's heart warmed at the woman's kindness. Two people would be for her tonight.

"Lord and Lady Blakemore."

Lady Greystone's other close friend and her husband entered and greeted the viscountess and the major. Lady Greystone summoned Anna with a gentle wave and presented her to her guests. The countess gave her a peck on the cheek and praised her appearance.

"Indeed, what a pretty little creature you are." The earl, a short, rotund man with a rim of dull brown hair around his bald pate, nevertheless presented a dignified presence. "We shall suffer no shame in introducing you about town."

Anna curtseyed. "I thank you, sir."

"Lord Greystone and Mr. James Grenville."

Lady Greystone gasped and turned away from the newcomers. "What is *he* doing here?" Her words came out on a hiss.

From where she stood, only Anna could see Lady Greystone's anguished expression. So this was Uncle Grenville, come at last to see the major, and his presence deeply distressed the lady. Anna raised a quick prayer that her employer would not faint, as she seemed about to do.

Beyond her, Lord Greystone and his uncle greeted the others. Mr. Grenville was a fine-looking gentleman of medium height, yet bearing a strong resemblance to his three nephews. His full head of white hair was pulled back in a queue, a style most men eschewed these days. And he wore a blue jacket and tan breeches, contradicting her assumptions about the attire of a barrister. Best of all, he shared a hearty handshake with Major Grenville and clapped him on the shoulder as if he were an intimate friend. Anna's heart lifted at the sight. According to the major, they had met only a few times during what he called his "unfortunate Season." She had never pressed him to elaborate.

Lady Greystone now trembled and her eyes reddened, causing Anna no little alarm.

"Madam, please let me summon—"

"No." She barely whispered the word, then pulled in a deep breath as if to steady herself. "Give me your arm, Miss Newfield." She turned to face her guests, leaning upon Anna as if she were an ancient.

His blue eyes glinting in the candlelight, Mr. Grenville crossed the room and stopped before them. "Good evening, Frances." The warmth in his voice hinted at a sincere fondness for the lady. "You look as beautiful as ever." He bowed, took her free hand and kissed it, then did not release her.

"James." Her voice broke. "You look well."

He gazed at her for several moments, admiration shining from his eyes. Anna could hear Lady Greystone swallow hard. One would think these two were awkward young lovers who had yet to declare themselves. That thought shocked her.

"And this is your protégée?" His bow over Anna's hand was as elegant as the one he had offered Lady Greystone, but his gaze had turned paternal.

Anna curtseyed as best she could while still supporting the viscountess. "How do you do, sir?" Too late she realized her employer had not presented her to him. But Lady Greystone did not scold. Instead, she slowly regained her regal bearing.

"This is Miss Newfield, granddaughter of the late Sir Reginald Elgin." Her voice cracked again. She cleared her throat. "As to whether she will be my protégée, I will decide once I learn more about him."

"Ah. Then perhaps I can be of service." He reached into his coat and pulled out a letter sealed with a red wax wafer stamped with a *G*. He glanced at Lady Greystone before handing the missive to Anna. "Miss Newfield, as you read this, please remember that we cannot choose our relatives, only our friends."

Chapter Twenty-Eight

Her heart nearly bursting from her chest, Anna accepted the letter from Mr. Grenville. It fluttered in her hands and she realized she was trembling.

"Perhaps you should sit, Miss Newfield." The gentleman attempted to take her arm, but Lady Greystone blocked his hand and glared at him.

"Perhaps *I* should read this." She reached for the missive, although the address clearly stated *Miss Newfield*.

Mr. Grenville took her hand and gracefully spun her away as if they were dancing. "Frances, I should like for you to come and sit with me." He spoke as one talking to a child. "Miss Newfield is entitled to be the first one to read the news regarding her family."

To Anna's shock, Lady Greystone complied with his request, although she looked none too pleased.

Clustered in conversation near the marble hearth, everyone else seemed to be doing their best to ignore the scene that had just transpired. But the moment Mr. Grenville seated Lady Greystone on a chair in a corner, Major Grenville strode across the room.

"Are you going to read it?" His eyes sparked with interest, but he looked at her, not the paper.

Anna clutched it to her chest. "I would like to sit, please."

"Yes, of course." He escorted her to a settee, sat beside her and squeezed her free hand. "Have no fear, Miss New-field. We are all your friends, no matter what is written here."

As she snapped the seal and spread the paper across her lap, she longed to lean against his broad chest for comfort, but must settle for letting him read along with her. Taking a deep breath, she shook away her trepidation and held the page up so they both could see it.

Dear Miss Newfield:
May I congratulate you upon your imminent intro-duction into Society, a position to which you are most undeniably worthy? As you know, your mater-nal grandfather was Sir Reginald Elgin. I am most pleased to provide additional information that should settle all of your concerns about your pedigree. Sir Reginald was a baronet of some fortune who lived a quiet life in Cornwall and rarely came to London. Despite his lack of important connections, he secured the hand of Miss Hamilton, daughter of Lord Ham-ilton, a baron. Their only child was, of course, your mother. With that information in hand, we need go no further in regard to ensuring your place in Soci-ety, should you decide to accept Lady Greystone's offer to sponsor your introduction. No one of note will consider you anything less than worthy to mingle with the *ton*.

In addition, having been in London during your mother's sole Season, I am privy to some in-formation that may help you understand why you knew nothing of your connection to Sir Reginald and why your mother was not the beneficiary of his fortune. Lord Greystone has informed me that you know Miss Elgin married against her father's wishes and was subsequently disowned. What you may not know is that Miss Elgin was extraordinarily popular and received many proposals, more than one from distinguished peers. Sir Reginald, a man whom most people found utterly disagreeable, ordered her to accept an equally disagreeable and entirely scandalous earl. She refused. He threatened her, to no avail. A lady of virtue and faith, she would have her gentleman vicar and no one else, for she loved him as Juliet loved Romeo. We who were young in those days (and now are old) found her choice wildly romantic. Few of us had the courage to do the same.

I pray this information does not distress you. It is never a good thing when a family is riven by strife. But I felt you should know that your mother was a virtuous lady admired by all.

Yours, James Grenville, Esq.

"Does this settle your mind?" The major's rumbling voice beside her suggested he was experiencing emotion as deep as her own.

"Yes." Anna refolded the letter and let it lie upon her lap. "I understand now why *Mamá* and *Papá* taught Peter and me to follow God's leading, why *Papá* permitted Peter to become a soldier and never tried to find a husband for me. They trusted our decisions regarding such important matters."

"I am pleased your father did not find you a husband." His voice took on a hint of ardor and his eyes shone with— dare she think it?—admiration.

A pleasant shiver swept down her back. But how could

he be so bold when his mother sat across the room? "Lady Greystone wishes to read this." Anna started to rise, but he placed a hand upon her arm.

"We should not interrupt." He tilted his head toward Lady Greystone and Mr. Grenville.

Even in the dim candlelight, Anna could see the two in deep conversation. How curious that all this time the lady had not wanted to see her husband's brother, yet now she leaned close to him as one did when confiding in a dear friend.

"Well, Miss Newfield?" Lord Greystone wandered over, a beverage in his hand. "What news do you have for us?" His playful grin suggested he already knew the contents of the letter.

A good-natured spirit smote her, as well. "Why, nothing of import, my lord."

"Nothing of import?" He chuckled. "Only information that will change your life considerably." He glanced toward his mother and uncle, then gave the major a significant look. "No more need to hide your feelings, eh, Edmond?"

"Indeed not." The major set his large, warm hand over Anna's. "That is, if the lady agrees."

"If?" Lord Greystone's laughter filled the room. "Well, with that taken care of, I shall return to my guests." He sauntered away.

After a nervous glance over her shoulder, Anna tried to tug her hand free from Major Grenville's grasp, but he tightened his grip.

"No more need to hide our feelings, Miss Newfield." His intense gaze sent a thrill spiraling through her. "Unless you do not return the strong sentiments I have for you." He exhaled impatiently. "More directly, if you do not love me as I love you." Doubt darted across his brow, an anguished expression so charming that Anna longed to smooth it away. Yet she dared not.

"I do love you." As she spoke a weight seemed to float from her chest, a pressure she had not realized was there.

"Nonsense!" Lady Greystone approached the settee gripping her fan as if it were a weapon. "What do either of you know of love or duty or responsibility?" She scowled at the major. "Release her at once."

He gripped Anna's hand until she gently eased it away. His grimace twisted her heart.

"Really, Miss Newfield." Lady Greystone's angry expression turned conciliatory. "As my protégée, you can win a much bigger prize than a penniless third son. I will see you get a peer or nothing at all. That should compensate Society for your mother's grievous error."

"Frances!" Mr. Grenville grasped the lady's elbow and turned her to face him. "Have you lost all sense?"

Major Grenville stood and touched his uncle's shoulder. "Never mind, sir." He brushed a finger across Anna's cheek, then marched out of the room, not bothering to take his leave of the rest of the party.

"Now you have done it," Mr. Grenville murmured to Lady Greystone. "Will you never be satisfied until everyone is as disappointed with their lot in life as you are?" He walked the length of the long room, said his goodbyes to the others and left.

Lord Greystone bowed across the chamber toward his mother, then followed the other two men, leaving the three visitors to stare in bewilderment at the viscountess.

Longing to pursue the major, Anna took a step toward the door.

Lady Greystone gripped her arm and hissed, "You will not embarrass me in front of my guests." She straightened her posture and gave the others a tight smile. "Well, that was a prickly little scene, was it not?"

"Oh, Frances." Mrs. Parton bustled over to her. "What a shame this could not be worked out." She cast a kind glance toward Anna, then refocused on the viscountess. "We will make your excuses for you."

"Nonsense." Lady Greystone huffed out her favorite word. "Everything is fine."

As if to confirm it, Crawford stepped into the room and announced more guests.

For the next three hours Anna was forced to submit to inspection by a small segment of London's *haute ton,* some pleasant and others almost too haughty to bear. After the last guest finally left, Lady Greystone pronounced Anna a success.

"Tomorrow at Lady Drayton's ball, you will be all the rage." The viscountess looped her arm in Anna's as they ascended the staircase. "You must permit me to plan your dance card to your best advantage."

They reached the landing and Anna stepped away from her employer, now her unwanted benefactress. "But, madam, I do not know how to dance."

"All of this is my fault." Greystone stood in Edmond's bedchamber with Uncle Grenville at his side. "I should have gone to Uncle's office days ago instead of writing." He eyed the gentleman. "I thought perhaps your secretary neglected to give you my letters."

"No, no. He is quite dependable." Uncle's forehead furrowed. "I received all three letters and answered each time. If anyone is to blame, it is I. I should have grasped the tenor of your second and third missives and realized you had not received my replies. Still, you came today, and we addressed at least one of your concerns. Miss Newfield now knows who she is and can feel free to enjoy her debut." His arched eyebrows invited Edmond to respond.

"Indeed, if that is what pleases her." Edmond clenched his jaw, determined not to reveal what he suspected. He had not the slightest doubt but that Mother had intercepted the letters. If so, and if she'd had the audacity to read them, she no doubt knew his fondest aspirations contradicted her plans for him. Perhaps that explained her increasing rancor toward him these past days, her cruel remarks in front of Miss Newfield moments ago. Only God's hand upon him had kept him from replying in kind to his parent. And he could not dismiss the irony of Mother's twisted logic. Where only days ago Miss Newfield had not been good enough for him, now he was not good enough for her. So much for a man's permanent stratum on the Great Chain of Being.

"What I wrote was actually quite harmless to *your* cause, Edmond." Had Uncle read his mind? "I merely told Greystone I would visit at his convenience." He glanced across the room. "If only I had been aware of how bitter poor Frances has become over the years, I could have intervened long ago. But when your father died she insisted I must not attempt to see any of you." Regret shone in his eyes. "Because her father was still living and moved his residence to Greystone Lodge, I did not contest her guardianship of you boys. Now I deeply regret that."

"Ah, well." Greystone clapped him on the shoulder. "We have not turned out so badly, have we?"

"No. In fact—" Uncle shook his head. "Enough of that. Edmond, your brother has informed me of your interest in the law. Is this true?"

Edmond's pulse began to race. "Yes, sir. I studied law at Oxford in hopes of becoming a barrister. Had I not wasted that summer seven years ago, perhaps—" Even back then he had seen what a good man his uncle was, which had reinforced his desire to follow in the same occupation. Unfortunately, at the time, he had not been able to control his youthful impulses long enough to pursue any serious path.

"Stubble it, Edmond." Greystone nudged Edmond's shoulder with his fist. "You are forgiven. You have paid your debts. And now you can forget all of that and look to the future. Is that not so, Uncle?"

"Hear, hear." Uncle chuckled. "I would be proud to sponsor you at Lincoln's Inn. Have your man pack your things and come with me now."

Edmond eyed his brother, then his uncle, hardly believing what good fortune had landed in his lap. No, not fortune at all, but God's grace. Yet he felt one constraint upon his soul.

"If it will not inconvenience you, Uncle, I have a matter to tend to before I accept your kind offer."

"Of course. I understand. You must resign your commission."

"Yes, but something else—"

"Miss Newfield?" Greystone grinned broadly. "Ah, no man could ask for a fairer prize."

Edmond sent him a warning look. "She has already been spoken for, brother. But it does concern her." He gestured toward the chairs beside his hearth. "If you are not too busy to sit for a while, I will be happy to explain it all."

Chapter Twenty-Nine

"No, Miss Newfield, no." The dance master, a thin, pale man of some fifty years, pounded his staff on the ballroom floor. "It is skip, step, turn, step, then up on the balls of your feet." Mr. Turner sighed dramatically and turned to Lady Greystone, who sat in a wooden chair set against the wall. "Lady Greystone, one simply cannot teach a person to dance in one day, especially not someone lacking—" he looked at Anna up and down, stopping to stare at her slippers peeking out from beneath her gown "—natural grace."

Anna desperately wanted to laugh at his remark, but she was far too exhausted and did not wish to embarrass him. Earlier, when she had giggled over her numerous slips and stumbles, the poor man had winced and glanced at Lady Greystone in fear. But even though Anna had never cared to learn how to dance, she was trying very hard to do so. How did Lady Greystone expect her to have any strength left for this evening, much less to dance on these aching feet? And were all ballroom floors this slippery?

"Still at it, Mother?" Lord Greystone sauntered into the room, his eyes on Anna.

"Oh, Greystone." Lady Greystone echoed Mr. Turner's dramatic sigh. "I fear it is useless. The *gel* simply cannot do it." She took a turn staring at Anna up and down through her quizzing glass.

"Madam, may I sit?" Anna considered doing so even if the viscountess forbade her.

"By all means." Lady Greystone waved her hand in a dismissive gesture. "Give up before you have mastered the skill." She sniffed with indignation. "I had thought you were made of sterner stuff."

Too weary to be hurt by the remark—or was there a veiled compliment in the lady's words?—Anna brushed aside the curls that had loosened from her tightly bound hair and limped over to a chair beside her employer. As she sat, relief flowed up her legs and throughout her body.

"Mr. Turner, you may go."

Lady Greystone waved the dance master away as one would a fly. The man bowed and walked out, but not before casting another disparaging look at Anna's feet. She tucked them beneath her gown, still trying not to laugh. Everyone took this dancing business far too seriously.

Did every town house in London have a ballroom like Greystone Hall? This spacious room took up a third of the second floor and in the daytime was well-lit by tall windows on the south side. On the other three walls, elegant giltwood girandoles with their framed mirrors promised to magnify the light of the candles posted in the ram's head candleholders during nighttime balls. The floor was polished to a flawless, slippery sheen, while equally polished wooden chairs lined the walls. A dais for the musicians sat at the east end. An exquisite room, to be sure, but one that stood empty for all but a few days each year.

"Greystone," Lady Greystone said. "Do tell me your brother has gotten over his petulance and plans to attend the ball with me. Lady Drayton has promised to seek an advancement for him. I forbid him to miss this opportunity."

She stood, which of course meant Anna was required to stand as well. Pain shot up her legs and back which, oddly, made her wish to laugh all the more. Or perhaps cry. *Lord, please help me endure this nonsense.*

"Actually, Mother, Edmond has left." Lord Greystone stared at Anna even as her heart plummeted, all good humor gone. Further, she could not discern any meaning in the viscount's intense gaze.

"Left?" Lady Greystone's posture stiffened. "What do you mean, *left?*"

The viscount effected a casual pose, leaning against the wall and studying his fingernails. "Last night during your little soiree, he packed his belongings and moved out."

Anna dropped back into the chair, her head spinning. If Major Grenville had abandoned her at last, she could not blame him. How could anyone endure a mother like Lady Greystone? Guilt smote her conscience over such an uncharitable thought. The viscountess had taken her in despite her unusual arrival, and far more often than not, no bite ever followed her bark, at least where Anna was concerned. But the woman's cruelty to her own son could not be explained away.

"The very idea!" Lady Greystone paced across the ballroom floor and back again. "Do you know where he went? Is he planning to return to America?" She tapped her fan against her opposite hand. "We may yet turn this to our advantage." Her eyes fell on Anna. "You may go, Miss Newfield. This evening I shall make your excuses to the marchioness."

"But, Mother—" Lord Greystone brushed invisible lint from his sleeve "—I was so looking forward to escorting both of you ladies to the ball."

He managed a wink at Anna without Lady Greystone detecting it. That simple signal gave her a wisp of hope but was not sufficient to fully restore her optimism in regard to Major Grenville. If he was well and truly gone, she would have difficulty remaining in this house with the woman who had driven him away. Yet she had no other place to go.

"But she cannot dance." Lady Greystone's complaint was nonetheless spoken in the deferential tone she always used with her eldest son.

"Of course not." Lord Greystone shrugged. "She is in half-mourning. How would it look to present her to Society wearing grey and black and have her cavorting about the marquess's ballroom with every dandy who fancies her?"

"Ah!" Lady Greystone actually smiled. "You are truly brilliant."

She snapped her eyes to Anna, who waited for the next blow with more curiosity than dread. What more could she do after driving away the gentleman Anna loved?

"Not every young lady requires a formal debut," Lady Greystone said. "You will simply appear at my side this Season. If any gentlemen request an introduction, I shall choose carefully whom you may be presented to." She gave Anna the same careless wave she had used to dismiss the dance master. "You must go have a lie-down. I shall summon you when it is time to dress for the ball."

"Yes, madam." Anna rose and slipped out, well aware of Lord Greystone's sympathetic gaze. As much as she was grateful for his kindness, she longed to know where Major Grenville was and whether or not he would ever return.

"Oh, miss, you are lovely, truly lovely." Esther stood behind Anna, who was seated at her vanity table, and continued to adjust her elaborate curls, securing each with an ebony pin. "Every eye will be on you."

"Do not forget my mourning lace." Anna reached for the black scarf lying on the vanity, but Esther seized it first.

"Must you wear it tonight?" In the mirror Anna could see the disappointment on the lady's maid's face as she pinned the headpiece over her well-wrought handiwork.

"Yes, Lady Greystone will want me to." Anna took a strange sort of comfort in wearing her grey silk gown. Although she doubted any gentleman would request an introduction, the color alone was bland enough to discourage their interest. But then, what did she know or care of Society and its preferences? She could see in the mirror that her face reflected her mood, but it made no difference. Without Major Grenville at her side, this evening would be boring beyond words. How she longed for the days when she was simply Lady Greystone's companion.

"Where is she?" The viscountess's lilting voice rang outside of Anna's door. She sailed into the bedchamber waving a lavender handkerchief that matched her elegant gown. Her hair was topped with a darker purple turban adorned with an albino peacock plume. To complement the ensemble, the scent of lavender wafted about her. "Oh, no, no, no." She snatched the black lace from Anna's hair, pulling several curls loose. Esther rushed to repair the damage. "We do not wish to proclaim you a spinster not seeking a husband, but a debutante…of sorts." She placed one finger under Anna's chin and narrowed her eyes as if studying a scientific specimen. "Although of course you are well past the proper age for a debut and have not been presented at court." A dramatic sigh. "If only I'd had you in hand years ago." A dismissive huff. "No matter. I shall launch you as if you were the daughter I never had." Only the tiniest hint of sorrow shaded her words, but the tone revealed much.

At last Anna comprehended the lady's eagerness for this evening, her eagerness to sponsor Anna's debut at all. Last night James Grenville spoke of her disappointments. Perhaps she had just revealed one of them. The viscountess often boasted about giving her husband three sons to ensure his title's continuation. She once said that a daughter was an expensive luxury. Yet this pretty suite bespoke a longing for a daughter to nurture. Now Anna understood. God had sent her to minister to this unhappy woman, and she prayed she would discharge her duty well. She turned to Lady Greystone with a warm smile.

"Madam, I am honored beyond words by your kindness." She could not check the emotional pitch of her voice or her sudden tears.

Lady Greystone blinked and tilted her head in confusion. "Yes. Well." She swallowed hard. "Let us be off." She spun away, summoning Anna with a brisk wave over her shoulder.

The Marquess of Drayton's house stood apart from other St. James Square residences on a broad plot of land only a half mile from Greystone Hall. As the carriage rolled up the drive, Anna peered through the conveyance's window at the estate's impressive grounds. Immaculately kept emerald-green lawns with exquisite flower gardens stretched beyond the half circle drive leading to the mansion's front portico. Lord Greystone's landau, drawn by four matching black horses, provided comfortable seating for four people, but only three alighted from the elegant carriage.

Stepping from the conveyance, Anna counseled herself that Major Grenville may have confessed his love for her, but he had made no promises. After living with this family for almost seven months, she understood his need to support himself, so of course he was in no position to take a wife. Having resigned herself to spinsterhood long ago, she would suffer no loss by waiting for him other than loneliness for his company. In the interim before he returned—for she knew he would—two things lifted her spirits when they began to flag. Lord Greystone showed her unfailing, brotherly kindness. More important, the Lord reminded her of the one sure truth in her life: she was a servant of God sent to minister to Lady Greystone. She would do everything possible to discharge that duty well.

Green-liveried footmen and black-uniformed maids buzzed about the portico and massive entrance to the house, making certain every guest received proper attention. Inside, wraps and cloaks were surrendered, slippers brushed, coiffures straightened, so each visitor could make an entrance befitting his or her station in life. Lord Greystone offered his arm to his mother and they ascended the wide front staircase, with Anna following close behind. She had never seen such a crush of people and did not wish to get lost.

At the door of the ballroom the butler bowed to them, took the viscount's calling card and announced in clarion tones, "Lord Greystone. Lady Greystone. Miss Newfield."

Anna stopped the laugh trying to escape her. This was just a fancy party, and yet everyone made it into such a drama.

The fragrances of countless perfumes mingled in the air, nearly choking Anna. She also detected the aromas of roast beef and other culinary delights being prepared for the midnight supper. The spring daylight had faded into a red-and-purple sunset which appeared like a watercolor painting through the massive west windows. Hundreds of candles blazed in crystal chandeliers, with several servants carefully attending to the dripping wax lest it fall upon the guests.

As she followed her benefactors a merry tune met her ears, and she located the source, musicians on a dais in the far corner. In the center of the room, which was a much larger ballroom than Lord Greystone's, couples had lined up for the first dance. While she had no hope, or desire, to improve her dancing skills, she would watch them and try to discover how to do it.

"I will leave you ladies here in good company." Lord Greystone gestured toward a pleasant corner set off by a row of large potted plants and furnished with uphol-stered chairs, wherein sat several older ladies. The viscount bowed and turned to leave.

"Greystone." Lady Greystone set a hand on his arm.

"Yes, madam?" His patient responses to his mother never ceased to amaze Anna.

"Do be careful whom you speak or dance with, espe-cially—"

His deep chuckle sounded much like Major Grenville's. "Of course, Mother." He brushed a kiss across her pow-dered cheek, then sauntered away, clearly in no hurry to speak or dance with anyone.

"Do sit down, Frances," Mrs. Parton called merrily from her chair. "You are blocking my view."

"And good evening to you, too, Julia." Lady Greystone found a chair and motioned Anna to one beside it, form-ing a half circle with Mrs. Parton. "Is anyone interesting here tonight?"

"Why, yes. And she is seated right next to you." Mrs. Parton gave Anna a warm smile. "Good evening, Miss Newfield."

"Good evening—"

"Oh, come, now, Julia." Lady Greystone sniffed. "Some-one of rank, of influence. Beyond Lord and Lady Drayton, of course."

Anna wanted to laugh. Oh, how she wanted to laugh. One moment she was about to make her debut. The next she had no significance at all. Goodness, how this lady did shift her opinions to suit the moment.

Mrs. Parton leaned toward Lady Greystone. "I have heard that Prinny may put in an appearance and may even bring the French king. They are said to be eager to begin celebrating Louis's upcoming coronation."

"Ah." Lady Greystone's eyes narrowed. "If that should happen, perhaps we can arrange an introduction for Miss Newfield. Prinny's notice would grant her great significance."

The idea gave Anna no pleasure. Even in her little village of Blandon, the Prince Regent's reputation for profligate living had become a cautionary tale for children. She would just as soon not receive his notice.

The two ladies put their heads together and gossiped about this and that. Anna ceased listening, concentrating instead on the movements of the dancers. The musicians played with great skill, and their merry tunes set her feet to tapping. How easy her lesson would have been with music. She would keep that in mind in case Lady Greystone arranged another session with poor Mr. Turner.

For the next hour or more Anna continued to survey the scene. Never before had she been given the opportunity to watch other people at play in such a grand way. Other matrons gathered in the chairs around her, clucking like hens. Young ladies in gowns of white or light colors were invited to dance by men both old and young. Some matrons in darker colors took to the floor with great energy. All appeared to be having a grand time. Lady Drayton brought her husband, the marquess, for an introduction and granted Anna a reprieve not to participate in the gaiety until her mourning was over.

Just as Anna began to weary of the scene, she spied a flash of crimson near the ballroom door. Her heart leapt into her throat, but only briefly. Instead of a fine head of dark brown hair, the young officer sported curly golden locks. Try though she might, she could not dispel a gathering gloom. What if Major Grenville did not return? How could she bear it if he was gone from her life forever?

Chapter Thirty

Edmond paced the small, unpretentious parlor in Squire Beamish's residence, trying to maintain a calm exterior even as his temper rose. No doubt the man had kept him waiting so he could gain the upper hand. But Edmond would have none of it. He would discover what had happened to Miss Newfield's inheritance, whatever it took. Both Greystone and Uncle Grenville assured him of their support. Edmond carried the inventory list from the vicarage, and Greystone had even penned a threatening letter, should the man refuse to cooperate.

The walls sported dark paneling, contributing to Edmond's mood. The furniture likewise was all browns and greys. A collection of some fairly valuable whatnots decorated the room: figurines of horses, a bust of Julius Caesar and shields bearing unremarkable crests. While every object appeared to have been dusted recently, the chamber had an atmosphere of disuse. In all his imaginings about the squire, he never considered that the man might live this modestly. But that did not give him an excuse for stealing a young lady's meager funds.

Just as he was about to march from the room and search for the squire, the door opened and a short, thin man of perhaps sixty years scurried in. His long, pointed nose gave him the appearance of a mouse. Perched upon that nose were thick-lensed spectacles, which magnified his round black eyes and completed the picture of a rodent. His dull brown suit, made of cheap wool, was frayed at the collar and cuffs. A thin line of dust extended down the length of one sleeve. A cobweb clung to the side of his dark grey hair.

"Major Grenville, sir." He held out his hand. "Forgive me. My manservant said you have been waiting for over an hour while he searched for me." He laughed, a squeaking sound much like the animal he resembled. "I was busy in my workroom, you see, and I think he failed to see me because of some boxes in the way. Ah, the perils of being a small man."

Edmond shook his hand, even as his conscience smote him for his uncharitable thoughts about the man's appearance. "Squire Beamish."

"Well, my goodness, do sit down, sir, and tell me what brings a cavalry officer to my humble abode." He gestured toward a chair and took the one across from it.

Once seated, Edmond felt his anger slip away. No doubt this gentleman's size often put him at a disadvantage. But a vision of another small man came to mind, one who had rocked all of Europe on its heels and had been defeated only last week. While Beamish might be just a country squire, he still had a small kingdom to rule, and Edmond had the duty to make certain he had not oppressed his subjects.

"My occupation and uniform have little to do with this visit." Except to intimidate, if necessary. "Although, when I returned to England from America October last, I visited Blandon to report the news of Lieutenant Peter Newfield's death to his family."

"Ah, yes. Poor Peter. What a fine lad and a sad loss." The squire's forehead furrowed. "And of course Mr. Newfield died as well. My, my, what a loss to everyone." He squinted at Edmond. "And worst of all, for Miss Newfield to go off as she did with some passing soldier. Why, we always thought she was such a fine Christian miss—"

"What?" Edmond leaned forward, almost rising to his feet until he thought better of it. He did not wish to frighten the squire. "What are you saying? Where did you hear such a thing?" So his instincts about Danders had been correct from the beginning. He had tried to tarnish Anna's reputation out of sheer maliciousness.

"W-why—" The man pressed back into his chair. "My solicitor, Mr. Danders, told me all about it, his charming wife confirming it. The very day the vicar was laid in the ground, the girl stole some valuables from the church and ran off with a—" His pale face turned whiter. "Sir, are you that soldier?"

"I am."

"And there is more to the matter?"

"There is. Miss Newfield's disappearing inheritance."

"Oh, my." The squire's mouth gaped, and his eyes darted here and there as if he was at last comprehending some great matter. Finally he slumped further down in the chair and repeated "Oh, my" on a whisper.

Edmond did not have the heart to berate the man, even though he had failed to ensure that his minion had properly performed his duty. But Edmond still had to complete his investigation. "On the day Mr. Newfield was buried, I had the misfortune of meeting your solicitor and his *charming* wife. When they were determined to toss Miss Newfield out to the wolves, I accompanied her—with the seamstress Mrs. Brown as our chaperone—to my mother's house, where she has found a satisfactory position as Lady

Greystone's companion." *Until I can marry her.* "Did you never speak to Mrs. Brown about this matter?"

"Oh, no, no. With all of my experiments, I never manage to get to the village." He coughed out a strange little laugh. "Always mean to, you understand. But Mr. Danders takes care of everything for me and tells me not to trouble myself." He grimaced. "I pray it is not too late to make amends." Then he stood and straightened his shoulders like a good soldier. "Major, will you kindly come to my office where we will sort out the details?"

"Truly, madam, I do not need another bonnet." Anna resisted the urge to squirm under the scrutiny of Lady Greystone, Mrs. Parton and the modiste. Seated in front of a vanity mirror in the Bond Street millinery shop, Anna had endured trying on at least a dozen lovely creations this morning, but not one pleased her benefactress.

"Nonsense." Lady Greystone walked from one side of Anna to the other, studying the grey satin bonnet through narrowed eyes. "Look at me." She guided Anna's chin in the right direction. "Hmm. No, not this one."

"I see what you mean." Mrs. Parton moved to the other side and directed Anna's chin toward herself. "One cannot deny that these lighter greys reflect an appealing silver in her eyes, but they seem to dull her brown hair."

"Indeed," Lady Greystone said. "Now if her hair were black, the contrast would—"

"Madam." The modiste purred in a rich French accent as she draped a length of delicate brocade across Anna's shoulder. "If you would consider a tint to ze lady's half-mourning, thees light green will complement both ze eyes and ze hair."

"Oh, how divine." Mrs. Parton clapped her hands.

"Yes, yes, a divine color." Lady Greystone continued to

study Anna as if she were an inanimate object. "Giselle, instead of a bonnet, you must use this fabric to make her a ball gown, and we must have it tomorrow."

Anna released a quiet sigh. Once again they were discussing her as if she were not present or, at the least, had no opinion worth regarding. For the entire week since the marchioness's ball, the two older women had dragged Anna about London, visiting some of the finest homes and introducing her to wealthy, aristocratic friends. Of course, everyone else was doing the same thing with their unmarried charges. Thus, after some deliberation, Lady Greystone, Mrs. Parton and Lady Blakemore decided Anna *could* be considered marriageable, as a parent's death generally demanded only six months' mourning, not a full year.

On Wednesday, the day after Parliament opened, Lady Greystone had been "at home" to receive visitors. Some ladies of the older generation, remembering Anna's mother, had come to meet her out of curiosity. Others, those with marriageable sons, had come to find out if she was a worthy bride. While some had shown interest, none had made an offer, which relieved her more than words could express. Should Lady Greystone settle upon a match for her, Anna would be forced to refuse. Only one gentleman would suit her. If she could not have him, she would remain a spinster.

In addition to making plans for Anna, Lady Greystone also searched for a match for her eldest son. Thus far not one young lady had sparked her interest. Too young, too silly, no sense of style, insufficient influence or dowry and, most important, the father lacking a title. All reasons not to give notice to the bevy of aristocratic debutantes who had flocked to London for the marriage competition. When Lady Greystone focused her attention on her son's prospects, Anna felt a profound sense of reprieve.

During this time, with her daily dance lessons and shopping trips, she had no chance to speak privately with Lord Greystone to ask after Major Grenville, and he seemed disinclined to offer her any information. Instead, from time to time he merely gave her that mysterious smile, which had ceased to comfort her days ago. Once Parliament opened he was rarely at home. When he was, Lady Greystone commanded his attention.

No one mentioned the major, so Anna could only wonder whether he had abandoned his dreams of becoming a barrister and returned to his regiment in America. Was he even now on a ship in the middle of the Atlantic Ocean? Anna prayed many times each day for his safety and, if the Lord willed it, that he would return home unharmed and enter the career to which he aspired. With each prayer, Anna added a post script: *Lord, if it is Your will, please grant that Major Grenville and I may marry one day.*

Chapter Thirty-One

"Now, Greystone." Lady Greystone set a hand on her eldest son's arm to delay his departure from the chaperones' corner of the ballroom. "You must ask Miss Newfield to dance, but only once. And you must choose an early dance so the other gentlemen may see she is, for lack of a better word, *out*."

"Yes, of course, Mother." Merriment lit the viscount's handsome face. "Miss Newfield, do you have a preference? Shall it be the minuet or the Sir Roger de Coverley?"

"Oh, no, my dear," Lady Greystone said. "Lady Blakemore's balls always open with a minuet and close with the Sir Roger de Coverley." She tapped her chin thoughtfully with her fan. "If you begin your evening with her, everyone of note will think you favor her. And the last dance will provide no opportunity for her to receive other offers. It should be—"

"Any country dance, my lord. I thank you." Anna's nerves fluttered like a covey of trapped birds. Although Lord Greystone had shown her nothing but kindness, she could not help but long for his youngest brother to be her partner for her first public dance.

With a bow the viscount took his leave. Anna joined

Lady Greystone in the corner where older ladies sat to oversee the festivities and younger ladies found refuge when they had no partners. Anna had long ago decided she would much prefer to sit here than to put herself on display on the dance floor.

Couples lined up for the first set, with Lady Blakemore's married daughter and a marquess leading the minuet. Anna noticed several crimson uniforms sprinkled among the brightly colored finery of the guests, but after a fortnight she had ceased looking for the only soldier who held her interest. For the most part, her eyes were fastened on the footwork of the dancers and her mind desperately reviewed Mr. Turner's many instructions. This floor had been dusted with chalk to keep the revelers from slipping on the polished surface, and so Anna could dismiss one fear. She still must remember the steps.

Her day of reckoning had come. There was no escape. Unlike her training for the canceled foxhunt, her dance lessons would be put to use at any moment. Her one consolation was this lovely gown, her favorite of Giselle's creations. More light green than grey, the brocade was comfortable for dancing, with its high waist not too confining over her stays and its underskirt sure to protect it from the chalk. Anna held no scruples in regard to the color. *Papá* had never made much of clothing particulars and would never scold the poor people of Blandon over a failure to wear mourning apparel. Still, Anna wondered what he and *Mamá* would think to see her so gaily clothed *and* at a ball.

After the guests had enjoyed several dances, but still too soon for Anna, Lord Greystone approached, his blue eyes twinkling. "You cannot escape your sentence, Miss Newfield." He held out his hand. "Time to perform." The brotherly tone in his challenge reminded her of Peter urging her to join him in some bit of harmless mischief.

"Oh, well." She placed her hand in his and stood. "What's the worst that can happen?" She had not played that game with herself in months. Even now it held little appeal. With no one to laugh with over life's absurdities, she found it more and more difficult to laugh at all.

"*Miss* Newfield," Lady Greystone almost growled. "You will not embarrass my son."

"Yes, madam." Anna released a helpless sigh.

The viscount's warm chuckle and supporting hand provided some reassurance as they journeyed to their places, hers near the bottom of the ladies' line and his across from her. The music began and the top couple danced their way through a series of figures. Anna watched closely, dreading the moment when she would do the same with the viscount. Yet as each couple executed their turns and they moved up the line, her own confidence grew. When Mr. Turner had brought a young man to play the piano for her lessons, the Mozart tune now playing had been her favorite. Her feet began to feel lighter, as if they were ready to take flight.

Her turn came. She turned to face her partner…and her knees threatened to buckle. "Major Grenville!"

The object of Anna's love stood opposite of her, a broad smile lighting his dear face and a spark lighting his dark eyes. "Miss Newfield." He gave her an elegant bow, but she dared not curtsey or she would surely fall over. The room and everyone in it seemed to disappear and she could see only the man of her heart.

"Move on, young lady." The older woman next in line nudged her. "'Tis your turn."

The major gripped her hand and spun her into the first figure. As Anna's awareness returned, her feet remembered their patterns while her heart did a dance of its own.

Their movements made it impossible to talk, but Anna felt no need to do so. His eyes communicated all she had hoped for.

At the end of the set, he offered his arm and they strolled out of the ballroom down a long hallway toward the refreshment room. He gazed down at her with tenderness. She smiled up at him, hoping he would see in her expression all that she felt for him. Conversation buzzed around them, but she heard only him, saw only him. He had not left her. And somehow she felt certain, this time, he never would.

After dreaming of her lovely face and sweet presence for nearly a fortnight, Edmond ached to take Miss Newfield into his arms and kiss her right here in front of everyone. How beautiful she looked in her pale green. How he wished to shout to all who would hear that he was madly in love with the most beautiful young lady in the world. Yet too many things must happen before he was free to give in to his yearning. He could, however, reassure her about one important matter.

He directed her toward the beverage table. "Will you have some lemonade?"

"Yes." She clutched his arm as if it were a lifeline as they walked.

Then, with glasses in hand, they found two chairs by the wall.

"Where have you been?" Biting her lip, she stared down at the floor. "Forgive me. I should not have asked."

Edmond's heart twisted. Just as he feared, she had worried he would not return. "Of course you should ask. You may ask me anything." He tried to use a light tone to encourage her. Her sudden, trusting smile revealed he had succeeded. "I had several business matters to take care of.

I believe everything is now settled. But before I make any final decision, I must repeat my question of several weeks ago. If I should change my occupation, will you miss this, ahem, *dashing* uniform?" He injected a modicum of playfulness into his tone.

"Not for a moment." Her instant response encouraged him.

"Well." Just for emphasis, he exhaled an exaggerated sigh. "That makes it much easier to report to you that Uncle Grenville has agreed to sponsor me at the Inns of Courts. I shall be under his tutelage until I have, as they say, *eaten my dinners* in the presence of the barristers there. And before you ask, that simply means I have spent enough time in suppertime fellowship with the gentlemen to prove my knowledge and ability."

"Oh, Major—" She blinked and her lips quirked prettily to one side. "Why, however shall I address you now? I will now count three Messrs. Grenville on my growing list of acquaintances. Why, la, how shall I distinguish amongst you?" Her lilting voice echoed the silliest young misses in the *ton*.

He shook his head sadly. "Ah, poor little thing, with so much on her little mind. Perhaps you will find it easier to distinguish me from my uncle and brother Richard if you call me by my Christian name."

"Hmm." Her smooth forehead wrinkled as if she were pondering the issue. Then she pinched her lips together as if trying not to laugh. "Was that Edward? Elton? Elbert?"

He bent down and whispered in her ear. "Edmond."

"Oh," she said breathlessly. "Yes, of course."

He really should not tease her this way, but could not resist. Again, he bent close to her ear. "May I call you Anna?"

She glanced down the hallway toward the ballroom,

then stood like an army private when an officer came into view. "Only when Lady Greystone is not present."

"What—?" He turned just in time to see his parent striding toward them. As he rose to greet her, his stomach clenched.

"There you are, Miss Newfield." Mother glared at him up and down. "And you, Edmond, not on your way to America, after all." The disappointment in her voice was clear.

Yes, here he was. And he had wasted precious moments with his beloved without telling her his most important news.

"Lord Winston has requested an introduction." Lady Greystone's displeasure was written across her face and resounded in her words.

Anna cringed inwardly but maintained her posture. "Lord Winston?" The young man, whom Mrs. Parton had pointed out earlier, was passably handsome but seemed quite arrogant toward his several dance partners. Hardly someone Anna wished to meet.

"You cannot know what this means, Miss Newfield. To receive the notice of a baron whose title bears an ancient patent is a great honor. You must not miss this opportunity. I have invested entirely too much in—"

"Madam, please." Major Grenville…*Edmond* reached out toward his mother, but she stepped away. With a heavy sigh, he turned to Anna, all good humor gone. "Do you wish to meet Lord Winston?"

She tried to smile at him, but it felt more like a grimace. "No, I do not." Her benefactress gasped, so Anna hurried to add, "However, Lady Greystone has been generous to a fault in preparing me for Society. I am pleased to…please her." She prayed he would understand. "Will you excuse me?"

Edmond grasped her hand. "Only if I may claim another dance this evening."

"Of course."

"No." Lady Greystone took Anna's other hand.

Anna stiffened. Then she laughed. "Do you both realize how foolish you look, as if you were playing tug-of-war and I am the rope?"

Lady Greystone gasped—*again*. But Edmond snorted out a laugh, then released her and brushed a kiss across her cheek.

"Go. Enjoy your dance with the baron. I shall be waiting when you finish." He stared at his mother. "Or, circumstances preventing that, I shall visit you tomorrow at my brother's home."

Anna sensed what he was saying. Lady Greystone often spoke of *her* home, but in truth, the town house belonged to her eldest son. And Lord Greystone had made it clear that Edmond would always be welcomed there.

Lady Greystone's eyes narrowed, but before she could speak, Edmond strode away. Anna's heart went with him.

Chapter Thirty-Two

"Without qualification," said Mrs. Parton, "I proclaim Miss Newfield's introduction into Society a success." She popped a bite of currant tart into her mouth and chased it with a sip of tea.

"Indeed." Lady Greystone wore a smug smile. "I look forward to Lord Winston's visit this afternoon. The *gel* has lived up to the better part of her breeding."

"I cannot think why the baron favored me." Anna had tired of the way they talked about her as if she were not present. After speaking with Edmond last night, she had made up her mind to be more forthright, especially in regard to her own future. While she could not keep the pompous peer from visiting, she could try to defuse his interest. "I found him rather boring."

"Why, my dear." Mrs. Parton's merry laughter filled the room. "That very disinterest attracted his attention, a decidedly clever ploy."

"Why, I hardly—"

"Indeed." Lady Greystone poured herself another cup of tea. "Disinterest will always set a young lady apart from the coy, simpering debutantes."

Hiding a sigh, Anna gazed toward the drawing room

window and thought about her favorite dance partner. Edmond had left shortly after his mother's crushing censure, but Anna looked forward to his promised visit today. She prayed he would arrive before the baron.

As if summoned by her thoughts, Edmond strolled into the drawing room wearing a stylish black suit with a spotless white shirt. How well they complemented his dark hair and eyes. How important the message they conveyed. "Good afternoon, ladies." He bowed to each. "This is a beautiful day, is it not? Everyone should be out for a carriage ride."

Anna's heart leapt. He did not need a uniform to present the most distinguished appearance of any gentleman she had ever seen. "What a wonderful idea." She gave Lady Greystone a hopeful look.

"Certainly not." The viscountess harrumphed rather forcefully. "The baron will be here at any time. I will not have him disappointed."

"Oh, but, Frances—" Mrs. Parton stopped nibbling her tart. "Parliament will not adjourn until late this afternoon, what with having to deal with the American war. Winston will be in the thick of that, you can be sure. Do let us go for a ride and see who is in Hyde Park. If we wait until Sunday we will have to mingle with every London tradesman taking his day off." She leaned toward the viscountess and lifted one eyebrow. "You never can say who will be there today. Lady Everton has a grandson—"

"Edmond!" Lady Greystone's jaw dropped as she stared at him. "*What* are you wearing?"

He glanced at Anna and smirked. "Why, madam, just some old rag my valet pulled from the wardrobe to replace my uniform." His voice held a note of triumph, and his use of "valet" instead of "batman" bespoke a significant change for both Matthews *and* his employer.

Anna also noticed Lady Greystone's wince.

* * *

The hurt on Mother's face cut into Edmond. In the instant before her eyes narrowed into their usual glare, he realized for the first time in his life that he could cause her real pain, not merely displeasure. Mother had always been angry, and her anger often focused on him. But that did not give him license to be less than a gentleman. Regret flooded into him, doubled by what he had learned from Uncle Grenville last night. Tripled by the fact that Anna had witnessed his failure to honor his mother by using such an impudent tone.

"Forgive me, madam." He prayed Mother could hear the honest contrition in his voice. "I know you will be disappointed, but I know of no way to soften the blow. Uncle Grenville has agreed to sponsor my residence at Lincoln's Inn. This morning I resigned my army commission."

Her eyes flared and she stared away from him, her elbow propped on the chair arm, her chin resting on her fist, her jaw clenched. Uncle had helped Edmond understand so much, yet in their first meeting after his resignation he failed to take it all into account. He had hurt her again.

"You have chosen poorly, Edmond." Mother looked at him, but her expression now held indifference. "If you had followed my advice and permitted my friends to open doors for you, you might have been made a duke, like Wellington. You do know the Prince Regent has granted him a dukedom?"

"Yes, madam, I heard the news." What she failed to consider, or perhaps even admit, was how many years it had taken the man to reach that position, how many years he had been forced to wait to marry the lady he loved. While Edmond knew his own lady's faith would undergird her constancy, he had no wish or patience to face the future without her. "But history does not favor many men that way."

"Humph." She offered him a dismissive wave of her hand. "Well then, go enjoy your day."

Anna's hopeful smile emboldened him. "Miss Newfield, would you honor me by accompanying me?"

"Yes—"

"Indeed *not*." Mother moved to the edge of her chair. "I forbid it."

Edmond could see the battle in Anna's face, but he had no idea what to pray for. As much as he longed for her company, he longed for her to follow God's will even more. After last night, one thing was certain: they had a future together. But would it begin today, or be delayed?

"Madam." Anna stood, causing Edmond's hopes to soar. "I should like to go with Major...Mr. Grenville."

"There. You see?" Mother sneered at Edmond. "How much more impressive it sounds to be addressed as 'Major.'" She turned her quizzing glass on Anna. "If you go with him, you will no longer be in my employ."

Anna's sweet face crumpled. "I should be very sad for that to happen, madam, but I must follow my heart."

"So this is your true character revealed at last. Just like your rebellious mother." Mother dismissed her with a wave like the one she had given Edmond. "Go on, then. Follow your heart." Her tone was laced with sarcasm. "But if you do, you may not return to this house."

Doubt filling her, Anna looked at Edmond. "I—I have no other place to go."

"Nonsense." This time Mrs. Parton used Lady Greystone's favorite word. "I shall give you a place of refuge until... hmm, what shall it be, Major, eh, Mr. Grenville. Goodness, it will be difficult to remember that change." She shook her head, causing the purple plume on her orange turban to flutter. "Will you marry the girl?"

"Julia!" Lady Greystone dug her fingernails into the arms of her blue brocade chair. "Will you betray me this way?"

"My dear Frances, if you are so foolish as to not recognize or appreciate true love when you see it, I hold no hope for your happiness."

"True love? Happiness? What nonsense! Why—"

"Oh, hush." Mrs. Parton stood, bustled over to Anna and took her hand. "Now, Miss Newfield, should you decide to marry this charming young soon-to-be barrister, you may live with me for the three weeks while the banns are cried. Should you decide not to marry him, you may have a position teaching my little charges at St. Ann's Orphanage, where I am a patroness."

Anna stared at the dear woman, unable to speak. She owed so much to Lady Greystone and despaired of coming between these two close friends.

"Close your mouth, dear." Mrs. Parton giggled. "And send that footman over there to tell your lady's maid to bring your bonnet and spencer. There may be a breeze in the park."

Anna looked at Edmond, then at Lady Greystone. The viscountess's glower was nothing less than a warning, and yet Anna knew what she must do.

"Edmond, if you will give me a moment, I will be delighted to accompany you."

"Uncle Grenville loaned me his phaeton." Edmond made a quick study of the black carriage, lest it had picked up too much dust on the trip from Uncle's house. To his relief, the conveyance passed inspection. "Shall we ride, or walk?"

Anna's trusting smile, which had given him such courage the night before, warmed his heart once again. "Whichever you prefer."

"As the distance is over a mile, I believe we should ride."

He handed her into the phaeton and climbed in beside her. At his direction, the mare set off on a moderate walk toward Piccadilly Street, with Edmond answering Anna's questions about the scenery. They passed Burlington House in all its Palladian beauty, then moved toward the shopping district. Usually Edmond noticed only the stray dogs, pickpockets and evidence of horses. Today his attention was drawn more to the pristine buildings and attractive shops. Among the crowds were elegant ladies accompanied by maids and bewigged footmen carrying wrapped purchases. Well-dressed gentlemen rode sleek steeds. And, as always, costermongers haggled loudly with customers over prices.

Observing the clashes, Anna frowned. "I am dismayed to think Mrs. Parton has destroyed her friendship with your mother on my account." She clasped her hands together in her lap.

"Have no fear, my darling." Speaking the endearment for the first time gave him more joy than he ever imagined. Yet he had a few things to tell her before they discussed their love. "My mother owes her life to Mrs. Parton."

"What?" Her horror-stricken expression gave him pause. Just how much should he tell her?

"Uncle Grenville did me the courtesy of explaining some of Mother's...oddities." He cringed inwardly, thinking of all she had endured, but Anna need not know the whole of it. "My father, who died when I was so small I do not remember him, was less than kind to her."

"I gathered that from conversations among the three ladies."

"But when his *unkindness* became so severe her life was threatened, Mrs. Parton and her husband gave her refuge."

"Ah." She was silent for a moment. "That was very brave of them."

"Yes. Crossing a peer is never advisable."

Anna's eyes reddened. "Perhaps I should not say this, but I do so wish to understand her unhappiness."

"What is it, my darling?" He leaned against her arm, wishing he could embrace her.

"I suspect she and your uncle have strong feelings for one another."

"I agree." Edmond easily reined the mare around a broken cart. Unfortunately, his mother and uncle had no such easy way around their broken relationship. English law forbade a widow to marry her late husband's brother. Had she chosen the wrong brother to marry simply because of his title and suffered for her decision? Was this the source of her bitterness? Such questions helped him understand and forgive her, even when she punished him for her unhappiness.

They wended their way past Whitehall and sunlight flooded the phaeton, filling Edmond with joy. Enough about Mother. At last he and Anna were free to decide their future. "I have something important to tell you."

"Oh, dear. What is it?" Worry clouded her grey-green eyes.

"Shh. Don't fret." Her bonnet kept him from kissing her cheek, so he bent at an angle and placed a quick peck beside her mouth. Then sat back and enjoyed her blush. "You asked me last night where I have been these past weeks."

Her eyes cleared. "Yes?"

"I traveled to Blandon to find your Squire Beamish."

"Ah." The clouds returned, then dispersed again. "Did you see any of my friends? How is Mrs. Brown?"

He chuckled at the direction of her thoughts. "She is

well and sends her love, as does Mrs. Pitcher." He paused for effect. "And the good squire sends his kindest regards."

"Hmm. How kind of him." She seemed less than cheered by his last remark.

"Dearest, I shall not keep you in suspense any longer. The long and the short of it is that the squire left all too much in Mr. Danders's hands, and the man cheated you out of your inheritance."

"My inheritance? Do you mean to say I actually did inherit something from *Papá?*"

"No, not from your father. As a country vicar, he had little to save or invest. Or for his son to buy a commission."

"But Peter did buy his commission."

"Yes, but the funds came from another source."

She tilted her head prettily. "Another source? But who?"

"Your grandfather."

"But—" she looked away, a frown furrowing her brow "—we were told Sir Reginald disowned *Mamá.*"

"He did, and he never surrendered his bitterness toward your parents. However, in his old age, he apparently wanted to do something for his only grandchildren. While he did not change his will entirely, he bequeathed sufficient funds for a modest future for both you and your brother." Renewed sorrow for young Newfield's death wrenched Edmond's soul. "He arranged the matter through Squire Beamish, with instructions that your parents—and you—would never know where the money came from. The good squire informed your father of a mysterious benefactor whose identity he could not disclose.

"Being a prudent man, your father did not inquire further. After all, you and your brother would now have the future he could never promise you. At the age of eighteen, your brother was to receive three hundred pounds to establish a career. At your father's death, you were to receive fifty pounds annual. Unfortunately, the squire left the execution of it all to Danders. Because your father expected the inheritance for Peter, Danders had no choice but to surrender the funds for his chosen profession. However, when your father died, the solicitor must have decided an unprotected young lady was easier to rob, even with a brother expected to return from America."

Edmond hurried on to avoid delving too deeply in that last inference. "Now that Danders's treachery has been uncovered, he has confessed all and is in the care of the constable. *And* your fifty pounds annual inheritance has been secured."

To give Anna time to sort out all he had disclosed, Edmond turned his full attention to driving. They rode in silence, and soon he spied his destination ahead.

After several minutes she slipped one arm through his and rested her head, or rather, her bothersome bonnet, against his shoulder. "You did all of that for me?"

"Of course." His longing to give her a true kiss made his chest ache, but with that silly bonnet in his way he settled for caressing her cheek. "My purpose was to give you peace of mind about your father's promises, but—"

"Edmond!" Anna sat up and squeezed his arm. "Do you realize what this means?"

"Why, yes." He chuckled to see such unfettered joy brightening her lovely face. "You do not have to depend upon Mother—"

"No, not that. It means you will have the funds to support you as you study law." A bright pink blush crept up her cheeks. "That is, if we…if you…" She huffed out a breath and stared away.

"Dearest." He gently gripped her chin and redirected her gaze back to him. "Always thinking of others. But do not be concerned about my expenses. God has already arranged everything. Uncle Grenville's offer of sponsorship provides more than my place at the Inns of Courts." Eager to complete an important task, he tugged the mare to a stop, jumped from the phaeton and helped her disembark. "We have arrived, my lady."

"Westminster Abbey?" She gazed up at the edifice, then at him, trust emanating from her beautiful emerald eyes.

Her sweet innocence melted his insides. How he longed to kiss her. But not in public. Not in front of this holy building. He had brought her here for another reason entirely, something he had longed to do since the day he met her. Despite their trials, despite Society's ridiculous rules, they had overcome every barrier, and nothing prevented him from making her his bride. His heart overflowed with love for her, and he laughed for the joy of it.

"Yes, Westminster Abbey. I consider this the most beautiful church in London." He glanced off to the right at the Palace of Westminster, where even now Greystone and his fellow lords were making decisions concerning the American war, something he no longer needed to worry about. "With my brother's influence, I believe we can arrange to be married here."

Chapter Thirty-Three

Anna's sense of mischief drove her toward a teasing reply, but the hopeful look on Edmond's face sobered her. Somewhat.

"Am I to take this as a proposal, Mr. Grenville?" Though she tried to sound nonchalant, her voice wavered with the joyful emotion pulsing through her.

He scrunched his face into a comical confusion. "Why, Miss Newfield, I do believe that is what it was."

"Well, then, I accept."

"My darling—" He gripped her hand and bent to kiss it.

"But—" Even through her gloves she felt a pleasant sensation streak up her arm, a feeling at odds with her thoughts. "I fear such a grand cathedral will overwhelm me. Could we not consider a small country church?"

"Hmm." Edmond stared up toward the cathedral's two square towers, his brow furrowed. At last he shrugged and gazed down into her eyes, causing a lovely flutter in the vicinity of her heart. "My darling, we can marry wherever you wish. That is, as long as it is in a house of God, for I believe this will set the course for our lives. Just say you will be my bride."

Never had Anna been more certain of God's direction. "Yes, my dear Edmond. I will marry you."

His intense gaze on her lips increased her own longing for his kiss, which had begun the moment they stepped into the phaeton at Lord Greystone's town house. But this was hardly the place. She swallowed her unruly sentiments, for once lamenting her strong sense of propriety. Not about the denied kiss, but about what they must do before she could in all good conscience marry this wonderful man.

She reached up and toyed with his ruffled cravat, admiring the lace edging. "Edmond, we must make amends to Lady Greystone for her disappointments." He started to speak, but she put a finger on his lips to stop him. "She did not have to take me in, yet she did. She did not have to sponsor my introduction into Society—"

"Such as it was."

"Shh." Again she touched his lips. "But she did."

He grimaced. "Very well. What will you say?"

"I have not thought that far ahead, but for now we should return to your brother's town house."

He sighed, then narrowed his eyes. "Very well. But I will not permit her to intimidate you."

She offered him a playful smirk. "Nor will *I* permit her to intimidate *you*."

They climbed aboard the phaeton and wended their way home by way of Green Park, chatting more freely than they ever had. Anna learned of Edmond's preference for country living, which bode well for her choice of a place to marry. She informed him of her preference of lamb over beef. They both enjoyed long walks, and now that his leg had nearly healed, they would take them often.

In the middle of the park they bought cups of fresh milk from one of the famous Green Park milkmaids. After they slaked their thirst, Edmond took a few winding turns around the flowerbeds, avoiding the children who chased about under the watchful eyes of their nursemaids.

All too soon they arrived in Hanover Square at Lord Greystone's town house. They found the viscount at home entertaining Lord Winston in the drawing room. Both Lady Greystone and Mrs. Parton appeared not to have moved from their chairs, but the viscountess had assumed the more pleasant demeanor she wore in company.

As Anna and Edmond walked toward the room's occupants, he put an arm around her waist. "This should tell the baron everything he needs to know."

Indeed Lord Winston's blond eyebrows arched upward, and his warm expression grew distant.

After greetings all around, the baron addressed Lord Greystone. "You will excuse me, my lord." He stared at Anna and Edmond, then gave them a haughty sniff. "I must be off." With proper adieus, he departed.

Anna quietly sighed, but her relief was short-lived. Lady Greystone refused to look her way. On the other hand, warm approval filled Lord Greystone's and Mrs. Parton's expressions.

"Madam." Anna sat next to the viscountess and put a hand on her chair arm. "Please know that I will be forever grateful to you for all you have done for me."

"Humph." The lady still would not look at her.

"You have just cause to be disappointed in me."

That brought a disapproving grunt from Edmond. In the corner of her eye, Anna saw Lord Greystone nudge Edmond's arm.

"For your comfort, I will accept Mrs. Parton's offer to live with her and work at her orphanage until Mr. Grenville and I can arrange our marriage."

"What?" Now Lady Greystone turned an angry glare

on her. "If you actually think I will permit a daughter-in-law of mine to *work,* you do not know me at all."

She stood, strode to the hearth and stared up at the large painting of Greystone Lodge. For several moments no sound could be heard in the vast room. Anna wondered if the others were holding their breath as she was, awaiting whatever explosion might emanate from Lady Greystone.

At last the viscountess spun around and faced them. "Now, Edmond, we must invite the cream of the *haute ton* to the wedding, for it will advance your law career, if you insist upon pursuing such a course. We will book St. Paul's for the ceremony and have the wedding breakfast here in the ballroom. Lady Blakemore will—"

"We thank you, Mother." Edmond walked over to her, holding up one hand. "However, we prefer Westminster Abbey, and you need not go to the expense of a breakfast."

Anna saw a hint of disappointment in the lady's face. Hurt, actually. She hurried over and looped her arm in Edmond's. "But, my darling, perhaps it would be wise to advance your career." Never mind that she still preferred that simple country wedding.

But her words had already done their job. Lady Greystone's expression warmed—ever so briefly, but sincerely. Anna could hardly contain her tears of joy. Looking at Edmond, she could see a bit of a shine in his eyes, too, accompanied by a smile that made her knees go delightfully weak.

Holding his prayer book, Richard Grenville faced Anna and Edmond. Beside Edmond, Lord Greystone grinned like a proud older brother. At Anna's side, Mary Grenville beamed at her husband as he conducted his first wedding ceremony. Behind them, dozens of members of the *haute ton* filled the pews. But it was Edmond's strong, handsome face Anna focused on at last as Richard began to speak.

"Dearly beloved, we are gathered together here in the sight of God, and in the face of this congregation, to join together this man and this woman in holy matrimony, which is an honorable estate…" Richard's deep baritone voice, so like his two brothers', echoed throughout the vaulted sanctuary of Westminster Abbey.

Anna could have recited the beloved ritual with him, having watched *Papá* join together countless couples through the years. But growing up in the remote village of Blandon, she had never expected to be a bride herself. This truly was the happiest day of her life, despite the size of the cathedral.

Although she had wished to marry in her childhood church, Anna had willingly surrendered her preference so Lord Greystone could celebrate the event with them. With his duties in Parliament, the three-day travel time each way would have prevented his attendance.

A Blandon wedding also would have prevented Lady Greystone hostessing the wedding breakfast, another concession Anna had decided was important to establishing peace within the Grenville family. While she found the event a bit overwhelming, she could see many of the influential guests sought Edmond out not only to congratulate him but to chat about law. It seemed that even the wealthy required the services of a barrister from time to time, which boded well for his law career. As for Anna, she had eyes only for her handsome husband, and he returned more of those knee-melting smiles.

In the days before and after the wedding, the rift between Lady Greystone and Edmond appeared to have healed, which was more than could be said for the viscountess and poor Richard and Mary. Rather than wait for the living at Greystone Village, Richard had accepted a church in Cornwall, far from his mother's controlling reach. Anna and Edmond agreed the less said about that matter, the better.

On the other hand, they both took delight in Lady Greystone's next project. She was determined to find a bride for Lord Greystone, and in their own happiness, they were more than pleased to help her. Then Mrs. Parton insisted *she* would find a match for the viscount. Anna and Edmond watched with amusement to see who would win the competition.

A week after becoming man and wife, they moved the last of their belongings from the town house into a large apartment Uncle Grenville owned in St. James Square. The old gentleman welcomed them with gifts of a full pantry and two servants to tend their needs. Of course Matthews still served as Edmond's valet, but Anna had yet to decide upon a lady's maid, for Lady Greystone would not release Esther.

"'Tis an excellent address," Uncle assured them. "Edmond will have a short walk to my office at Lincoln's Inn, and you will have your privacy."

As if to emphasize that privacy, he wished them happiness and bade them goodbye.

"What shall we unpack next?" Edmond had been very attentive, giving Anna her every preference.

She eyed the few remaining boxes. "I suppose I should look through *Papá*'s things. I have postponed the chore long enough."

Seated beside her beloved and leaning against him for support, she rummaged through the box of papers and letters. Among them she found some of her first efforts at sketching and painting, which sent a nostalgic twinge through her heart. When the Lord granted her children, she would save every precious memento like these.

Next she pulled out a familiar page. "This is the only letter we received from Peter after he went to America." The twinge in her heart became a painful pang. After all these months of hearing nothing, not even from the army officials, perhaps she must finally accept that her brother was indeed dead.

"May I read it?" Edmond reached for the missive and quickly perused it. "Ah, his excellent wit fills the page."

"And not a mention of bloody battles or fears of dying for king and country."

Edmond set the letter down and pulled her into a comforting embrace. "He was the best of men." He kissed her temple, then reached into the box. "This one has an unbroken seal. I wonder how it escaped Danders's greedy tentacles."

Absorbing the strength of his arms, Anna studied *Papá*'s name on the missive. "I do not recognize the handwriting. Is it all right to open it?"

He chuckled softly, sadly. "Your father will not mind."

She snapped the seal and unfolded the page. For a moment she could not comprehend the words, but at last they began to make sense. "Peter!" Unable to say anything more, she held out the letter.

"What?" Edmond seized it. "'Dear Father and sweet Anna, No doubt you will be surprised to hear from me, especially if you received reports that I met my end on the battlefield. A friend is writing this letter for me, as my right arm has been injured. After being separated from my regiment for most of the winter, I have at last made contact and will soon return home to you.'" Edmond choked and set down the page to swipe a hand across his eyes. "He will be devastated to learn of your father's death, but at least *he* is alive."

"There is no way to soften the blow, but knowing Peter, his faith will be his strength." Anna buried her face in Edmond's shirt front. "Oh, my darling, God has given me back my beloved brother. I have a family again."

He withdrew a linen handkerchief from his coat pocket and dried her tears. "And a new family who loves you, too." A teasing grin appeared. "Well, if you do not count my mother."

Pleased at his attempt at humor, Anna sat up and gave his arm a playful smack. "I forbid you to say anything about my mother-in-law. She is—"

Edmond stopped her with a kiss, halting her defense of Lady Greystone, indeed, removing the viscountess entirely from her thoughts. But as her husband's kiss deepened and her feelings warmed, Anna did not complain.

* * * * *

Dear Reader,

Thank you for choosing *A Proper Companion,* the first book in my LADIES IN WAITING series. I hope you've enjoyed this journey back to Regency England. This is my first full-length Regency book, and I have absolutely fallen in love with this unique and fascinating era, the setting for Jane Austen's timeless novels.

One of the tricky things about writing these stories is getting all of the details right. The social structures of the Regency era were quite strict and confining, but true love could always find a way to cross social lines. By the way, if you're a diehard Regency fan and find an error, please let me know! And please know that I tried to get it right!

As with all of my stories, beyond the romance, I hope to inspire my readers always to seek God's guidance, no matter what trials may come their way.

I love to hear from readers, so if you have a comment, please contact me through my website: http://blog.Louisemgouge.com.

Blessings,
Louise M. Gouge

Questions for Discussion

1. In the beginning of the story, Anna receives one piece of bad news after another, any one of which could have defeated her. How does she respond? What Biblical character did she try to emulate?

2. For all the romance of the Regency era, English society of the time would consider Anna a spinster at age twenty-three. How have social norms changed? How are the lives of young women different today?

3. In spite of his own infirmities, Edmond makes an unusual offer to Anna to rescue her from destitution. What does this say about his character? Do you think he fits the image of a "hero"? Why or why not? What is your definition of a hero?

4. From the moment Edmond meets Anna he admires her, but considers her beneath him socially. Why? Do you think this reflects upon his character? What causes him to change his opinion over time?

5. What sort of person is Lady Greystone? Why does she regard Anna as "insignificant"? Are there people today with that attitude toward certain people?

6. What expectations did Lady Greystone have of Edmond and Richard? Why were her expectations different for Greystone? Considering the times, was she justified in trying to force Edmond into an advantageous career?

7. Why doesn't Edmond want to remain in the army? Do you think his reasons are valid? Why or why not?

8. This was an age in which the aristocracy ruled and held all of the privileges. As much as we romanticize the era, would you like to travel back in time for a visit? At what level of society did your ancestors live?

9. Both Anna and Edmond are Christians. Which one changes the most in the story? In what ways did each one mature and become stronger? In what ways did they stay the same?

10. In the Regency era there were no televisions or movies, and families had to make their own evening entertainment. Each member and each guest was responsible to help pass the time in a pleasant way. What does your family do in the evening to spend time together?

INSPIRATIONAL

celebrating 15 YEARS

COMING NEXT MONTH
AVAILABLE JULY 2, 2012

WOOING THE SCHOOLMARM
Pinewood Weddings
Dorothy Clark
Schoolteacher Willa Wright has given up on romance—
until Reverend Matthew Calvert sneaks his way into
her heart.

THE CAPTAIN'S COURTSHIP
The Everard Legacy
Regina Scott
London's whirlwind season would seem manageable to
Captain Richard Everard...if it hadn't reunited him with the
lady he'd once loved.

THE RUNAWAY BRIDE
Noelle Marchand
Childhood rejection closed Lorelei Wilkins's heart to Sean
O'Brien. Is a forced engagement love's chance to finally
conquer them both?

HEARTS IN HIDING
Patty Smith Hall
Beau Daniels is captivated by Edie Michaels, but can love
withstand the ultimate test of loyalty when he discovers
her family ties to Nazi Germany?

Look for these and other Love Inspired books wherever books
are sold, including most bookstores, supermarkets, discount
stores and drugstores.

LIHCNM0612

REQUEST YOUR FREE BOOKS!

2 FREE INSPIRATIONAL NOVELS
PLUS 2
FREE
MYSTERY GIFTS

Love Inspired
HISTORICAL
INSPIRATIONAL HISTORICAL ROMANCE

YES! Please send me 2 FREE Love Inspired® Historical novels and my 2 FREE mystery gifts (gifts are worth about $10). After receiving them, if I don't wish to receive any more books, I can return the shipping statement marked "cancel". If I don't cancel, I will receive 4 brand-new novels every month and be billed just $4.49 per book in the U.S. or $4.99 per book in Canada. That's a saving of at least 22% off the cover price. It's quite a bargain! Shipping and handling is just 50¢ per book in the U.S. and 75¢ per book in Canada.* I understand that accepting the 2 free books and gifts places me under no obligation to buy anything. I can always return a shipment and cancel at any time. Even if I never buy another book, the two free books and gifts are mine to keep forever.

102/302 IDN FEHF

Name	(PLEASE PRINT)	
Address		Apt. #
City	State/Prov.	Zip/Postal Code

Signature (if under 18, a parent or guardian must sign)

Mail to the **Reader Service:**
IN U.S.A.: P.O. Box 1867, Buffalo, NY 14240-1867
IN CANADA: P.O. Box 609, Fort Erie, Ontario L2A 5X3
Not valid for current subscribers to Love Inspired Historical books.

Want to try two free books from another series?
Call 1-800-873-8635 or visit www.ReaderService.com.

* Terms and prices subject to change without notice. Prices do not include applicable taxes. Sales tax applicable in N.Y. Canadian residents will be charged applicable taxes. Offer not valid in Quebec. This offer is limited to one order per household. All orders subject to credit approval. Credit or debit balances in a customer's account(s) may be offset by any other outstanding balance owed by or to the customer. Please allow 4 to 6 weeks for delivery. Offer available while quantities last.

Your Privacy—The Reader Service is committed to protecting your privacy. Our Privacy Policy is available online at www.ReaderService.com or upon request from the Reader Service.

We make a portion of our mailing list available to reputable third parties that offer products we believe may interest you. If you prefer that we not exchange your name with third parties, or if you wish to clarify or modify your communication preferences, please visit us at www.ReaderService.com/consumerchoice or write to us at Reader Service Preference Service, P.O. Box 9062, Buffalo, NY 14269. Include your complete name and address.

LIH11B